TRAIL OF SIN

'The website,' I began, unbuttoning my blouse. 'Will it be
. . . I mean –'

'People will pay to become a member of the site,' Don
cut it. 'Your pics will be available to members only, not to
the whole world.'

'I just hope my mother doesn't see the website,' I said
softly as I slipped out of my jeans.

'You've never mentioned your mother before. Does she
live locally?'

'She . . . she lives up north.'

'Oh, right. OK, we'll start off with a few shots of you on
the couch in your bra and panties.'

Settling on the couch, I gazed at the camera lens as Don
clicked the shutter. He told me to smile and lick my lips
provocatively, and I did my best to comply. I felt
awkward, uncomfortable and . . . This just wasn't me at
all. But the money was excellent and it wasn't as if I was
completely naked. As Don clicked the camera, I followed
his instructions and moved about on the couch. Legs open,
one foot on the couch, legs crossed . . . I quite enjoyed
playing the role of a model, until he asked me to take my
bra and panties off.

TRAIL OF SIN

Ray Gordon

This book is a work of fiction.
In real life, make sure you practise safe, sane and
consensual sex.

First published in 2008 by
Nexus
Thames Wharf Studios
Rainville Rd
London W6 9HA

A catalogue record for this book is available from the British Library.

www.nexus-books.com

Typeset by TW Typesetting, Plymouth, Devon
Printed and bound in Great Britain by
CPI Bookmarque, Croydon, CR0 4TD

Distributed in the USA by Macmillan, 175 Fifth Avenue,
New York, NY 10010, USA

The paper used in this book is a natural, recyclable product made from
wood grown in sustainable forests. The manufacturing process conforms
to the regulations of the country of origin.

ISBN 978 0 352 34182 2

1 3 5 7 9 10 8 6 4 2

Symbols key

 Corporal Punishment

 Female Domination

 Institution

 Medical

 Period Setting

 Restraint/Bondage

 Rubber/Leather

 Spanking

 Transvestism

 Underwear

 Uniforms

One

I saw this young guy looking at me through the newsagent's shop window. He smiled and waved, but I ignored him. I'd only popped out to buy a magazine for my mother, and the last thing I wanted was to be chatted up in the street by a stranger. He was in his late twenties and not bad-looking. He was also very persistent. After tapping on the window and making a series of odd facial expressions, he finally came into the shop.

'Hi, Ali,' he said, grinning at me. 'I haven't seen you for ages – how are you doing?'

'I'm sorry?' I breathed, wondering how he knew my name. 'Do I know you?'

'Do you know me?' He chuckled and looked down at the cleavage of my firm young breasts. 'We know each other intimately,' he said. 'Or have you forgotten our nights of passion?'

'If that's the best chat-up line you can manage, you won't get anywhere,' I replied.

'Chat-up line?' He frowned and brushed his dark hair away from his forehead. 'Why are you playing games? I'm Rod, Rod Davis. Why make out that you don't know me?'

I quickly paid for the magazine, left the shop and walked the short distance home. Rod Davis?

1

I wondered, glancing over my shoulder now and then to make sure that he wasn't following me. Nights of passion? He'd obviously mistaken me for someone else, although it was odd that he knew my name. I closed the front door behind me, went into the lounge and looked through the window. Thankfully, he wasn't hovering outside the house.

'What are you doing?' my mother asked me. 'What are you looking at?'

'Nothing, I . . . I thought I was being followed,' I said, turning and facing her.

'You watch too many films, young lady,' she sighed. 'Did you get my magazine?'

'It's there,' I said, pointing to the couch. 'A man came up to me in the shop and . . . He seemed to know me, but I've never met him before.'

'It's about time you found yourself a nice young man,' she said, obviously not listening to me as she flicked through the magazine.

'I'm not going out with a stranger who chats me up in a shop, mum.'

'You should have stayed with Sam. He was a nice lad.'

'He was married, mum. He lied to me about . . . Anyway, I'm only eighteen. There's no rush.'

My mother seemed to think that I should settle down and make wedding plans, but I wasn't ready for that. Besides, I hadn't yet met anyone I wanted to spend the rest of my life with. But she was right about Sam: he *was* very nice. But he was married and I was nothing more than his bit on the side. Our relationship didn't last long because, apart from him having a wife at home, I was a prude. He wanted crude sex, and . . . well, I wasn't that way inclined. But I really did like him.

* * *

2

The next puzzling incident happened when I was in a local pub one evening. I'd arranged to meet a girlfriend there and was sitting at a table sipping a gin and tonic when a young man came over to me. He sat opposite me, plonked his pint of beer on the table, and asked me how I was getting on. He knew my name, but I'd never seen him before. Was I going mad? I wondered as he smiled and winked at me. When he asked me whether I still shaved my pussy, I felt my face flush. What a bloody nerve, I thought angrily. I ignored his crude comments about my being a blow-job queen and, when he invited me back to his place for a good spanking, I made my anger clear.

'I don't know who the hell you are,' I hissed angrily. 'But I want you to leave me alone.'

'Ali, it's me,' he said, frowning. 'Your old friend and lover – you know, Rick.'

'I've never met you before,' I retorted. 'And you're certainly not an old friend and lover. Please go away.'

'I . . . I don't understand. We parted on the best of terms, Ali. What's happened to make you like this?'

'You've obviously mistaken me for someone else. I don't know you, and I don't *want* to know you.'

'OK, well . . . We'll leave it at that, then.'

He walked to the bar, turned and gazed at me. He frowned again, looking genuinely confused as he half smiled at me. He was very good-looking and I wished that I did know him, but he was a complete stranger. I sipped my drink and pondered on his comment about me shaving my pussy. I'd never shaved my pussy. One or two boyfriends had asked me to shave it, but I'd hated the idea. As for spanking . . . Apart from an occasional whack on my bum from my dad years ago when I'd been a naughty child I'd never been spanked.

I finished my drink but didn't want to go to the bar for another in case Rick, or whoever he was, started

3

chatting to me again. He was leaning on the bar, glancing in my direction every now and then as he sipped his beer. Where the hell was my friend? Jackie had never let me down before, and she'd never been late. Finally plucking up courage, I grabbed my handbag and took my empty glass to the bar. Rick said nothing, but I knew that he was watching me as I ordered another gin and tonic. I'd hoped for a relaxing evening with Jackie, but I felt uneasy with Rick staring at me.

Returning to the table, I thought about leaving the pub once I'd finished my drink. Jackie obviously wasn't going to turn up, so there was no point sitting there alone with a stranger constantly eyeing me. Would he follow me home? I wondered anxiously. Was he some kind of weirdo? What if he was a sad pervert? I was eighteen and attractive. I should never have worn such a short skirt, I realised as he smiled at me again. If he followed me and –

'Sorry I'm late,' Jackie said, breezing into the pub and dumping her handbag on the table. 'Mum was going on at me and I couldn't get away.'

'You don't know how pleased I am to see you,' I breathed in relief. 'That man over there – he's been chatting me up.'

'Lucky you,' she said, glancing at Rick. 'He's not bad-looking.'

'He asked me whether I still shave my pussy.'

'What?' Jackie gasped, her dark eyes wide as she stared at me. 'Do you know him, then?'

'No, I've never met him before. He also invited me back to his place for a good spanking. And he knows my name.'

'A good spanking?' She grinned and giggled as she took her purse from her bag. 'That sounds interesting.'

4

'He keeps looking at me, Jackie. I didn't think you were going to turn up and I wasn't sure what to do.'

'He fancies you, that's all.'

'But he knows my name.'

'Maybe he's seen you in here before, heard someone call your name and . . . I wouldn't worry about it. I'll go and get a drink.'

Jackie was probably right, I thought as she walked up to the bar. But that was the second man within a week who'd known my name and had chatted to me as if we were old friends. Two coincidences in seven days? The first man had commented on nights of passion, and then Rick had asked me whether I still shaved my pussy. It was all rather odd but, as Jackie sat opposite me with her drink, I tried to forget about it.

'What was your mum going on about?' I asked her.

'The usual stuff,' she sighed. 'When are you going to get a job, you should have gone to university, nag, nag, nag . . . She knows that I'm looking for a job. It's not my fault if I can't find one.'

'University is great, Jackie. Look at the situation I'm in. I've got two months off for the summer, I have some money –'

'A student loan has to be paid back, Ali.'

'I know, but I earn money too.'

'You have your job at the DIY store, which means that you earn a *little* money, sure. But you don't really have two months' summer holiday because you're working.'

'I enjoy the job. Anyway, it's only part-time.'

'Do you reckon that's where that man knows you from? You wear a name badge at the store. He might have been there and seen you.'

'I hadn't thought of that. Yes, that must be it. There was another man the other day. He came up to me in

5

the paper shop and started chatting as if he knew me. He knew my name too so . . . You're right, they must have been into the store and seen me there. That explains it.'

'There's usually a simple explanation to a mystery.' Jackie cocked her head to one side and grinned. '*Do* you shave your pussy?'

'What?' I gasped, holding my hand to my mouth.

'You said the man over there asked you whether you still shave your pussy.'

'Oh, right. Er . . . no, no, I don't. Do you?'

'I used to. Do you remember that idiot Brian who I went out with? He got me to shave my pussy. I quite liked it but . . .'

I wasn't really listening to Jackie. I was watching Rick from the corner of my eye and when he waved at me I foolishly turned my head to look at him. He pointed to his glass and then pointed at me, obviously offering me a drink. I shook my head and turned my gaze back to Jackie. She was going on about her smooth pussy lips and how Brian used to love licking her hairless crack. Jackie was a lovely girl, but she had sluttish tendencies. I'd never shaved 'down there'.

There was one boyfriend I'd had who . . . He'd been into bondage and I'd allowed him to tie my hands to his brass bedstead. Then he ran a length of rope beneath the bed and tied the ends to my ankles. Naked, with my feet pulled down at either side of the bed and my thighs parted wide, I was unable to move as he licked my vagina. I wasn't sure that I liked being tied down – it wasn't really my thing. I felt like a whore, but I was still glad that I'd tried it.

I finished my drink while Jackie answered her mobile phone. I wondered what she was going to do with her life. She was beautiful with her long black hair and huge dark eyes. She should have been a model, I mused, gazing at her petite firm breasts that were clearly outlined by her tight top. I'd have liked to have been a model, but I didn't have the looks. What was *I* going to do with *my* life? I wondered as she slipped her phone into her handbag. I was studying nursing at university. The problem was that I didn't want to be a nurse.

'I have to go,' Jackie sighed, finishing her drink.

'Already?' I asked her.

'It's my mum. I thought she'd been acting funny recently and now I know why. Dad's just walked out on her.'

'God, no.'

'He's gone off with some younger woman, apparently. I'd better get home and be with her.'

'Yes, of course.'

'I'll ring you later, OK?'

'OK.'

I'd forgotten about Rick but when Jackie left he wandered over to my table, holding a gin and tonic. He smiled and pulled up a chair, raising his eyebrows as if silently asking whether he could join me. I wished that I'd left with Jackie as he sat down opposite me. I was about to go when I decided to ask him about the DIY store. I didn't want to get into a conversation with him, but I was intrigued.

'I've never been to the place,' he replied. 'Besides, we met at John's party last year.'

'Who the hell's John?' I asked him.

'Ali, I don't know what you're playing at. Making out that you don't know me and –'

'Rick, I have never seen you before,' I cut in. 'I'm not playing games. I honestly have no idea who you are.'

'In that case, you must have a double.'

'A double, with the same name? That's highly unlikely.'

7

'How else do you explain it?' Rick looked at my hair and frowned. 'I preferred you with dark hair,' he said. 'Blonde doesn't suit you. When did you change the colour?'

'About two weeks ... How did you know I'd changed my hair colour?'

'The last time we met you had dark hair.'

'When did you last see me? I mean, when did you last see my lookalike?'

'Must be about three weeks ago.'

'And where was that?'

'You came ... *she* came back to my place after we'd spent the evening here. Ali, I'm confused.'

'*You*'re confused? What do you think *I* am? What's this girl's address? Where does she live?'

'I don't know. She was looking for a flat and staying with a friend in the meantime. I don't know the address. Why not come back to my place and –'

'Rick, I don't want to know you. I know that sounds rude, but I'm not available.'

'I wasn't trying to chat you up, Ali,' he sighed. 'It's just that I find the whole thing incredible. Are you sure you don't have a twin sister?'

'I'm an only child. Look, I must be going. I'm sorry I'm not who you thought I was.'

I smiled back at him as I left the table. I knew that he hadn't been trying to chat me up. He'd seemed genuinely confused, as I was. As I walked home I thought again about his comment concerning my hair. I'd always been dark and had decided to go blonde a couple of weeks previously. It was quite a coincidence that he not only knew my name but knew I'd changed my hair colour. Coincidence, or ... or what? I'd always been prone to neurotic behaviour, according to my mother, so I decided to try to forget about the incident before I became obsessed with the mystery.

8

But I *couldn't* forget it. Being chatted up by two men within a week had got me thinking. In my bed that night I pondered on my previous relationships. I'd never really had a sex life, apart from the time when I'd been tied to a bed and licked. I'd had sex but . . . I suppose I'd always been shy, and prudish. I'd thought that the bondage episode might have brought me out of my shell, but it hadn't. If anything, the loveless act had left me cold. What's the point in tying someone to a bed? I'd have allowed him to lick my pussy without being tied down. There again, *would* I have agreed to him licking me? I'd never had an orgasm because I hadn't been able to let go. I'd come close when he'd tied me to the bed and tongued me, but I'd been concerned because I was vulnerable and defenceless. There was no way I could have relaxed and allowed my climax to explode.

Curiosity was getting the better of me and I went back to the pub the following evening. I was hoping to bump into Rick as I wanted to talk to him, ask him some more questions, but he wasn't there. I was standing at the bar sipping my drink when another young man came over to me. He asked me where I'd been and said that he hadn't seen me for over a week. I was stunned, and a little frightened. He knew my name, and I realised that this was no coincidence.

'I've been here and there,' I replied, deciding to play along with him in the hope of discovering what was going on.

'Screwing around, as usual?' he said, with a chuckle.

'Maybe. What have *you* been up to?'

'Nothing much. Ali, have you given any more thought to the photographs?'

'Photographs?' I echoed.

'The ones we talked about.'

'Oh, er . . . no, no, I haven't.'

'Is it the money? I could offer you a little more, if that's the problem.'

'I've been busy,' I said softly, wishing that I knew his name and what he was talking about.

'You've got too many men on the go,' he sighed. 'We'd both do well from the photos. When will you give me an answer?'

'I . . . I don't know.' I hesitated, wondering what to say. 'Tell me more about it.'

'You know what it's about. It's nothing bad, just nude shots. And some naughty shots of your lovely pussy, of course. I've got the studio set up. All I need is for you to agree.'

'It's not the sort of thing I'm into,' I said, trying not to look shocked.

'That's a laugh, coming from someone who's screwed half the guys in town.'

'I'm not a slut,' I retorted.

'Ali, you *are* a slut. You've always said that you're a slut.'

'Yes, well . . . I'd better be going.'

'Already?'

'I have things to do.'

'Two hundred pounds, Ali. That's the best I can offer you at the moment. Once the money starts coming in I'll give you more. At least come round and see the studio.'

'Where is it?' I asked him, hoping I hadn't given the game away.

'You're hopeless, Ali. I suppose you've lost my card?'

'I have it somewhere.'

He reached into his jacket pocket. 'Here's another one.'

I took his card and read his name. 'OK, Don. I'll come and take a look sometime.'

'When?'

'Maybe tomorrow. Tomorrow evening, OK?'

'The idea's good, Ali. A website with a members' area – we'd make a fortune.'

'I'll come round tomorrow.'

'I'll be waiting for you. Make it early, about seven. And don't let me down.'

'I'll be there, Don.'

I finished my drink and left the pub, relieved to have escaped. Nude photographs, a website ... What the hell did this man think I was? He thought I was a slut, I reflected as I walked home. Three men, I thought anxiously. Three men who seemed to know me and ... A lookalike? I mused. It was highly unlikely. A lookalike with the same name? Although I was totally confused, Don had got me thinking. Two hundred pounds. That was a lot of money for a few photographs. I earned very little at the DIY store and I could have done with some extra cash. But he wanted nude photographs. Who on earth was this other girl called Ali?

I'd worked at the DIY store all day and had earned forty pounds. Two hundred for a few photographs was incredibly tempting, but there was no way I was going to strip naked in front of a stranger wielding a camera. I was in two minds about going to Don's studio, but I decided that I had to discover more about my lookalike. Who was she? Where did she live? I had no intention of agreeing to be photographed, and I was a little apprehensive, but I thought I might learn something about the other Ali.

Reaching the address I looked up at the old house and wondered whether it had been converted into flats. There was only one doorbell – I couldn't believe that Don owned the huge property. He opened the door and grinned at me, obviously pleased that I'd turned up. He was wearing jeans and a white T-shirt and seemed relaxed, even laid-back, as he invited me in, which made me feel a little easier. He talked about the photo shoot as I followed him through the hall to a back room, and I felt apprehensive again. After all, he was a complete stranger. Apart from that, he wanted to take nude photos of me. There was an old couch in the room and a camera mounted on a tripod that was surrounded by lights. But what caught my attention was a corner table littered with vibrators and dildos of various shapes and sizes.

'I got your message,' Don said, looking down at my legs. 'That's the first time I've seen you in jeans. You usually wear skirts so short that –'

'What message?' I asked him.

'The one you left on my answerphone earlier. I'm really pleased that you've decided to go ahead with the photos.'

'I didn't leave a message,' I murmured, realising that the other girl must have phoned him. Then, 'Oh, maybe I did,' I said hurriedly, not wanting to confuse the matter still further.

'You can't remember?' Don chuckled and brushed his dark hair away from his forehead. 'Anyway, you're here now so get your kit off and we'll get started.'

'Have you got my address?' I asked him. 'I mean . . .'

'You know I haven't,' he replied, frowning at me. 'Are you all right, Ali? You seem to be confused.'

'It's been a long day. I . . . I've been forgetting things lately.'

'I realise that. You've never given me your address. You've always made a point of telling me to sod off when I've asked you where you live.'

'I'm losing my memory,' I sighed. 'Perhaps I'm going mad.'

'You're probably tired. You said it's been a long day, so you're probably tired. What have you been doing, shagging all day?'

'No, no, I . . . Tell me all you know about me.'

'What?'

'Seriously, Don, I think I'm losing my memory.'

'Fucking hell, Ali. I think you *have* gone mad. Tell you all I know about you?'

'Where did we meet?'

'Where did we meet?' He shook his head and grimaced. 'Are you serious?'

'I'm very serious.'

'We met in a bar and then I fucked you senseless in the park. Are you having me on, Ali?'

'I'll have to be honest,' I mumbled, sitting on the couch. 'I've never met you before.'

'Ali, you've come here to do the pics. Don't give me all this crap. You left a message earlier saying that you'd decided to go ahead with the shoot.'

'Do you have my phone number?'

'You changed your mobile phone, if you remember. You haven't given me your new number. Shall we get on with this? I want to go out for a drink later, not spend the whole evening here.'

'I can't do it,' I blurted out.

'What? Christ, Ali . . . Look, there's two hundred on the table. You agreed, for fuck's sake. It's only nude shots, nothing more.'

I bit my lip as Don left the room. I didn't know what to do. I'd made a fool of myself, got myself into a corner, and didn't know how to get out of it. Don returned with a large gin and tonic and frowned at me again. I took the glass, knocked back the drink and then gazed at the money lying on the table. Two

13

hundred pounds was a lot of cash, but I wasn't going to take my clothes off.

'Have you forgotten about these?' Don asked me, grabbing a folder from a shelf. 'Don't say that you can't remember the time I took these pics of you in the park.'

I gazed at the photographs as he opened the folder – I couldn't believe my eyes. It was me, wearing nothing but bra and panties. My hair was slightly different, and the photographs weren't very clear, but it was definitely me. But I'd never met Don before, I hadn't been to the park and stripped down to my underwear . . . For a moment, I honestly believed that I *had* gone mad. There was no denying the existence of the photographs.

'I need another drink,' I said shakily as Don closed the folder.

'Come through to the kitchen,' he told me, tossing the folder onto the shelf. 'You *do* remember the park?'

Following him through the hall, I didn't know what to say. 'I told you, I've lost my memory,' I sighed.

'All right, I'll play along with you.' He poured a large gin and tonic, passed me the glass and grabbed a can of beer from the fridge for himself. 'We went to the park and I had my small camera with me. You were pissed, as usual. You took your clothes off and I took a few shots. That was when we talked about doing a proper shoot and starting a website.'

'I *must* have been pissed,' I said, forcing a smile. 'I can't remember a thing about it.'

'Photographs don't lie, Ali. Now, are we going to do this shoot or not?'

I followed him back to the studio, feeling as confused as hell. I'd never had too much to drink, let alone got so pissed that I couldn't remember what I'd done. And yet, the photos were there. *Photographs don't lie*. Don fiddled with the camera and went on about my drinking, suggesting that I change my lifestyle before I totally messed up my head. I wasn't mad, I decided. I was confused, but not mad. I must have had a lookalike, a double. I recalled meeting Rick in the pub and remembered his words. *Are you sure you don't have a twin sister?* I couldn't understand why I hadn't thought about it before. I was adopted and could easily have had a twin sister. It would be one hell of a coincidence. A twin sister with the same name, living in the same town, going to the same pub . . . Was it possible?

If that was the case, I could go ahead with the photo shoot and, if anyone recognised me in the shots, I could say it was my twin sister. Eyeing the cash on the table, I thought again that it was money for jam. I wasn't a slut, but two hundred pounds for a few photographs really was easy pickings. Never in a million years would I have dreamed that I'd even be contemplating posing nude in front of a camera, though. There again, Don already had photos of me, or at any rate of a girl in the park who looked like me, so a few more wouldn't matter. Still, earning two hundred pounds might be fine but my real aim was to find the other Ali.

'The website,' I began, unbuttoning my blouse. 'Will it be . . . I mean –'

'People will pay to become a member of the site,' Don cut it. 'Your pics will be available to members only, not to the whole world.'

'I just hope my mother doesn't see the website,' I said softly as I slipped out of my jeans.

'You've never mentioned your mother before. Does she live locally?'

'She . . . she lives up north.'

'Oh, right. OK, we'll start off with a few shots of you on the couch in your bra and panties.'

Settling on the couch, I gazed at the camera lens as Don clicked the shutter. He told me to smile and lick my lips provocatively, and I did my best to comply. I felt awkward, uncomfortable and . . . This just wasn't me at all. But the money was excellent and it wasn't as if I was completely naked. As Don clicked the camera, I followed his instructions and moved about on the couch. Legs open, one foot on the couch, legs crossed . . . I quite enjoyed playing the role of a model – until he asked me to take my bra and panties off.

'I have to go,' I said, getting up from the couch and grabbing my clothes.

'You've changed, Ali,' Don sighed, shaking his head. 'You used to be game for anything, but now . . .'

'We'll do another shoot some other time.'

'It'll only take five minutes, Ali. To be honest, two hundred pounds for a few underwear shots is a hell of a lot of money. Whip your bra and panties off and I'll take no more than five minutes.'

'Well, I . . .'

'I'll just change the batteries in the camera and then I'll be ready.'

I didn't know what to do as he fiddled with the camera. To pose completely naked would be highly embarrassing and . . . He was right, two hundred was a silly amount to pay for a few shots of me in my bra and panties. Was I following in the footsteps of my twin sister? I wondered. She'd agreed to do it but she was a slut. Was I treading the path towards becoming a slut? I had to do it, I knew as I glanced again at the cash lying on the table. Don knew nothing about me, he didn't have my address or phone number, so I had nothing to lose. In fact, if I stripped naked I'd be two hundred pounds the richer.

I reached behind my back and unhooked my bra, allowing the cups to fall away from my firm breasts. Don smiled as he focused on my erect nipples rising from the darkening discs of my areolae. I was only eighteen and I had a good figure. Would he want more than photographs? I wondered as I slipped my panties down my long legs. He gazed at the sparse black hairs veiling my pussy crack and licked his lips. He believed that we'd had sex in the past. *We met in a bar and then I fucked you senseless in the park.* Was that what he hoped to do again?

'You look great,' he said as I sat on the couch. 'You've lost weight. You look really good.'

'I'm skinny,' I murmured, trying to relax.

'Your tits seem different,' he muttered abstractedly. 'They look smaller and much firmer.'

'Not *too* small, I hope?'

'They're perfect, Ali. OK, lie back with your legs slightly parted.'

Reclining, I parted my thighs a little and smiled as he took several shots. Strangely, my embarrassment faded as I parted my thighs wider and exposed the tight crack of my pussy. I was actually enjoying posing naked, but I couldn't think why. I hoped that I was coming out of my shell but I knew in my heart that I was still a prude. I'd never had men after me before. Now I had Rick and Don and ... How many more men would mistake me for another girl? More to the point, where would it all lead?

I thought that it would be fun to play the role of my twin sister the next time I went to the pub. I could be more sexual, open-minded and ... and sluttish? This was an opportunity, I decided. This was an opportunity to play the role of a slut and have some fun. I'd be Ali the prude by day and Ali the slut at night. The notion excited me. When I was Ali the slut, I could tell people about my prudish sister. When I was Ali the innocent, I could slag off my sluttish sister.

Feeling more confident now, I followed Don's instructions and opened my thighs wide. He took more photographs and, since I was Ali the slut, I parted my pussy lips for him and exposed my vaginal hole. He grinned and praised me, saying that now I was the dirty Ali he knew and loved. He took the camera off the tripod and knelt between my feet to take some close-up shots of my yawning pussy. My stomach somersaulted and I felt my clitoris swell and my juices flow as my libido heightened. This wasn't me at all, but I was gripped by excitement and arousal.

'That's more like it,' Don said, with a chuckle. 'I don't know what happened to you earlier but you're back to normal now. We're going to make a fortune, Ali.'

'I hope so,' I said, smiling at him as he took a close-up photo of my erect clitoris.

He finally placed the camera back on the tripod and knelt again before me. 'What happened to you earlier?' he asked me. 'Surely you didn't really lose your memory?'

'I was playing about,' I replied. 'I do have a twin sister and I've been having fun with some friends, making out that I'm her.'

'I assume she's nothing like you, then? Apart from your looks, I mean.'

'We're identical twins but she's a prude.'

'Fuck me, Ali. You had me going earlier. I really thought you'd lost the plot.'

'Sorry about that – I was just having a laugh. My sister went into the pub the other evening and a friend of mine thought she was me. Apparently, he asked her whether she still shaved her pussy and she was shocked.'

'I'll bet she was. Actually, that's an idea. Why don't you shave your pussy for the next photo shoot? The website punters will love it.'

'OK,' I said, my excitement rising as I imagined posing with my bald pussy on show. 'Right, I'd better be going. I have things to do this evening.'

'No quick fuck, then?' Don asked.

'Well, I . . .'

He parted my knees, moved forward and kissed the swollen lips of my pussy. It had been so long since I'd had sex, but I didn't want to go with a man I'd only just met. The feel of his wet tongue running up and down my crack sent quivers through my young womb and I thought again of the other Ali. What would *she* have done? I wondered. I knew very well what she'd have done, so I opened my legs wide and gave Don better access to the most private part of my teenage body.

If I was to embark on a game of playing the role of my twin sister, then I had to behave like her. Although I'd never met her and knew nothing about her, I did know that she was a slut. The game might be dangerous, I mused as Don parted my fleshy vaginal lips and licked the sensitive tip of my erect clitoris. Dangerous – but extremely exciting. As Don sucked my clitoris into his hot mouth and drove a finger deep into my contracting vagina, I felt my heart race and my hands tremble. It had been so long since I'd been loved, I reflected again. But I knew that this wasn't love. This was cold sex for the sake of sex.

'You taste as good as ever,' Don murmured. 'I'd like to meet your sister and give her a good licking.'

'There's no way she'd let you do that,' I said. 'She's never taken her knickers off for a man.'

'I'd still like to meet her, Ali.'

'Maybe I'll arrange something.'

19

His tongue delved deep into my contracting vagina and I thought it might be fun if Don met Ali the prude. But I was losing sight of my quest. Playing games would be entertaining, but first I had to meet the other Ali. I'd ask my mother about her, I decided, closing my eyes as my clitoris pulsated and my juices squelched with the beautiful fingering of my tight vagina. I hoped that I was about to experience my first orgasm. To my delight I found that now I was able to relax and let go. That was the answer, I thought as Don slid a second finger into my yearning vagina. Playing the role of my twin, I realised that I could loosen up and allow my pleasure to come.

Don slipped his fingers out of my pussy and, before I knew what was happening, he had thrust his solid penis deep into my hot sheath. I gasped, opening my eyes to stare at his veined shaft as he withdrew and thrust into me again. What the hell was I doing? I wondered as Don pushed my knees further apart and repeatedly drove his rock-hard shaft deep into my contracting vagina. The game wasn't a good idea, I thought, suddenly panic-stricken: I didn't want a stranger screwing me, I didn't want –

'You're so tight and hot,' Don breathed, his dark eyes shining with lust. 'I'll bet your virgin sister is even tighter. I'd love to force my cock into her snug cunt and fuck her senseless.'

'She'd never allow you,' I murmured. 'Ali would never do that.'

My clitoris was being massaged by his thrusting shaft and I could feel the birth of my orgasm building within my contracting womb. I needed an orgasm, I thought as Don gasped and increased his shafting rhythm. My lower stomach rose and fell as his cock repeatedly thrust into my spasming vagina. My naked body went rigid and I let out a cry as my pioneering climax erupted within my pulsating clitoris. I could feel Don's sperm gushing, flooding my tight vagina as his swinging balls battered the rounded cheeks of my bottom. In the grip of my amazing ecstasy, I shook uncontrollably as my eyes rolled and my pulsating clitoris transmitted wave after wave of pleasure deep into my pelvis.

Never had I experienced such arousal, such immense pleasure, as my naked body rocked with the beautiful thrusting of Don's penis. His sperm overflowed from my quim, splattering my inner thighs, and I thought that I'd never come down from my sexual heaven as my orgasm reached new heights. My vagina rhythmically contracted, sucking the sperm from Don's throbbing knob, and I basked in the pleasure flooding through my teenage body.

My orgasm finally faded and I watched as Don slipped his deflating penis out of my sperm-drenched vagina and sat back on his heels. I gazed at the spunk oozing from my gaping vaginal entrance and realised that I'd behaved like a common whore, a slut. I might only have been playing the role of the other Ali, but I couldn't come to terms with the fact that I'd allowed a virtual stranger to fuck me. I must have been crazy, I thought, leaping to my feet and grabbing my clothes. I dressed hurriedly, just wanting to go home and forget the sordid incident.

'How about tomorrow?' Don asked me. 'About the same time?'

'No,' I answered, moving to the door. 'I'm . . . I'm busy tomorrow.'

'OK – give me a ring when you're free.'

'Yes, yes I will.'

I went through the hall, left the house, and breathed in the warm evening air as I walked home. I could feel Don's sperm oozing from my inflamed vagina and filling the crotch of my panties, a stark reminder of the crude act that I'd committed. The game was ridiculous, I decided as I reached my house. I didn't want to know who the other Ali was – I had no interest in her. And I certainly wasn't going to play the role of my sluttish twin sister again.

Two

Swamped with guilt and shame as I sat at the breakfast table the following morning, I still couldn't believe what I'd done. I'd stripped naked and let a man take photographs of my young body and close-up shots of my open pussy. And then I'd allowed him to fuck me. I'd played the role of my twin sister admirably, but I didn't want to be like her. I began to wonder whether I really did have a twin and, as my mother placed a plate of toast on the table, I asked her about it.

'Not as far as I know,' she replied as she sat opposite me. 'Why do you ask?'

'I told you about that man in the paper shop, the one who knew my name. Well, since then two other men have chatted to me as if I'm an old friend. They both knew my name and ...'

'They must have seen you working in the DIY store,' she proffered.

'That's what Jackie said, but one of the men reckoned that he'd never been to the store. Besides, they knew things about me.'

'There was no mention of a twin when we adopted you, Ali. I suppose it's possible, but ... A twin with the same name living in the same town? I don't think so.'

'Neither do I,' I said. 'So who are these people?'

23

'Did you ask them about it? A few simple questions should clear it up, surely?'

'Yes, I did ask one of them. He even showed me photographs of this other girl. She looks identical to me.'

'They do say that we all have a double.'

'A double with the same name, living in the same town?'

'There's a very easy way to get to the bottom of this, Ali.'

'How?'

'Meet this other girl. If these people know her, get them to arrange a meeting.'

'She seems to be elusive. The man with the photographs doesn't know where she lives, he doesn't have her phone number or —'

'Give him your phone number and, the next time he sees her, he can ask her to ring you.'

'That's a good idea, and it would have worked if I hadn't . . .'

'Hadn't what?'

'I pretended to be the other girl. I know it was silly, but . . . Oh, I don't know.'

'What's she like? Did he tell you anything about her?'

'She's a . . . she's just a normal girl.'

'I'd be honest with this man and ask him to give her your phone number.'

'Yes, maybe I will.'

After a long day at the store, I decided to go to the pub and try to discover more about the other Ali. I might even bump into her, I mused, as I dressed in a miniskirt and a revealing top. Although I'd vowed not to play the game again, I couldn't help myself. The excitement, the danger, the intrigue . . . The sex? Just one more time, I thought as I went into the pub and walked up to the bar. I'd pretend to be the other Ali just one more time.

'Hi,' Rick said, joining me at the bar as I ordered a drink. 'Are you going to pretend that you don't know me, or –'

'Of course I know you,' I cut in. 'What are you talking about?'

'You denied all knowledge of me the last time we met, Ali.'

'Ah, so you've met my sister?' I said, with a giggle.

'Your sister?'

'My twin sister. I heard that she'd been in here.'

'You said that you ... I mean, she said that she didn't have a sister.'

'We were split up at birth and both of us were adopted. We didn't know about each other until recently.'

'Ah, that explains everything.' Rick looked down at my cleavage and grinned. 'I asked her whether she still shaves her pussy,' he said, chuckling.

'I'll bet that went down well. She's a right prude.'

'So I gathered. How come you both have the same name?'

'I have no idea. You'd have to ask my biological mother, whoever she is.'

'You're identical,' he murmured. 'It's incredible.'

'Identical twins *are* identical, Rick. Or didn't you realise that?'

'Yes, no, I mean ... I've never met identical twins before.'

'Well, you have now. Has anyone else been in this evening? Anyone I know?'

'No, but John said that he might be in later. Is he still pestering you for sex?'

'Er ... yes, yes, he is.'

'So, your twin sister. How did you meet up with her?'

'She tracked me down. We've met up a few times and we're getting to know each other.'

'I hope you haven't said too much about yourself.'

'Such as?'

'Well, I don't think it a good idea to tell her that you have sex with other girls. She wouldn't want to discover that her sister is a lesbian.'

'A lesbian?' I gasped, staring at him.

'Unless she's a lesbian herself,' he said, chortling wickedly. 'You two could get together. Incestuous dykes – now there's a thought.'

'Don't be disgusting,' I said, grinning at him.

'You know how much you love licking Amy's pussy. Why not lick your sister's?'

'Rick, you get worse,' I said softly, sipping my drink.

The revelation had shocked me, but I dared not show even a glimmer of surprise. It had also made me even more determined to meet the infamous Ali. But I was going to have to be careful. If Amy, her lesbian lover, came into the pub . . . Thinking again that the game wasn't a good idea, I imagined another girl kissing me and wanting to have sex with me. Never in a million years would I have had sex with another girl. I was sure that I'd be caught out at some stage. If the other Ali walked into the pub . . . She was bound to hear about me before long, I thought anxiously. If Rick met her, then he'd talk about her twin sister. But if she really was my twin, then I wanted to meet her.

'I would take you back to my place for a good spanking and a fuck,' Rick said. 'But I have to go soon.'

'You men are all the same,' I said.

'And you love it.'

'Have you seen Rod recently?' I asked him, recalling the man in the paper shop.

'Rod?'

'Rod Davis.'

'Never heard of him.'

'Oh, I thought you'd met him. He's a friend of mine.'

'A *fuck* of yours, you mean. Talking of which, why don't you give John what he wants? You know the situation with his wife. He could do with a bit of fun on the side.'

'Maybe I will,' I replied, wondering who the hell John was.

'As I said, he should be in later. I know that he's an old man, but he fancies you rotten.'

'Yes, well . . .'

'Right, I'd better get going. I'll see you around. Or your sister, of course.'

'OK, Rick, I'll see you soon.'

Rick finished his beer and left the pub, and left me wondering what the hell I was playing at. The problem was that the other Ali would realise that I'd been making out that I was her. She was bound to speak to Don, and he'd talk about the photo shoot and I'd be exposed as a fraud. There again, I had tried to tell Don that I wasn't the girl he'd thought me to be. I could feel a mess brewing but, after thinking about it, I decided it wasn't my fault that people had mistaken me for someone else.

I ordered another gin and tonic and returned to my musings. I knew that I couldn't give up playing the game. It was fun and it had been very enlightening – not to mention the money I'd made. I decided to sort out a set of clothes for Ali the slut. I'd buy her some new outfits: very short skirts and revealing tops that only she would wear. Ali the innocent would wear

27

longer skirts and conceal her cleavage with decent tops. The more I thought about playing the role of the other Ali, the more excited I became.

'Hi, Ali,' a man in his sixties said, joining me at the bar.

Hoping that it was John, I smiled. 'Hi, John,' I said. 'How are things?'

'Same as usual,' he sighed. 'You look stunning, as always.'

'I know what you're thinking, John,' I said, wondering how a girl of my age could go with a man in his sixties.

'I'm thinking how nice it would be to get my hands inside your knickers,' he replied, chuckling.

'How's your wife?' I asked him, hoping I wasn't putting my foot in it.

'No change, I'm afraid. They reckon that she won't come out of the home.'

'Oh, that *is* bad news.'

'So, I'm a single man with a nice bungalow – and a cock longing for a tight little teenage pussy.'

'You're not going to give up, are you?'

'I'll never give up, Ali. I know how free you are with your body and how much you like sex. But what I don't understand is, why not have a little fun with me? I might be old, but I can still fuck.'

'I'll think about it,' I murmured, wondering what else to say.

'Let me get you another drink. What is it?'

'Gin and tonic, please.'

I did feel sorry for him, and he looked good for his age, but I couldn't have sex with a man older than my father. It seemed that even the other Ali wasn't keen, so I decided just to chat with him and, hopefully, discover more about my twin sister. I sipped my drink as he ordered a beer. How dull my life had been before

I'd been mistaken for Ali the slut, I mused. Working at the DIY store, going to university, staying at home and rarely going out ... Things were changing. But were they changing for the better?

'I haven't seen you for a while,' John said. 'What have you been up to?'

'I've got a twin sister,' I announced proudly. 'We were separated at birth when we were adopted and we've just met up after all these years.'

'Really? I'll have to meet her.'

'She's been in here once or twice. We're identical twins so you won't be able to tell us apart.'

'With identical pussies?' he asked, laughing and winking at me.

'Presumably,' I said. 'I've never seen her pussy so I wouldn't know for sure. By the way, if you meet up with her, I should warn you that she's a prude. I thought I'd better mention that in case you try to get your hand inside her knickers.'

'What's her name?'

'Ali, same as me.'

'That's odd, isn't it?'

'Yes, but it wasn't my doing. So, who have you seen recently? Anyone I know?'

'I saw Barry the other day.'

'Oh, how is he?'

'He wants to get back with you, as you know. It was a shame you two split up.'

'Yes, yes – it was a shame.'

'Ali, would you like to come back to my place for a drink?'

'Well, I ... I don't know, John.'

'It's only a five-minute walk. It's just that ... I'm lonely, Ali.'

'All right,' I said, smiling at him. 'But only for a drink, OK?'

'OK.'

Finishing my drink, I thought it might be a good idea to leave in case the other Ali arrived. I also wanted to learn more from John. He seemed like a nice enough man, and I was sure that I'd be safe with him. We left the pub and walked the short distance to his bungalow. What I really wanted to know was where the other Ali lived. Someone must know her address or phone number, I thought. John opened the front door of his home and led me through the hall to the lounge.

Looking around the room at the expensive furniture, I realised that John had money. He poured me a large gin and tonic and went into the kitchen for some ice as I made myself comfortable on the huge Chesterfield sofa. It must be nice to have money, I reflected. I'd made two hundred pounds, but that was a one-off. My prospects were pretty grim. After university, I'd be working as a nurse. I didn't want to go into nursing, but I had no idea what else to do.

'Thanks for coming back with me,' John said, passing me my drink. 'I get so lonely here sometimes.'

'That's OK,' I said, smiling at him. 'I wish I had a nice home like this.'

'Your place was nice enough. Have you moved into another flat yet?'

'Er . . . no, not yet. I'm still staying with a friend. So, you liked my old place?'

'I know it wasn't the best of areas, above that shop in the high street, but it was very nice.'

I was learning something, I realised. But I had to be careful not to say the wrong thing. 'The flat was OK, but the shop was . . . Did you ever go into the shop?'

'No, I didn't. Why do you ask?'

I had to find out which shop it was. 'I just wondered whether you'd met the people there,' I persisted.

'I'm not into women's clothing,' he said, with a chuckle.

Now I knew where Ali's old flat was, I hoped to be able to find out where she'd moved to. The people in the shop might have a forwarding address, I thought, as John eyed my naked thighs. If I could track her down and . . . and what? She probably had no idea that she was a twin. Besides, she might not want to know. She might be happy with her life and not want the past dragged up. She might not even know that she was adopted.

'Ali,' John said softly. 'Is there any chance that we might . . . What I mean is . . . Do you need money?'

'I always need money, John.'

'As you know, I'm pretty well off financially. How about . . . If I gave you fifty pounds, would you . . .'

'Would I what? Give you a wank?'

'Yes.'

I could hardly believe what I'd said. John grinned at me. I wasn't a whore, I reminded myself. There again, if I was playing the role of Ali the slut . . . But how far was I prepared to go? Fifty pounds, I mused. If I did wank him, he'd probably want me to call round again. I might even make fifty pounds every week. If he only wanted me to wank him, then it would be easy money.

'What were you thinking?' he asked me. 'You were miles away.'

'I was thinking that I'm not a prostitute,' I said.

'Don't look at it like that, Ali.'

'That's what it is, isn't it? It's prostitution.'

'It's just helping out an old man. You could do with a boost to your income. Where do you work, by the way?'

'I . . . I'm not working at the moment.'

'There you are, then. You could come round on a regular basis and –'

'How regular?' I cut in.

'That's up to you. Two or three times a week would suit me.'

'All right,' I said, wondering what the hell I was getting into.

As John unbuckled his belt and lowered his trousers, I felt my heart race and my hands tremble. Wank an old man for fifty pounds? God, I must have been mad, I reflected as he stood before me with his erect penis hovering only inches from my face. I'd only just met him – and he was older than my father. Wrapping my fingers around the solid shaft of his huge penis, I imagined giving up my part-time job at the store. I was Ali the slut, I mused as I cupped his heavy balls in my free hand. This was how Ali the slut would earn money.

John said nothing as I ran my hand up and down his hard shaft and fondled his full balls. This might have been easy money, but worrying thoughts flooded my mind as I wanked him. What would my mother say if she discovered that I was a prostitute? What would Jackie say? How much further would John want me to go? Would he want full sex in return for his cash? Trying not to think about prostitution, I watched his purple glans appear and disappear as I stroked and pulled his rock-hard penis. Where would his sperm go? I wondered as he breathed heavily. All over my blouse and skirt?

'It's been so long,' John gasped, jutting his hips forward. 'I've wanted to ask you to do this for weeks but –'

'You like it?' I asked, my own arousal heightening as I waited in expectation for his sperm to jet from his swollen knob.

'God, yes. Make it last, Ali. I don't want to come yet.'

Slowing my wanking rhythm, I kneaded John's balls and tickled his scrotum as I imagined calling round to his bungalow three times each week and earning fifty pounds. I realised again what a dull life I'd led as I squeezed his hard shaft in my hand. My life was now exciting and profitable and . . . But this *wasn't* my life. This was the life that Ali the slut led. I was really getting into playing the role of my twin sister. I felt as if I could do anything, get away with anything, and it had nothing to do with me.

John gasped as his sperm shot out of his throbbing knob and splattered my blouse. I wanked him faster and watched his male liquid jetting from the tiny slit of his glans, but it wasn't only my outer clothing that was getting wet. My knickers were soaking up my pussy juice, and I knew that my arousal was running high. This was a business arrangement, I thought as my clitoris swelled. I couldn't go any further with John, with a man older than my father. No matter how much money he offered me, I couldn't . . .

'That was amazing,' he breathed as his sperm-flow stemmed. 'God, I needed that.'

'I need a tissue,' I said, watching his creamy spunk running down the front of my blouse.

John pulled his trousers up and took a handkerchief from his pocket. 'Use that,' he said. 'That really was amazing, Ali. Thank you so much.'

'You're welcome,' I murmured as I cleaned my blouse.

'There's the money.' He tossed the notes onto the sofa beside me. 'Are you free tomorrow evening?'

'I'm not sure. Give me your phone number and I'll ring you.'

'OK, I'll write it down.'

The whole thing was over so quickly. I don't know what I'd expected but, as John passed me a piece of paper, I decided to go home. Slipping the paper and the cash into my handbag, I finished my drink and stood up. It was only eight o'clock, but I didn't want to hang around. I'd earned some cash and discovered where Ali's old flat was, and it was time to leave. John wanted me to stay, but I told him that I'd see him the following evening at seven.

My parents were out when I got home. I sat in my bedroom feeling bored and frustrated, and I wondered what I was going to do for the rest of the evening. I didn't fancy walking into town and looking at Ali's old flat. Besides, I wouldn't learn anything as the clothes shop would be closed so there was no point. Changing into a knee-length skirt and high-necked blouse, I had an idea. I changed my hairstyle as best I could, washed my make-up off – and decided to go back to the pub as Ali the innocent.

I was hooked on the game, I knew as I neared the pub. My initial interest had turned into an obsession, and I felt a wave of excitement roll through me as I walked up to the bar and ordered a drink. I looked around me but couldn't see anyone I recognised and I began to feel despondent. Don might turn up, I thought as I sipped my drink. What if the other Ali arrived? I'd bump into her at some stage, I was sure of that. I had to remember which Ali I was, I reflected as I sat at a corner table. The last thing I needed was to put my foot in it and ruin the game. My heart jumped into my mouth and I stared wide-eyed at John as he walked into the pub. I hadn't expected him to come back. What the hell was I going to say? I had to remember that I didn't know him. As he walked over to me with his drink, I felt sure that I was going to mess things up.

'Hi again,' John said as he sat down opposite me. 'I thought you'd gone home?'

'I'm sorry,' I said, frowning at him. 'Do I know you?'

'You must be Ali's sister. I was in here earlier with her and –'

'Oh, you're a friend of my sister's,' I cut in, smiling at him. 'It's OK, no one can tell us apart.'

'God, the likeness is incredible.'

'We are identical twins,' I said, chuckling as he stared at me.

'Wow, it's amazing. Anyway, I'm very pleased to meet you. I'm John, by the way.'

'It's nice to meet you, too. I was hoping that my sister would be here.'

'She was here earlier with me. She came back to my place for a drink and then she went home. I came back because . . . well, I live alone and I get pretty bored.'

'Has she told you that we've only just met up?'

'Yes, yes, she did tell me. She's a lovely girl.'

'She's a . . . I mustn't be rude about her. Are you one of her men friends, if you know what I mean?'

'Well, er . . . I suppose so.'

'Tell me all about her. I haven't had the opportunity to have a proper chat with her yet. What she's like, where she's been living and –'

'I don't know a great deal about her,' John said, much to my disappointment. 'She used to live in a flat in town but now she's staying at a friend's place until she finds another apartment. She's quite an elusive girl. She'll be around for a week or two and then disappear for a while.'

'How long have you known her?' I asked him.

'I've known her for a few months. I met her through Barry, a friend of mine. He was her boyfriend and they were living together but then they split up.'

'Why was that?'

'She was always out with other men. Barry's a nice chap. He's good-looking – dark hair, dark eyes, a great sense of humour . . . It was a shame they split up. I shouldn't be talking about her like this, but she is a bit of a . . . well, she's a –'

'A slut? It's all right, I do know that much about her. She said that she's not working at the moment. Has she *ever* worked?'

'I don't know. As I said, she's elusive, she comes and goes. I may not see her for a few weeks, and then she'll be around all the time. She keeps herself to herself. I don't think anyone knows a great deal about her.'

'She has a lot of friends, I suppose?'

'Yes, yes, she has. Apart from Barry, I think Don knows more about her than most. He's a photographer, of sorts, and she's always been well in with him.'

'Has she ever mentioned her parents?'

'No, never. So, where do *you* live?'

'I . . . I'm staying with friends at the moment. I haven't seen much of Ali because . . . well, I've only just moved down here and, like you said, she's looking for a flat. We haven't had any time together properly.'

'I'm really pleased that we've met. Your hair is slightly different and you don't wear make-up, but the likeness is amazing. I've never known identical twins before.'

'We're identical in our looks, but not in our thinking. I don't carry on with men the way she does.'

'She did say that . . . that you weren't like her in that respect. Do you have a boyfriend or –'

'No, no, I'm single. I'm at university, studying nursing. I don't have time for boyfriends.'

'You're a good-looking girl, Ali. You must have all the boys chasing you.'

'No, not really. Could you give me Ali's phone

36

number? She did tell me to write it down but I've lost it.'

'Sorry, but I don't know it. Ali is the sort of girl who doesn't want people calling her. She calls them, if she wants to. Thinking about it, I've never met anyone as elusive as her.'

'You might not see her for a while, then?'

'She's coming to my place tomorrow evening. Just for a drink and . . . and a chat. When are *you* seeing her again?'

'It was supposed to be this evening, but she's obviously got other things to do. Anyway, I'd better be going. It's been nice meeting you, John.'

'Yes, and you. Is there any chance of us meeting again some time? Just for a drink, I mean.'

'Yes, I'd like that. Give me your number and I'll ring you.'

As he wrote his number down, I felt guilty. This was a huge con, and I didn't think that I'd be able to carry on with it. I'd done pretty well so far, but it was a risky game. To make matters worse, I hadn't really learned anything about the other Ali. Don was the man I needed to speak to, but I could hardly turn up at his house as Ali the innocent. I was getting nowhere fast, I thought as John passed me the slip of paper.

'Thanks,' I said, slipping the paper into my hand-bag. 'I'll ring you, OK?'

'It will be nice to get to know you, Ali. You're a lovely girl, and good company.'

'I've enjoyed talking to you, John. I'll ring you and —'

'Guess who's just walked in,' he interrupted.

I followed his gaze and saw a young man heading for the bar. 'I don't know. Is that Barry?'

'It is. Would you like to meet him?'

'Well, yes, I would.'

'I'll go and talk to him, I'll tell him that you're Ali's twin. Would you like another drink?'

'Yes, please. Gin . . . *vodka* and tonic, please.'

Watching John join the man at the bar, I felt that I was plunging deeper into a mess that I wouldn't be able to get out of. Barry looked at me and frowned, and I half smiled. This was very awkward, I thought as I finished my drink. If the real Ali walked in . . . But I was Ali the innocent, I reminded myself. If my twin sister arrived, things would be fine. We'd meet and talk and get to know each other and everything would be OK. I took a deep breath as Barry brought my drink over to my table. This was it, I thought apprehensively as he passed me my drink.

'Hi,' he said as he sat down opposite me. 'I'm Barry. John tells me you're Ali's twin sister.'

'That's right. I'm pleased to meet you.'

'God, you look identical. Ali never mentioned a sister.'

'We were parted at birth. Have you met her parents?'

'No, I haven't. So, were you adopted?'

'Yes, I was.'

'Presumably Ali was adopted too. This is amazing.'

'I've only just met her after all these years.'

'There *are* differences,' he said, studying my face.

'I don't think identical twins are necessarily *completely* identical,' I said stupidly. 'Do you have her phone number? Only, I had it but I've lost it and –'

'She changed her mobile phone. I don't have her new number. Aren't you in touch with her, then?'

'Yes, yes, I am. We were supposed to meet here this evening. I just thought I'd call her and see where she's got to.'

'I'm off now,' John said as he approached our table. 'I'll leave you two to chat. Call me tomorrow, Ali.'

'Yes, I will,' I replied.

'See you around,' Barry called as John left. He looked at me and smiled. 'Ali never said that she was adopted.'

'Does she have any other brothers or sisters?'

'No, I don't think so. We lived together for a while, but I never met any of her family. I say that we lived together but she wasn't there half the time. She was always out having fun. Are you free? I mean, no boyfriend or anything?'

'I'm single,' I said, gazing into his dark eyes.

'That's a bit of luck. Do you live locally?'

'I live up north. I'm staying with friends at the moment. I've only come down to meet Ali.'

'Are you *sure* you're identical twins?' Barry asked. 'There are a few differences, like I said.'

'Yes, as far as I know.'

Our conversation was stilted and I thought that Barry seemed to be suspicious as he stared at me. I began to wonder whether the other Ali really was my twin sister. If I hadn't said that I'd met Ali I could have been honest with him. Had he realised that I was lying? I'd asked for Ali's phone number, asked about any other brothers and sisters. He must have thought me rather suspicious. Playing the role of both sisters was confusing, and I thought again that I should stop playing the game. But I was in too deep to turn back now. Besides, I rather liked Barry and wanted to get to know him better. I reminded myself that I was Ali the innocent and changed the subject, hoping to break the ice by asking him what he did for a living.

'I buy and sell on the internet,' he replied. 'I'm an entrepreneur.' He seemed more relaxed as he chuckled. 'I suppose I should say that I *hope* to be an entrepreneur. I make a living, but that's about all. How about you?'

39

'I'm at university studying nursing, but I don't want to be a nurse.'

Barry laughed again. 'That's different,' he said. 'Studying for something that you're not interested in is . . . Why don't you leave uni and do something else? Why not take up modelling? I know a photographer who'd be interested in a good-looking girl like you.'

'Yes, I've met . . . I did meet a photographer once.'

'Ali wanted to get into modelling. I'll put that another way: Ali wanted to get into porn. I haven't seen her for a while. Where's she living now?'

'She's staying with friends, I think.'

'You don't seem to know much about her. You don't have her phone number, you don't know where she lives – hasn't she told you anything?'

'We haven't had a chance to chat very much. She's very difficult to track down.'

'You can say that again. Would you like another drink?'

'No, thanks. I'd better be going soon.'

Barry was obviously suspicious, I thought as he finished his beer. I was supposed to have met up with Ali after all these years, and yet I knew nothing about her. If Barry ever came into the pub when I was playing the role of my twin sister he'd realise immediately that I was a fraud. I'd have to keep my role of Ali the slut well away from the pub, I decided. I'd be the slut at John's house and at Don's studio, but nowhere else.

'I'll walk you home,' Barry said, rising to his feet.

'No, don't worry.'

'Fancy a coffee at my place?' he persisted as we left the pub.

'Well, I suppose . . .'

'It's only around the corner. Come in and I'll show you some photographs of your sister.'

Barry had a nice flat, but I knew that I shouldn't have been there. This was a dangerous game, I thought again as he filled the kettle. He started questioning me again as he made the coffee. When was I going to see Ali? Would I get her phone number for him? Would I give him her address? I tried to change the subject several times but he wouldn't give up. In the lounge he passed me several photographs of the other Ali. The likeness was amazing, and I was sure that she was my twin sister.

'May I keep one of these?' I asked him.

'Keep them all,' he sighed. 'Ali and I split up and I don't really want to be reminded of her.'

'I must remind you of her,' I murmured.

'Yes, of course you do. In fact, you could be her sitting there on my sofa. It's uncanny.'

'Maybe it's not a good idea for me to be here, Barry. Perhaps it would be best if I –'

'No, no – I want you to stay. You see, I'm still in love with Ali. I know that you're her sister, but I feel that I'm in love with you too. I'm sorry, that doesn't make any sense.'

'Yes, it does. I understand what you're saying.'

'I feel as if . . . I feel as if I should be next to you on the sofa. We should be kissing, loving and –'

'Barry, we've never met before.'

'I realise that, Ali. It just seems so strange with you sitting there the way your sister used to.'

'Sit next to me, if you want to,' I said softly, wondering as I uttered the words what the hell I was playing at.

He joined me on the sofa, held my head and kissed my full lips. I felt my stomach somersault as he slipped his hand up my skirt and pressed his fingertips into the swell of my Venus mound beneath my tight knickers. This wasn't what I'd expected or wanted, but I

41

couldn't push him away, I had no will-power to stop him. His fingers pulled the edge of my knickers aside and he massaged my swollen pussy lips as he slipped his tongue into my mouth. I breathed heavily through my nose, my heart racing, my young body trembling, as he drove a finger deep into my contracting vagina. What the hell was I getting myself into? I wondered apprehensively. I should never have gone back to the pub. I should have gone home and . . . I should never have played silly games.

Barry slid off the sofa, kissed my naked thighs and pulled my knickers down. I wanted to stop him as he slipped the scrap of cloth off over my feet and parted my legs wide. Before I'd had time to think straight he was kissing the fleshy lips of my pussy and licking my wetting sex valley. I let out a rush of breath as he repeatedly licked the sensitive tip of my erect clitoris, but I wasn't relaxed. This was a stranger, I thought as he thrust two fingers into my tight vagina. How could I relax and enjoy his intimate attention?

Don had taken photographs of my open pussy and he'd fucked me, I'd wanked John in exchange for cash, and now I was allowing Barry to lick and finger my pussy. My life was taking a new direction – and I wasn't sure that I liked it. I liked the money and the attention, but – oh, I didn't know *what* I wanted as Barry's fingers slipped out of my wet hole and he drove his tongue deep into my tightening vagina. I could hear him slurping, sucking out my juices and swallowing hard. I didn't want this, I thought again. I didn't want this, but my arousal was reaching frightening heights.

As Barry sucked again on my solid clitoris and fingered my contracting vagina, my orgasm came like an explosion and rocked my young body. My eyes rolling, my heart banging hard against my chest, I shook uncontrollably as my clitoris pulsated and pumped waves of pure sexual pleasure throughout my body. I knew that he was going to fuck me as he sustained my amazing orgasm. I knew that, once my orgasm had faded, he'd drive his hard penis deep into my young pussy and fuck me hard. Was that what I wanted? I wondered as my orgasm peaked. Ali the innocent wasn't supposed to get herself fucked, I reflected. What the hell was I doing?

My eyes closing, I quivered as he withdrew his fingers and thrust his solid penis deep into my young body. My vaginal muscles hugged his huge shaft and I gasped as his swollen knob pressed hard against my cervix. I'd fucked Don, I'd wanked John, and now I was fucking Barry. I hardly knew these men, I thought as Barry repeatedly rammed his rock-hard penis deep into my contracting vagina. What the hell would my mother say if she discovered the shocking truth about her sweet little daughter?

'You're bloody tight,' Barry gasped. 'Much tighter than your sister.'

Again and again he rammed his huge penis deep into my trembling body. Then his sperm gushed into me, lubricating our coupling, and he threw his head back and let out a low moan of pleasure. I could feel his swinging balls battering the rounded cheeks of my bottom as he made his final thrusts into my sperm-flooded vagina – I couldn't believe that I was being fucked by yet another man I hardly knew. My orgasm receded and I could feel his male cream running down to the tight ring of my anus as he withdrew his semi-erect cock and sat back on his heels. What the hell had I done? I asked myself as he grinned down at me.

'You were amazing,' Barry said, watching his sperm oozing from my gaping vaginal entrance.

I closed my legs and smiled at him. 'So were you,' I said quietly. 'I'd better be going now.'

'I'll see you again, I hope?'

'Yes, yes, you will.' I grabbed my knickers from the floor, slipped them on and adjusted my skirt. 'I'll ring you, if you like?'

'Here's my phone number.' He leaped to his feet and pulled his trousers up. 'And my card,' he said. 'Barry the entrepreneur.'

'Thanks.'

Barry escorted me to the door, spun me round on my heels and kissed me. I finally pulled away and left his flat. My quest to track down my twin sister was going terribly wrong, my life was changing direction . . . I didn't know what I wanted or what I was going to do. At least no one knew my phone number or my address, I thought as I walked home. I could feel Barry's sperm filling the crotch of my knickers. A stark reminder of what I'd done, I reflected as I reached my house.

Three

I rang the DIY store the following morning and said that I had a family crisis and wouldn't be going back to work. I thought it best not to tell my mother that I'd left the store because she'd start asking questions, and I could hardly tell her about my new job at John's house. Prostitute: the word loomed in my mind as I hid the money I'd earned behind my wardrobe. Prostitute, slut, whore . . .

I went shopping and bought some new clothes for the slut. A microskirt, a few thongs, stockings, a suspender belt . . . I tried them on in my bedroom and I was amazed by the transformation. I looked like a right little tart. I'd never worn stockings before, but I quite liked the feel of them against my skin. The thong barely covered my pussy and I reckoned that I should have bought a larger one.

As the evening approached I felt confused. I didn't know what I was going to do. I'd given up my job so I had to visit John regularly. But what was I going to do about Barry? Should I go to John's place and wank him off and then go round to Barry's flat and have sex with him? No, I couldn't bring myself to do that. This situation was ridiculous. John knew me as Ali the slut who wanked him for cash, he also knew me as my true self. Then there was Barry and Don and . . . This was quickly becoming a mess.

As I closed my bedroom door and went downstairs I knew that my visit to John's bungalow was going to be easy. I was Ali the slut and no one else would be there to confuse things. My mother frowned at my short skirt and make-up as I left the house, but she didn't say anything. Was she suspicious? I wondered. Had she guessed that her young daughter was a prostitute? As I walked along the street I felt like a whore – I certainly looked like one. Men stared at me and one shouted something from his car as he drove by.

'You look stunning,' John said as he opened his front door and invited me in. 'You look like –'

'A slut?' I cut in, with a giggle.

'Well, no, I didn't mean . . .'

'I *am* a slut, John. You know it, and I know it.'

'Yes, well . . . Would you like a drink? Gin and tonic, isn't it?'

'Yes, thanks.'

'I saw your sister last night.'

'Oh? Where was that?'

'After you left I went back to the pub. We had quite a chat.'

'I'll bet she slagged me off.'

'No, not at all. She's a lovely girl, Ali. Nothing like you, of course.'

'Are you saying that I'm not lovely?'

'You're gorgeous, Ali. So, are you going to do a strip for me?'

'John, the deal was that I should wank you off for fifty pounds.'

'I know, but I'd like to take a look at your sweet pussy.'

'It'll cost you more.'

'How much more? Hang on, last night you said that

you weren't a prostitute. To hear you talking now anyone would think –'

'I'm not a prostitute,' I interrupted him. 'I'm a sexy teenage girl doing you a favour. And you're paying me. One hundred, and you can have my body for half an hour.'

'It's a deal,' he said eagerly.

I knew that I must have been mad as John stood in front of me, reached out and unbuttoned my blouse, but there was no denying that the money was excellent. Apart from the cash, I was really getting into the role of Ali the slut. It was exciting, profitable – and incredibly arousing. Perhaps I wasn't mad after all, I mused as John lifted my bra clear of my firm breasts and encircled my erect nipples with his fingertip. Leading two separate lives was giving me the opportunity to discover my sexuality, my darker side, and yet was also allowing me the safety of playing myself, Ali the innocent.

As John leaned forward and sucked on each sensitive nipple in turn, I thought it was a shame that the other Ali existed. She was bound to appear at some stage and spoil my game. Had I dreamed up the fake existence of a twin sister I could have played both roles without having to worry about the real slut turning up at the pub. But I was safe enough at John's place, safe enough earning money in return for sexual favours.

'You have beautiful tits,' he breathed, kneeling in front of me. 'But it's your teenage pussy I want to look at.'

'Help yourself,' I said as he tugged my short skirt down and gazed at my thong.

'Have you shaved?'

'No, I haven't. You like shaved pussies, then?'

'Yes, very much.'

Yanking my thong down, John stared wide-eyed at the swollen lips of my pussy rising either side of my deep sex crack. I wasn't mad at all, I reflected, as he slipped his tongue into my wet valley. I needed money and a little excitement in my mundane life, and I was simply being resourceful. Looking down at his grey hair, I realised that his age didn't bother me any more. He was older than my father, but that didn't matter. As he murmured his crude words, my arousal soared and my juices flowed. *Firm lips, tight little cunt, wet hole* ... If only Jackie could see me now, I thought happily as John's tongue entered my snug and very moist vagina. But this was my secret life. She'd never know what I got up to in the guise of Ali the slut.

Moving behind me, John parted the rounded cheeks of my firm buttocks and licked my tight anal hole. No one had ever licked me there before. I was learning, discovering new pleasures, and I realised again what a prude I'd been. His tongue entered my hot rectum and teased my inner flesh as he simultaneously thrust two fingers deep into my dripping vagina. I felt dizzy with desire, with lust, and clung to his head as my legs trembled. Never had I known such amazing sensations as he pushed his tongue further into my fiery anus, and I knew that this was only the beginning of a rewarding relationship.

My body was alive with sex, my juices of lust were flowing, my clitoris was as hard as rock ... I felt like a naughty little girl with her knickers down as John moved his fingers in and out of my drenched quim and tongued my anal hole. This was another world, I thought as my heart banged hard against my chest and my pussy milk flowed down my inner thighs. A world far removed from university, the DIY store, Ali the prude ... This was a new and exciting world of sex and prostitution, and I was beginning to love it.

'Twenty minutes left,' John said, rising to his feet and slipping out of his trousers. Sitting on the sofa with his legs apart and his erect penis pointing to the ceiling, he grinned. 'Suck it,' he ordered me. 'I want to fuck your pretty little mouth.'

Kneeling between his feet, I gazed at the shaft of his solid penis, his rolling balls and his purple knob. I'd never sucked a man before. Ali the prude would never have committed such a crude act. But now I was Ali the slut and I knew that I had no choice. Leaning forward, I tentatively licked the silky-smooth surface of John's huge knob and tasted his salt. He gasped, his body twitching as I repeatedly ran my wet tongue over his bulging globe.

Clutching tufts of my long blonde hair, he rammed his knob deep into my mouth. I breathed heavily through my nose, my eyes wide as he rocked his hips and repeatedly drove his swollen cock-head to the back of my throat. Another first, I thought as he mumbled something again about fucking my beautiful mouth. I fondled his heaving balls, wondering whether he was going to pump his sperm down my throat or save it for my vagina. I'd never tasted sperm – the idea had always repulsed me – but now?

John once more muttered crude words as I gobbled on his thrusting penis. *Suck it, mouth fuck, cum-slut, swallow it . . .* His spunk jetted from his throbbing knob and filled my cheeks. I swallowed hard, gulping down his fresh cream as he gripped my head and pummelled the back of my throat with his swollen glans. My first taste of sperm, I mused as my mouth overflowed and the male fluid dribbled down my chin. Having sucked the last of his offering from his deflating knob, I finally slipped his cock out of my mouth as he released my head.

'Amazing,' he said softly. 'I've always wanted to fuck your mouth, Ali. And now I've done it.'

49

'I'm glad you enjoyed it,' I said, smiling at John as I stood before him. 'Now that you're happy, I'll take the money and –'

'I haven't finished yet,' he cut in, running his hand up and down his sperm-drenched penis. 'I haven't fucked your sweet little teenage cunt yet. Get down on all fours on the floor and I'll give you the fucking of your young life.'

Taking up my position, I was amazed to think that John could manage another erection. I'd always believed old men to be near-impotent, but I was obviously wrong. His knob slipped between my splayed inner lips and his rigid shaft entered me. I gasped as he grabbed my hips and rammed his fleshy rod fully home. The taste of sperm lingered on my tongue as my young body rocked back and forth and I rested my head on the floor as John repeatedly battered my cervix with his bulbous knob. I could feel his swinging balls meeting the rise of my mons as he fucked me, his wet shaft massaging my erect clitoris, and I knew that I'd soon be writhing in the grip of my second orgasm of the evening.

Wondering how many orgasms I could achieve as the squelching sound of my vaginal juices resounded around the room, I recalled Jackie talking about her vibrator. I'd only masturbated on a few occasions, and I'd never been able to reach a climax. Thinking that I might buy a vibrator of my own, I imagined lying in my bed at night enjoying one orgasm after another. John uttered more crude words as I pictured myself beneath my quilt with the soft buzzing sound of the vibrator filling my ears and my clitoris pulsating in orgasm. *Filthy whore, dirty little slut, cock-loving bitch . . .*

His words heightened my arousal and I knew that I was plunging deeper into the pit of depravity. I *was* a filthy whore, a dirty little slut, and the notion excited me beyond belief. I was eighteen years old with a good body, and yet I'd always been such a prude. I'd never really given sex a great deal of thought. Some of the girls at the university had talked and giggled about blow jobs and spunk and orgasms, and I'd thought they *were* sluts. They *were* sluts, I concluded. And so was I.

John let out a moan of pleasure as his sperm gushed from his huge knob and flooded my rhythmically contracting vaginal canal. I could feel his cream overflowing and running down my inner thighs, and I wondered again what Jackie would think if she witnessed my crude act with an old man. But I'd make sure that no one would ever discover the shocking truth. As far as John was concerned, even Ali the prude would know nothing about her sister's wanton whoredom.

My second orgasm erupted as John's thrusting penis massaged the sensitive tip of my pulsating clitoris. I shook uncontrollably and let out a cry of pleasure. A cocktail of sperm and vaginal milk streamed down my inner thighs as I writhed on the floor and listened to John's utterances about my tight little cunt. *Schoolgirlie cunt, wet cunt, hot little cunt . . .* I'd always hated the crude word but now it sent my arousal rocketing and intensified my amazing orgasm.

'You've got big cunt lips,' John breathed as he slowed his thrusting rhythm. 'Puffy, swollen . . . I want you to shave them, Ali.'

'Maybe I will,' I gasped as my orgasm receded.

'You're a damned good fuck, Ali. Worth every penny.'

'Your time's up,' I said as he yanked his deflating penis out of my inflamed vagina.

'But I haven't fucked your tight little arsehole. I want to fuck your –'

'You couldn't manage a third time,' I interrupted, giggling as I clambered to my feet and gazed at his limp penis. 'Besides, I don't want you up my bum.'

'I'll do your bum next time.'

'No, you won't. There are limits, John. I may be a slut, but I'm not a complete and utter whore.'

'Yes, you are.' He rose to his feet and laughed. 'I'll do your bum next time, I can promise you that. You're my complete and utter whore.'

'Don't you go telling my sister about me,' I said as I got dressed. 'She knows that I'm a slut, but she doesn't know I take money from dirty old men.'

'Less of the old,' John quipped, pulling his trousers on. 'I like you, Ali. We get on really well together.'

'You like my cunt, you mean?'

'Yes, of course I do. But I also like you as a person.'

'Don't be silly.' Fully dressed, I sat on the sofa. 'Go and get me a large gin and tonic,' I ordered him. 'I could do with a drink.'

'I thought you were a vodka and tonic girl? Your sister drinks gin, doesn't she?'

'Er . . . yes, yes, I know. I fancy a change, that's all.'

I was going to have to be more careful, I thought as he went out to the kitchen. Little slips like that could give the game away. The prude drinks gin, the slut drinks vodka, I reminded myself. It occurred to me that John wouldn't worry even if he did discover the truth. All he wanted was a teenage girl to fuck, and I was sure that he didn't care which sister opened her legs for him. As he returned and passed me my drink, I thought how happy he looked. His wife in a home somewhere, old age creeping up on him . . . It was nice to think that I could bring him some pleasure and excitement, even though I was charging him a small fortune.

'I've spunked all over your sofa cushion,' I said, really getting into the role of Ali the slut. Lifting my skirt and showing him my soaked thong, I giggled. 'See? There's spunk pouring out of my cunt.'

'You *are* a dirty little slut,' he replied, his face beaming. 'A dirty little lovable slut.'

'And you're a lovable dirty old man,' I replied as he passed me a wad of notes. 'That'll do nicely,' I said, stuffing the money into my bag. 'But you're not going to fuck my bum-hole.'

'Oh yes I am.' John grinned at me as he popped open a can of beer. 'I'll bet you've got the tightest, hottest little arse in town. And I want my cock rammed deep into it.'

'You are disgusting, John. Talking to an innocent young eighteen-year-old girl like that . . .'

'I'm talking to you, not to your sister. I wonder whether she'll be in the pub tonight? I might go along and see whether she's there.'

'She's seeing friends this evening,' I said, suddenly remembering that I was supposed to be going to Barry's flat as Ali the innocent. 'She's not really the pub type.'

'I have a quest in life,' John announced.

'Oh?'

'My quest is to fuck your sister.'

'You won't get anywhere near her.'

'Want to bet on it?'

'All right, one hundred says you won't even pull her knickers down, let alone fuck her.'

'You're on.'

I liked John, I mused as he sat in the armchair opposite me and sipped his beer. He was fun, good company, a good fuck . . . But he was also a damned sight older than my father. I could never have a long-lasting relationship with any of the men I'd recently met. I imagined introducing John as my boyfriend to my parents. Not a good idea, I thought, downing my drink. But this was only a game. Barry was fucking Ali the innocent, John was fucking Ali the slut . . . Nothing more than a game. No strings, no ties, no love . . . just a game of sex.

I asked John for another drink and decided against going round to Barry's flat. I'd have to change my clothes, change into Ali the prude, and I really couldn't be bothered. Besides, I was quite happy chatting with John and drinking his gin. He asked me whether I was into bondage as he passed me another gin and tonic. Ali the slut would be into anything, I mused. Into anything and everything, as long as she got paid for it. Anything and everything – apart from anal sex.

'You're a naughty old man,' I said.

'And you're a dirty little girl. I feel that I know you so much better now. We've known each other for a while, but you've never let me get anywhere near you. What changed things?'

'Money, John. Money talks.'

'I might have guessed. Tell me, when you do your disappearing act for a few weeks now and then where do you go?'

'Now that would be telling. Let's talk about you, John. Where did you get all your money from?'

'Now *that* would be telling,' he riposted, laughing. 'Mind you, now that you're calling round on a regular basis, I don't think my savings will last very long.'

'But I'm worth it, right?'

'It's not every man of my age who has a beautiful teenage girl calling round for hard sex. Yes, you're worth it.'

I felt good chatting to John and drinking his gin, but I had to work out my future. I was tempted to leave university, especially as I didn't want to become a nurse, but I knew that my parents would go mad. I couldn't let them think that I was still working at the store because they were bound to find out that I'd left. My dad often called in there so I was going to have to say that I'd got another job. I didn't want to lie to my parents, but I had no choice.

John offered me another drink, but I'd had too much already. I said that I was feeling dizzy and I could tell that my words were slurred, but he refilled my glass anyway. We chatted, joked and laughed and, quite apart from the money I'd earned, I felt that I was having a great evening. He poured me another drink, and another, until I was completely off my head. I had no idea what time it was as he knelt on the floor at my feet and pulled my thong off. He spread my legs, ran his tongue up and down my pussy slit and sucked on my clitoris. I quivered, closing my eyes as the room spun round and round and my juices flowed from my open sex hole.

'You'd like me to fuck you again, wouldn't you?' he asked me.

'I think I'd better go home,' I muttered. 'I feel totally pissed.'

'And *I* feel totally hard,' John said, thrusting two fingers deep into my contracting vagina. 'Come on, Ali, you know you can't resist a ruthless fuck.'

My mind reeled and I gasped as he massaged deep inside my wet vagina and licked my erect clitoris. He must have had amazing staying power, I thought as he parted my thighs wide and buried his face between my splayed pussy lips. I writhed on the sofa as my clitoris responded and my juices streamed from my bloated vaginal cavern. After he'd stretched my sex lips wide apart, he slipped his fingers out of my spasming sheath and teased the delicate tissue surrounding my anal sphincter. His fingertip entered my tight hole and I gasped as he drove it deep into my hot rectum.

My clitoris pulsated within his hot mouth as he fingered my bottom-hole and my orgasm erupted and shook my young body to the core. A second finger forced its way into my contracting rectal duct, heightening my amazing pleasure. I whimpered uncontrollably as my head lolled from side to side and my eyes rolled. John was good, I thought in my sexual delirium. He knew exactly how to please a girl.

My orgasm peaked, sending shock waves of pleasure deep into my young womb, and I knew that I was hooked on crude sex. John had not only brought me incredible pleasure, he'd roused something deep within my mind. I realised that I was all girl, that I had something that men wanted, that I could derive fantastic pleasure from my teenage body . . . John had woken sleeping desires. But where was I going in life?

As my orgasm faded, John slipped his fingers out of my bottom-hole and unzipped his trousers. I'd thought that he was going to drive his solid penis deep into my yearning vagina, but instead he pressed his bulbous knob hard against my anal inlet. Dizzy with alcohol, I slurred incoherent words of protest as his knob glided into my rectal duct and finally embedded itself deep within the heat of my bowels. I felt as if I was going to tear open as he withdrew partially and then rammed into me again. My tight anal tissue rolled back and forth along his veined shaft as his knob repeatedly drove deep into my forbidden hole. I felt my clitoris swell and my vaginal milk flow.

Although I'd sworn not to allow John to push his penis into my bottom-hole, I was amazed by the heavenly sensations that the illicit penetration produced. The inflating and deflating of my pelvic cavity as he fucked me anally sent ripples of illicit sex through my young body. Never had I known that I could derive such pleasure from my rectum, and I opened my legs wide to allow his prick to spear deeper into my once private duct.

Again and again his huge penis thrust hard into my hot sphincter, sending my arousal soaring as he gasped and neared his own orgasm. I really was Ali the slut, I thought happily as John's swinging balls battered the rounded cheeks of my naked buttocks. His fingers drove deep into my neglected vagina, massaging my hot and very wet inner flesh, and I closed my eyes as my own climax approached. I shook uncontrollably and then my body became rigid. I could feel John's sperm gushing into my fiery bowels as my clitoris erupted in orgasm against his thrusting fingers.

John lifted my feet high in the air, resting my legs on his shoulders as he fucked my tight bottom-hole and pumped his sperm into my bowels. His cream lubricated our forbidden union, his balls battered my naked buttocks, and he rammed his swollen knob into my rectum again and again. Flopping back and forth like a rag doll, I whimpered and writhed on the sofa in the grip of an orgasm so intense that I thought I'd pass out.

The squelching of sperm resounding around the room, the slapping of flesh meeting flesh filling my ears, I lost myself completely in my breathtaking pleasure. I knew that John would from now on be fucking my bottom every time I went to his house. My mouth, my vagina, my rectal duct . . . He'd be fucking my three holes and filling my young body with spunk every time I called round to see him. And he'd pay me for bringing me amazing pleasure.

'I said that I'd do your arse good and hard,' he breathed, finally slowing his thrusting rhythm. 'I said I'd do it.'

'That was heaven,' I gasped, trying to focus on his beaming face. 'That was absolutely amazing.'

'I suppose you'll want more money now,' he said, chuckling as he slid his deflating penis out of my inflamed anal duct.

'Of course,' I replied.

John sat back on his heels and smiled at me. 'Ali, I don't suppose . . . Would you move in with me?'

'*What?*' I said, thinking that I must have misheard him.

'You're looking for a flat, staying with friends and . . . Live here, with me.'

'No, I . . . I can't,' I stammered. 'As much as I like you, John, I can't live with you.'

'Christ, why ever not?'

'Because . . . God, I don't know, just because.'

'I want you, Ali. All or nothing, that's the way it is.'

'All or nothing? You don't even know who I am, John.'

'Yes, I do.'

'All or nothing of what? All of me?'

'Yes, I want all of you. All of you, or nothing.'

'Bloody hell, John.'

'OK, it was just a thought.'

'Look, I'd better be going.' Leaping to my feet and stuffing my thong into my handbag, I smiled at him. 'When would you like me to call again?' I asked him as I moved to the door. 'Or are you going for nothing now that I've turned down all?'

'Ali, I . . . Tomorrow, if that's OK?'

'Yes, that's OK. Don't worry about giving me more money. I don't want to break the bank.'

'You're wonderful, Ali.'

'I'm a dirty slut, and you know it. I'll see you tomorrow. Bye.'

'Ali, I just want . . . OK, bye.'

I left John's bungalow and wandered down the street with sperm oozing from the inflamed eye of my bottom-hole and coursing down my inner thighs. I felt like a whore as I cut through the park. I'd had my mouth fucked – and my vagina and my rectum – I had a wad of cash in my bag . . . I was a whore, I reminded myself as I sat on a bench watching the evening sun sinking behind the trees. Prostitute, dirty money . . . The park was deserted, peaceful, and I relaxed and thought about my future.

Move in with John? I wondered. There was no way I could do that. He was a lovely man, and he had plenty of money, but my real quest was to meet the other Ali, my twin sister. Mulling over the situation, my role-playing games, I thought that it might be best if I didn't meet her. If she appeared on the scene my games would have to end. There'd be confusion, difficulties. She'd want to meet my mother, she'd want to know who our real mother was and . . . She might not even know that she'd been adopted. It might be best if we never met, I thought again.

Still dizzy with alcohol, I wondered what I was doing sitting in the park with my wet thong in my bag and sperm oozing from my bottom-hole. Was this what I wanted? I had plenty of money, I was meeting new people and having amazing sex but . . . what should I do? I should have been at home. Normally, I'd be in my room studying or watching television with my parents. Now I was sitting in the park, naked beneath my very short skirt with sperm oozing –

'Hi,' a middle-aged man said as he approached me from behind. 'How are you doing?'

'Oh, er . . . hi,' I gasped, spinning round.

'What are you doing here all alone? It's getting dark.'

'Just relaxing,' I replied as he stood in front of me. I reckoned that he was another of Ali's friends as he looked down at my naked thighs. 'I might ask you the same question,' I said.

'I've been to the pub. I'm just on my way home.'

'Oh, right.' Wishing that I knew his name, I thought I'd better play things by ear. 'Were there many people in the pub?' I asked him.

'Only a few regulars. I saw you in the pub the other night. I was going to come over and say hello but you were with some man.'

'I always seem to be with some man or other,' I said, with a giggle.

'There's nothing wrong with that.'

'No, I suppose not. Well, it's getting late. I suppose I'd better be going.'

The man plunged his hand into his trouser pocket. 'This should be enough to make you stay for a while,' he said. He passed me a twenty-pound note and he grinned. 'Is that OK for a quick blow job?'

I stared at the bulge in the crotch of his trousers, wondering how many men the other Ali was playing around with. How well was she known in the area? I'd had no idea that she was a prostitute but she was obviously charging men for sex. This man was about forty and quite good-looking, but . . . He was around the same age as my father. I couldn't suck his penis. I wanted to pass the money back to him and go home. I'd had more than enough sex for one day, but . . . I was getting into the role of Ali the slut and didn't want to ruin the game. Whoever this man was, he knew Ali. He also paid her for sex.

'Isn't it enough?' he asked me.

'It's fine,' I replied, stuffing the money into my handbag.

'I was hoping to see you in the pub this evening,' he said, unzipping his trousers. 'It's a bit of luck bumping into you here. Were you looking for punters?'

'No, I . . . I was about to go home.'

'You can suck my cock and swallow my spunk before you go home.' Hauling out his erect penis, he grinned at me. 'Call it a nightcap.'

I wrapped my fingers around the hard shaft of his penis, pulled his fleshy foreskin back, and gazed at his purple knob. Was he married? I wondered, imagining his wife waiting at home for him. A middle-aged man's cock, I thought, wondering whether my father had ever been to a prostitute. Cock: I'd never liked the word. Cock, fuck, cunt . . . they were words that Ali the slut used.

I moved forward, sucked his purple knob into my wet mouth and breathed heavily through my nose. I'd had far too much gin, I thought as I tasted his salt. The drink had obviously blurred my thinking. What on earth was I doing? I wondered apprehensively. Sucking a stranger's knob in the park – Christ, I must have been mad. But he knew the other Ali, he'd hoped to see her in the pub and . . . If I'd turned him down I'd have ruined my games. Why was I so insistent on playing the game? I knew that it would lead to trouble, but I couldn't help myself.

I wanked his rock-hard shaft and ran my tongue over the velveteen surface of his bulbous knob as he clung to my head and gasped. I was thirsty for sperm, and I waited in anticipation for his cream to flood my gobbling mouth. I was changing beyond belief, I reflected. But this wasn't the real me. This was Ali the slut. Ali the innocent prude would wake up in the morning and chat to her mother over breakfast and . . . and then, at night, she'd turn into Ali the prostitute.

'Here it comes,' the man announced, rocking his hips and fucking my mouth. 'Swallow it all up like a good little whore.'

'Mmm,' I moaned though my nose as his sperm jetted from his throbbing knob. A good little whore. Was that what I was?

'Yes,' he gasped, repeatedly driving his orgasming knob to the back of my throat. 'Suck it hard, you dirty whore.'

I did my best to gulp down his creamy spunk, but my mouth overflowed and his male liquid dribbled down my chin, splattering my blouse and my naked thighs. Swallowing hard, drinking from his swollen knob, I knew that I couldn't kid myself. This was the real me. There was no point in pretending to be anything other than a filthy slut. I was playing the role of my twin sister, but there was no denying that *I* was the one who was sucking sperm out of a stranger's throbbing cock.

'You're good,' the man gasped, finally slipping his penis out of my sperm-flooded mouth. 'You're bloody good.'

'Thank you,' I said, licking my jism-glossed lips and wiping my chin with the back of my hand.

'It really was a bit of luck bumping into you. Have you got a mobile-phone number?'

'Er . . . well, I . . .'

'I'd like to meet you here again, become a regular customer.'

'I'm getting a new phone tomorrow. My old one doesn't work so . . . I'll give you the number when I next see you.'

'OK, that's great. I'm Ian, by the way.'

'Yes, right . . .'

'And you are?'

'I'm Ali,' I replied, suddenly realising that I'd made a big mistake. 'When you mentioned seeing me in the pub . . . I thought you knew me?'

'No, no. I've seen you in the pub a couple of times

62

and reckoned that you were on the game, but we've never met before. Anyway, I'll see you here tomorrow. Is the same time OK with you?'

'Yes, yes,' I sighed abstractedly as Ian walked away.

I wiped his sperm from my thighs – I couldn't believe what I'd just done. He'd never met me before, he'd thought that I was on the game and . . . and I'd taken twenty pounds in return for giving him a blow job. As I walked home, I hoped that my parents weren't still awake. My hair was dishevelled, my blouse was stained with sperm – I looked like a common tart. I couldn't carry on like this, I knew as I opened the front door and crept into the hall. I wouldn't play Ali the slut again, and I'd have to keep away from the pub. The game was over.

I could hear the sound of the television coming from the sitting room so I realised that my parents were still up. There was spunk oozing from my bum, seeping from my pussy, splattered down the front of my blouse . . . Did I smell of sex? I wondered as I crept up the stairs. The lounge door opened and my father looked up at me. He stared at my short skirt, my naked thighs, and frowned.

'Are you all right?' he asked me.

'Yes, yes, I'm fine,' I replied, hoping that he wouldn't see my naked pussy if he happened to look up my skirt.

'It's unlike you to stay out late. Where have you been?'

'I've been in the pub. I met a couple of friends and we got talking.'

'Are you *sure* you're all right?' he persisted. 'You look like you've been dragged through a bush back-wards.'

'I'm tired, that's all.'

'Come and have a cup of tea,' my mother said, appearing in the lounge doorway.

'No, I think I'll –'

'A man from the DIY store phoned earlier, Ali. Come and have some tea.'

I went back down the stairs and I followed my mother into the kitchen as my father went back into the lounge. Who the hell had phoned? I wondered, brushing my fingers through my long blonde hair as my mother filled the kettle. More to the point, what had they said? My mother took the milk from the fridge, turned and looked me up and down. I said nothing as she poured the tea. What could I say? I looked like a tramp.

'So you've left the store?' she finally said.

'Yes, I have another job,' I breathed. 'I wasn't going to tell you until –'

'What is this new job? Where is it?'

'Working for a . . . I'm going to work as a secretary. The money's a lot better.'

'That's good, Ali. For a moment, I thought that you . . . well, I wondered what on earth you were up to.'

'What do you mean?'

'Going out in that short skirt and looking like a . . . I just wondered what you were doing.'

'Jackie gave me the skirt,' I lied. 'What did you think I was doing, mum?'

'Nothing, I . . . I just thought it was odd that you should leave your job without telling us, and then go out dressed like that. You never stay out this late, Ali. And you've never dressed like that before.'

'The skirt *is* rather short. I didn't realise just how short it was when I put it on. I won't be wearing it again.'

'That's very wise. You don't want people thinking things.'

'What things, mum?'

'We've been worrying about you, Ali. You went out in that skirt, then we got the phone call, and you stayed out late. We were worried.'

'There's no need to worry, mum. I'm fine, honestly. I met some friends in the pub and we got talking and I didn't realise what the time was.'

'You would tell me if anything was wrong, wouldn't you?'

'Of course I would.'

'Have you met that other girl yet? The one who looks like you?'

'No, no, I haven't. I'll take my tea up to my room.'

'All right. Sleep well.'

I sat down on my bed and sighed. My mother was obviously suspicious, which didn't surprise me. I'd gone out dressed like a slut so it was no wonder that she was uneasy. At least she knew now that I wasn't working at the DIY store. But why hadn't she asked me more about my new job? I was going to have to change my life, I decided. No more games, no more short skirt and thong . . . No more Ali the slut.

Four

I went into town early the following morning and bought a new mobile phone. Although I told myself I wasn't going to prostitute my body, I did want to see John now and then and thought it best to give him my number. I needed the money but, apart from that, I enjoyed sex with him. He was good company, and I liked the way he satisfied me sexually. It *was* prostitution, I couldn't deny that. But I wouldn't be going with a lot of other men, and certainly not with strangers in the park.

I called into the clothes shop beneath the flat where the other Ali had lived and asked the woman behind the counter whether she knew where Ali was living. She shrugged her shoulders and shook her head. She seemed cagey, and I reckoned that she knew where Ali was but didn't want to tell me. Why was the girl so elusive, always in hiding? I wondered. I wasn't going to learn anything so I left the premises.

I passed a chemist's shop, stopped, retraced my steps, went inside and bought a tube of hair-removing cream. I didn't want a bald pussy, and I had no intention of using the cream. Why had I bought it? I asked myself as I wandered along the high street. What was happening to my thinking? John had asked me to shave my pubic hairs, but . . . well, I didn't want to look like a schoolgirl.

I felt that I was in a daze as I sat at a table in a café and ordered a cup of coffee. My life was a mess, going nowhere, and I couldn't seem to get myself back on track. I didn't want to go back to university, but I didn't want to take some mundane job and work from nine till five every day. What *did* I want to do? I mused, gazing through the café window and watching the people walking by. I leapt to my feet and held my hand to my mouth as I saw a girl walk past. It was Ali, the other Ali – my twin sister.

I dashed out of the café and looked down the street but I couldn't see her. She might have gone into a shop or . . . I ran along the street, not knowing where she might have gone. I checked the shops but she'd disappeared into thin air. This was ridiculous, I thought as I gave up and walked to the park. No one knew where Ali lived, no one knew her phone number . . . At least I'd seen her, I reflected as I wandered through the park. Although I'd only had a glimpse of her, she looked just like me. A twin sister living in the same town? I found the whole thing uncanny. Would I ever meet her? I wondered. Someone was sure to tell her about me. As I toyed with my new phone, I decided to give my number to everyone. Don, Barry, John . . . someone was bound to meet Ali and tell her about me, and give her my number.

The sun shone in a clear blue sky and I sat in the park for several hours. I'd told my mother that I was going to work so I could hardly go home. It was odd that she hadn't asked me anything about my new job, but I was sure that she'd question me about my first day as a secretary when I got home. I was wearing a dark blue knee-length skirt and a white blouse, which I'd hoped would convince my mother that I was working as a secretary. I was also wearing white cotton knickers rather than a thong. As my mind drifted and

I recalled sucking the middle-aged man's cock my knickers became very wet.

A sleeping desire had definitely been roused, I knew as I left the bench and walked into the wooded area bordering the park. My libido was rising, my clitoris stirring, and I knew that I'd have to masturbate. This was nothing like me, I thought as I settled on the soft grass in a small clearing among the trees. This wasn't just uncharacteristic, it was completely alien to me. Before I took on the role of Ali the slut, I'd never really thought about sex. I'd certainly never had the urge to masturbate, let alone in the woods.

On my back beneath the trees, with my skirt pulled up over my stomach, I lifted my buttocks clear of the ground and slipped my wet knickers off. Who was I now? I wondered as I ran a finger up and down my wet pussy slit and massaged the sensitive tip of my erect clitoris. Was I Ali the slut, or Ali the prude? I was myself, I decided as my young body trembled and my vaginal juices flowed from my opening sex hole. There was no clear-cut innocent Ali or distinct sluttish Ali. There weren't two separate people, there was only me.

Reaching beneath my thighs, I slipped two fingers into the wetness of my pussy as I massaged my solid clitoris. I needed an orgasm desperately, I knew as I looked up at the sunlight filtering through the foliage high above me. Fingering, massaging, attending my female needs . . . I felt feminine, sensual, as I masturbated in the woods. It was as if I'd discovered my body at long last, and I wanted to make the most of the pleasure that I could get from my pussy. It was as if I'd discovered myself.

I slowed my clitoral massaging and caressed my inner vaginal flesh gently – I didn't want to come too soon. Quivering, breathing deeply, I stroked my sensitive clitoris, teasing out ripples of ecstasy and inducing my sex milk to flow over my fingers. I'd changed since Ali the slut had arrived, and I was still going through changes. Crude words loomed in my mind: cunt, fuck, spunk, blow job, cocksucking slut ... My cunt, I thought as I caressed my clitoris and fingered my wet pussy. My beautiful cunt.

Although I tried to hold back, my orgasm exploded within the pulsating bud of my clitoris and shook my young body to the core. I felt alive with sex as I writhed on the ground. My whimpers of pleasure echoed around the trees and I massaged my clitoris faster to sustain my wonderful orgasm. Again and again, waves of ecstasy rolled through my body as I fingered my cunt and rubbed my solid clitoris with my fingertips. I could feel my pussy milk flowing, running down between my naked buttocks to the tight hole of my anus, and I realised just how hungry I'd been for an orgasm.

Finally coming down from my sexual heaven, I lay quivering and writhing on the grass. Suckling my quim-wet fingers, savouring the taste of my cunt juice, I realised that I was desperate to feel a hard cock driving deep into my yearning vagina. This was so unlike me, I reflected as my clitoris swelled again and demanded my intimate attention. I unbuttoned my blouse and lifted my bra clear of my firm breasts before pinching and squeezing my brown milk teats. I could feel my young womb contracting, my sex cream flowing from my vaginal entrance.

I had become a nymphomaniac, I thought as I pulled at my erect nipples. I needed a man, a rock-hard cock fucking me and spunking over my cervix. Reaching into my bag, I grabbed the tube of hair-removing cream and unscrewed the cap. I squeezed the tube and a swirl of white cream appeared. All I had to do was smear the cream over my pussy and my Venus mound would be bald within ten minutes, along with my vulval lips. I didn't want to do it but something deep inside my mind was urging me to.

I parted my legs wide, took a deep breath and held the tube over my quim. My fingers were wrapped around the tube but I tried not to squeeze it any more. There was a battle raging in my mind but I couldn't understand why. Then I tightened my grip, repeatedly telling myself that I'd regret it. But I had no will-power. The unguent was cold against the sensitive flesh of my outer cunt lips. I squeezed the tube harder and then massaged the cream all around my vagina. I felt confused as I lay on the ground beneath the trees. What the hell had I done?

After ten minutes, I grabbed my knickers and wiped the cream away. I sat up and gazed in horror at my bald pussy. I'd stripped away years along with my pubic curls. My outer lips were smooth and puffy, soft to the touch. They appeared to be fuller and my sex crack looked deeper. My inner lips protruded alluring-ly from my wet valley and I wondered what John would think of my new look. I also wondered what my mother would think if she discovered what I'd done. Was I a nymphomaniac?

The sensitive flesh of my pussy was stinging a little, and I knew that I should wash off the remnants of the cream. I stuffed my knickers into my bag, leapt to my feet and walked through the woods to the small stream where I had played when I was young. Squatting by the stream, I scooped up handfuls of fresh water and splashed the bald flesh of my pussy. The water cooled my swollen lips, sending my arousal soaring as I washed.

When I'd been younger and had played by the stream, I'd been happy, with no worries or concerns. Life had been simple, fun, exciting . . . Now that I was eighteen, life was complicated. I'd taken money in return for sex – I was playing the role of a whore. My blouse was still open, my young breasts on show, and I knew that I looked like a slut. I covered my breasts with my bra and buttoned my blouse as I walked away from the stream. Acutely aware of my bald pussy lips as I emerged from the relative darkness of the woods into the sunlit park, I thought that I was going through an identity crisis. Who the hell was I?

'Hi, Ali,' someone called.

I turned, hoping that it wasn't another of the slut's men, and said, 'Hi, Alan.' I sighed with relief as the boy who lived a few doors away from me approached. 'How are you?'

'I'm cool. What are you up to?'

'Just walking in the park,' I replied. I glanced down at his tight jeans and pictured his cock. 'Where are you off to?' I asked him. Why couldn't I stop thinking about his cock? 'Anywhere exciting?'

'I was supposed to meet my girlfriend here, but she hasn't turned up.'

'Have you known her long?' He was the same age as me, and I wanted his cock.

'A couple of months. We were going into town but . . . Never mind.'

'Do you remember when we used to play by the stream in the woods?' I asked him.

'God, that was years ago.'

'Want to go and take a look at the stream?'

'OK, seeing as I've got nothing else to do.'

As Alan and I walked across the park to the woods I knew that I'd have sex with him. I didn't want to but I had no will-power to fight the battle raging in my mind. I wanted a cock deep inside my cunt, fucking me hard, spunking me and . . . Such thoughts never entered my head when we used to walk to the stream and look for tadpoles. We never found any, but it was fun playing about with the water. I was going to the stream with Alan again, but it wasn't water I wanted to play with. If he knew that I wasn't wearing any knickers, that my pussy was bald and my tight cunt was yearning for a hard cock . . .

'It's nice here,' he said as we reached the stream. 'I used to love coming here.'

'And me,' I replied softly, eyeing the crotch of his jeans again and imagining his prick. 'I don't know why we stopped coming here.'

'We got older, Ali. We got older and found other things to do.'

I sat on the grass and smiled at him. 'How many girlfriends have you had?'

'Not many,' he sighed, sitting beside me. 'I've never had much luck with girls.'

'Why's that?'

'I don't know. I've been out with a few but . . . I must be going wrong somewhere.'

'Have you had sex with any of them?' I persisted.

'Only two, and both times were disastrous.'

'You have to know what you're doing,' I said, with a giggle. 'It's no good just fumbling about between their legs.'

'Well, I . . . I know what to do. At least, I thought I did.'

'You need some practice.'

As I lay back on the grass and lifted my skirt up over my stomach, he gazed wide-eyed at the bald lips of my pussy. His gaze caught mine, and we exchanged smiles. I didn't have to say anything – he knew that I was offering him my teenage body. He stroked my inner thighs as I parted my legs, and I felt my womb contract and my stomach somersault. We were safe in the woods by the stream. There were no prying eyes,

72

so I unbuttoned my blouse and lifted my bra clear of my firm breasts.

His finger parted my hairless lips and entered my vagina. He couldn't take his eyes off my pussy. He was learning, I thought as he slipped a second finger into my wet sheath. He needed a girl to practise on, a girl to play with, and I needed sex. I reckoned that he was too dumbfounded to say anything, to ask me why I'd shaved or why I wasn't wearing any knickers. Maybe he didn't want to know why. Maybe he was just happy to have my young body to himself.

His fingers probed deep within my tight vagina as he leaned over and sucked one of my ripe nipples into his hot mouth. I writhed on the grass, breathing heavily as he bit gently on my sensitive milk teat. Wondering why I'd never thought of Alan in a sexual way before, I also wondered why I'd never previously thought of *anyone* in that way. Had he ever looked at me and imagined my pussy or my tits? I mused as he sucked my other nipple into his wet mouth. Had he pictured my naked body when he'd wanked?

'You're beautiful,' he said gently, slipping my wet nipple out of his mouth.

'I'm not beautiful,' I replied, giggling.

'You are, Ali. You have a beautiful body.'

'My cunt, you mean?'

'Yes, no, I . . .'

'Have you ever licked a girl's cunt?'

'No, no, I haven't.'

'Lick mine for me, Alan. Lick my cunt and make me come.'

His fingers slid out of my hot vagina and he settled between my legs and ran his wet tongue up and down the open valley between my bald pussy lips. I quivered and writhed, breathing deeply as the tip of his tongue repeatedly swept over the sensitive tip of my solid

73

clitoris. Parting my fleshy lips with his fingers and opening my hole wide, he pushed his tongue inside me and lapped up my flowing milk. My vaginal muscles contracted and my clitoris ached for the relief of orgasm. I told Alan to stretch my lips open wider and push his tongue even deeper into my hot cunt. He followed my instructions, parting my sex lips so wide that I thought I'd tear open. I could feel his tongue deep inside me, licking, caressing . . .

'I want to fuck you,' he said unashamedly.

'I know you do. Is your cock stiff?'

'Very.'

'How often do you wank?'

'I . . . well, I . . .'

'Don't say that you never wank, Alan. How often do you do it?'

'Every day, I suppose.'

'Do you think of girls when you wank?'

'Yes.'

'Have you ever thought of me?'

'Yes, many times.'

'Well, now you can fuck me. Push your hard cock deep into my cunt and fuck me hard.'

Alan yanked his jeans off and positioned himself between my legs with his erect cock hovering above the hairless crack of my pussy. I gazed at his purple knob as he pulled his fleshy foreskin back. His cock was big, I observed as he slipped his bulging glans between the splayed lips of my pussy. His solid shaft entered me, opening my tight cunt wide, and I knew that I should have had him fuck me long ago. Had I not been such a prude, had I opened my eyes to my young body and the amazing pleasures waiting between my legs . . . It wasn't too late, I thought happily as his cock-head pressed gently against my creamy-wet cervix. I was only eighteen, I had years of sex ahead of me.

Alan withdrew his rigid cock and then thrust into me again. My young body jolted as he found his rhythm and began fucking me, and I gazed at his grinning face, the satisfaction plain to see in his dark eyes. We'd always been like brother and sister, I reflected. Going to the woods together, playing by the stream . . . Alan was right: we'd grown older and had found other things to do. I'd worked hard at college and had gone on to university, Alan was also at a university, and we'd drifted apart. Until now.

'You're big,' I breathed, listening the sound of my vaginal juices squelching as he repeatedly drove his beautiful cock deep into my yearning cunt. 'You're *very* big.'

'Have you been with many boys?' he asked me, obviously hoping that he was the first.

'No, I . . . I haven't had sex before,' I lied.

'So . . . how come you've shaved your pussy? You seem to know all about sex.'

'I've always used cream on my pussy. I don't like hairs there. I know about sex because I've been on the internet and learned things.'

'Wow – so I'm the first one?'

'Yes, yes, you are.'

Alan beamed and increased his pounding rhythm. I could feel my lower stomach rising and falling with each thrust of his rock-hard cock, my inner cunt lips rolling back and forth along his pussy-wet shaft. I was hoping that he'd last long enough for me to reach my orgasm, but he gasped and his sperm flooded my spasming sheath all too soon. He made his last lunge, grunting as his distended knob battered my spunked cervix. He collapsed on top of me, panting for breath, and asked me whether it had been good.

'It will be,' I said. 'It will be if you last longer next time.'

'I know it was quick,' he sighed, resting his weight on his hands and raising his body.

'Fuck me again in a minute, Alan.' His cock left my sperm-brimming vagina as he moved back. 'Fuck me again, and next time make it last.'

'I'm no good,' he said, shaking his head. 'That's why girls don't stay with me.'

'You're very good, so don't be silly. It was very nice – it's just that I didn't come because you were so quick.'

As he lay on his back on the grass I settled beside him and sucked his limp cock into my hot mouth and ran my tongue over his knob. I could taste his spunk and my pussy milk as I sucked and licked. A blend of sex, I thought, savouring the aphrodisiacal liquid. His cock soon stiffened and he gasped and writhed on the grass. I told him that I'd seen pictures of cocksucking on the internet. I also told him that I'd never seen a real cock before. I was becoming a truly wicked girl – and an accomplished liar.

Slipping Alan's silky knob out of my mouth, I ran my tongue up and down his hard shaft. He was ready to fuck me again but I wanted to enjoy the taste of his cock before he spunked my vagina once more. Licking his scrotum, lapping up the cocktail of sperm and vaginal juice, I felt my clitoris swell and my young womb contract. I was heavily into sex now, I thought. After years of denying myself the pleasures that my pussy had to offer I was now hooked on sex.

'Clean me,' I said, placing my knees either side of his head and lowering my dripping quim. 'Lick your spunk out of my cunt and clean me.'

'You're amazing,' he said softly as I sucked his solid knob into my mouth. 'Where do you get these ideas from?'

'The internet,' I replied. 'Lick my cunt out, Alan.'

His tongue entered my spunk-dripping vaginal hole and he lapped up his spunk as I sucked and gobbled on his beautiful knob. I could feel the hairless lips of my pussy pressing against his cheeks, my solid clitoris rubbing against his chin, as he sucked out the blend of sperm and girl juice from my hot vaginal sheath. Rocking my hips, massaging my sensitive clitoris against his wet chin, I bobbed my head up and down and fucked my mouth with his hard cock.

Where *did* I get these ideas from? I wondered as my young body began to quiver. Was it instinctive? Or was it that I wanted to be as crude and dirty as possible? My mother had once talked to me about sex. She'd said that sex shouldn't be dirty, it should be a loving union between a married couple. I was neither married nor loving. I was single, a slut, and very dirty. I was using Alan for my own sexual satisfaction. Just as John and the other men had used me for crude sex, I was using Alan.

My womb contracting, my clitoris pulsating, I could feel my orgasm coming as Alan licked and sucked the wet flesh between the swollen lips of my pussy. Desperate for his spunk to flood my mouth, I gobbled on his bulbous knob and wanked his solid shaft. His body grew rigid and I knew that he was about to pump out his cream as my own orgasm welled and erupted within my solid clitoris. Our young bodies trembled and writhed as Alan pumped his fresh sperm into my mouth and we clung to each other, locked in our act of wanton lust as our climaxes gripped us.

As I drank from Alan's throbbing knob and he swallowed my flowing pussy milk, I knew that he'd want to see me again. He'd probably pester me to go out with him, to meet him in the woods and have sex with him. I'd have to keep my other life secret, I reflected as his sperm-flow ceased and his cock began to deflate. As I rolled off his trembling body and lay on my back beside him, I knew that I had to make sure that he never discovered Ali the slut.

'You get better,' he said softly, turning his head and smiling at me.

'So do you,' I said, licking my sperm-glossed lips. 'I want you to fuck me again in a minute.'

'I'll fuck you every day, Ali. How about going out for a drink this evening? We could go to the pub and –'

'I'm studying this evening,' I cut in. 'I have to study most evenings, I'm afraid. But we'll have plenty of time to see each other during the days.'

'I could come round to your house,' he persisted. 'I have some studying to do too, so we could . . .'

'I can only work alone, Alan. Not even my parents are allowed to come into my room when I'm studying. Do you go to the pub very often?'

'I don't really like drinking, to be honest. I prefer to go to the cinema. Maybe we could see a film sometime.'

'Yes, maybe we could. Now relax for a while and, when your cock is hard again, I want you to fuck me senseless.'

'You're an amazing girl,' he sighed.

I *was* an amazing girl, and I very much doubted that Alan would meet anyone else like me. But I knew that he was going to be pestering me daily. He lived just a few doors away and he'd be calling at my house and . . . I'd known that living two separate lives wasn't going to be easy, but I hadn't expected Alan to appear on the scene. It was my fault, I reflected. I should never have seduced him. But I'd wanted his cock, and I couldn't help myself. I'd wanted him fucking me and spunking in my tight pussy and my mouth and . . . and now he thought that we were an item.

I sat up, reached over and grabbed his flaccid cock. I wanted Alan fucking me, I wanted to reach my orgasm as he reached his and pumped out his spunk. I ran my hand up and down his prick, rubbing my thumb over his slimy-wet knob as his shaft began to stiffen. When he was fully hard, I licked his knob and ran my tongue up and down his solid shaft. He was ready to fuck me to orgasm.

I knelt astride his young body and eased his beautiful cock deep into my spunk-bubbling vagina. Alan breathed heavily as I rested my naked buttocks on his legs and impaled myself completely on his shaft. I could feel his knob against my cervix, my pussy lips stretched tautly around the base of his cock. I threw my head back and I looked up at the trees as I tightened my vaginal muscles and squeezed his young organ. He gasped again as he reached up, and kneaded my firm breasts and tweaked my erect nipples. I sat still for several minutes, allowing his knob to absorb the heat of my cunt as my clitoris swelled against his solid shaft.

Raising my body until the petals of my inner quim lips lovingly hugged his knob, I then lowered myself until his cock once more impaled me completely. Moving slowly up and down, fucking myself gently on his lovely prick, I breathed heavily as my arousal heightened. My clitoris was massaged by his wet cock as I quickened my bouncing and I hoped that Alan wouldn't pump out his spunk until my orgasm came and shook me. We had to come together, we had to fly up to our sexual heavens as one.

'Is that nice?' I asked him as I bounced up and down.

'Yes, yes,' he gasped, his eyes rolling, his head lolling from side to side. 'It's amazing, Ali.'

'Are you pleased that your girlfriend didn't turn up?'

'*You*'re my girlfriend now.'

'Yes, yes, I am.'

I was everyone's girlfriend, I thought, looking down at my hairless pussy, my bald lips opened wide to accommodate Alan's solid shaft. I recalled John's huge cock fucking me, and wondered again whether he'd like my naked pussy. He'd asked me to shave for him and I was sure that he'd like my new look. Listening to the squelching of my vaginal juices as I bounced up and down on Alan's beautiful cock, I thought that the situation was becoming more complicated. I was Ali the prude, Ali the slut, and now I was Alan's girlfriend. The poor boy thought that he'd taken my virginity.

The day was sure to come when the truth stared him in the face and hurt him. I didn't want to hurt him – I didn't want to hurt anyone – but I knew that I was only using him for my own sexual pleasure. He was a nice lad, but I could never love him. Could I love anyone? I wondered as my womb contracted and my clitoris ached for the release of orgasm. I'd enjoyed too much cold sex to find love. Did I even *want* to find love?

Alan gasped as his spunk flooded my tight vagina and my clitoris exploded in orgasm against his sex-slimed shaft. I bounced up and down faster, whimpering as I once more threw my head back and rode the crest of my climax. This was real sex, I reflected. Crude, dirty, loveless – sex for the sake of sex. I was a slut, a whore, but Alan thought I was the sweet teenage girl from down the road. He'd believed that I was a virgin, but I'd been fucked by several men and had even had a rock-hard cock fucking my tight little bottom-hole.

I felt no guilt or shame, which was most unlike me. I'd always been an honest girl, a good girl. The worst thing I'd ever done before was agree to be tied down by a boyfriend. Now that incident paled in significance. I was far from a good girl now. Discovering the other Ali had led me to discover the *real* me, the sexual deviant lurking deep within myself. My job at the DIY store was history, university would soon become nothing more than a memory. I had my new and exciting life – *two* lives – now.

'No more,' Alan gasped as his cock deflated within the heat of my sperm-frothing vagina.

'You were good,' I gasped as my orgasm faded. 'You were very good, Alan.'

'Are you satisfied now?' he asked me, with a chuckle.

'I'm never satisfied – I thought you'd realised that.'

'You're insatiable. For a girl who's never seen a cock, let alone had sex, you seem to be incredibly experienced.'

'It's instinct,' I said, sliding off Alan's wet cock and settling on the grass beside him. 'And I've been looking on the internet.'

'I'd like to see you this evening, Ali. I know that you're studying, but I'd like to see you for a little while.'

'I don't know,' I sighed. 'If I finish my work early, then maybe I'll see you for a bit.'

Finish my work early? My so-called work was to satisfy John. And Alan reminded me of John in a way. John had said that he'd wanted all or nothing, and Alan was persistent about seeing me. I didn't belong to anyone, I thought as I covered my young breasts with my bra and buttoned my blouse. I was my own person, my life belonged to me and . . . Or did my life belong to Ali the slut? She'd pushed me aside and taken over. I had to keep a balance, I concluded. I couldn't allow the slut to rule my life completely.

After watching Alan pull his trousers back on, I stood up and straightened my skirt. I could feel his spunk pouring from the entrance of my inflamed vagina and streaming down my inner thighs. It seemed that every time I walked home now I had sperm pouring down my legs. My knickers were in my handbag, my pussy had no hair, and my sex hole was oozing with jism. I was a slut, I thought as I walked through the woods with Alan. A complete and utter whore.

When I reached my house I said goodbye to Alan and promised to see him that evening if I finished my work early. He was insistent, saying that he'd come round anyway. I had to be firm with him, and he finally wandered off. The last thing I wanted was my mother telling him that I'd gone out. Perhaps I shouldn't have seduced him in the woods? I thought again as I went into my house.

'What sort of secretary are you?' my mother asked me, frowning as she gazed at my dishevelled hair, my dirty blouse. 'You look as though you've been rolling about on the ground.'

'I was clearing out an old storeroom,' I lied. 'There are files that have been there for years and –'

'Where is the office? Is it in town?'

'No, no . . . it's a private house. The chap works from home. His wife works with him.'

'Oh, I see. Well, you should tell him to warn you in advance if you're going to get dirty. Then you could wear your old jeans. What sort of work does he do?'

'He's . . . he's working for the government. I'd better go and get changed.'

'Dinner won't be long. You're not going out this evening, are you?'

'Yes, I'm seeing some friends later.'

'What about your work, Ali? You're supposed to be studying.'

'I study every day, mum. An hour this morning before I went out, an hour at lunchtime, and I'll spend another hour or two when I get in tonight.'

'That's good. By the way, there's a package for you on the hall table.'

'Oh, thanks,' I said, grabbing the small box before I went up to my room.

I sat on my bed, opened the box and stared open-mouthed at a pink vibrator. I had no idea who'd sent it to me. It must have been one of the men I'd met, although no one knew where I lived. But *someone* knew, I thought anxiously. Someone must have followed me home and . . . This was all I needed. Was it John? I wondered. Had Don followed me home? Some man must have seen me leave the pub one evening and they had followed me home.

I hid the vibrator beneath my pillow and went into the bathroom where I slipped out of my crumpled clothes. I caught my reflection in the mirror as I stepped into the shower. My bald pussy lips were puffy and inflamed from fucking. My crack was gaping open and sperm was oozing from my sex hole. Previously my pubic hairs had veiled my slit but now everything was on show. I looked like I had when I'd been younger, I thought, wondering again whether using the hair-removing cream had been a good idea.

I washed away the spunk and vaginal juice and wrapped a towel around my naked body before returning to my bedroom. I locked the door and dropped the towel to the floor. I looked again at my reflection in the mirror. My outer sex lips were still full and puffed up, while my inner lips protruded slightly from my deep slit. I glanced at my pillow and thought about using the vibrator. After checking that I'd locked the door properly, I grabbed the vibrator and lay on my bed.

The soft buzzing resounded around the room as I parted my bald lips and pressed the tip of the vibrator against my expectant clitoris. The wonderful sensations immediately transmitted deep into my contracting womb and I let out a rush of breath. I'd never known anything like it as I writhed and whimpered on my bed. Stifling my gasps in case my mother heard me, I ran the tip of the vibrator around the base of my solid clitoris. My naked body shook, my thighs twitched, and I felt my vaginal milk spewing from my opening hole as my climax neared. I couldn't stop shaking as my clitoris began to pulsate. My heart banged hard against my chest and my breathing became fast and shallow. I cried out as my orgasm erupted within the swollen bulb of my clitoris.

Again and again, shock waves of ecstasy rocked my young body to its core. My eyes rolling, my nostrils flaring, I threw my head back and arched my spine as a second wave of intense pleasure gripped my trembling body. I didn't know what was happening to me as wave after wave of bliss rolled through my naked being. I didn't realise that I was experiencing my first ever multiple orgasm. Delirious, my mind blown away, I felt as though I'd left my body as my pleasure peaked again.

Whoever had sent me the vibrator must have known that it would blow my mind. As my climax finally began to fade, leaving me panting for breath, I wondered again who had discovered my address. My clitoris aching, my inner thighs splattered with my orgasmic juice, I drifted into a deep sleep as I imagined John using the vibrator on my clitoris. His cock ramming into my bottom, the vibrator teasing my clitoris . . . I dreamed my dreams of obscene sex with a man who was older than my father.

Five

I got to John's house at seven-thirty and apologised for being late. He looked down at my short skirt and grinned as he invited me into the lounge. Luckily, I'd managed to leave my house without my parents seeing how I was dressed. But I had to get back in later without being noticed. I'd cross that bridge when I came to it, I decided as I sat down on the sofa and John passed me a large gin and tonic.

'You look stunning,' he praised me, eyeing my naked thighs.

'Thank you,' I said.

'Ali, I was wondering whether you'd . . .'

'What is it this time?' I asked him. I smiled at him and giggled. 'You want to do my arse again?'

'No, I mean yes . . . It's the money.'

'Can't you afford me?' I frowned at him. 'Aren't I worth it?'

'Yes, of course you're worth it. It took me long enough to get you to agree to have sex with me, and I'm very grateful. The thing is . . . I don't know how to put this.'

'Just say it, John,' I sighed, hoping that I hadn't lost my job.

'I have a friend. I thought that, if you want a hundred pounds every time you come round, I might share the cost with my friend.'

'Share my body with him, you mean?'

'Well, yes.'

I couldn't believe what I was getting into as John gazed at me with expectation reflected in his dark eyes. Share my body? Did he mean that I was to have two men at once? Two old men groping and fucking me? I should have been shocked, but in fact I felt excited at the prospect. I'd gone through changes since I'd discovered Ali the slut, but I'd never thought that I'd be excited by the thought of having two old men groping my teenage body. The problem was that I'd given up my job at the store and I had to earn money. I had no choice, did I?

'I . . . I suppose so,' I muttered hesitantly, trying to conceal my enthusiasm.

'Really? That *is* good news, Ali.'

'Hang on, hang on. Do you mean, you both want me at the same time?'

'Well, yes, if that's OK?'

'I don't know, John. I'm a slut, but there are limits.'

'One hundred pounds every time you come round? Several good orgasms and more spunk than you can swallow and –'

'Well, all right,' I conceded finally, my stomach somersaulting as I imagined having two hard cocks to enjoy. 'When do you want to . . .'

'Now, if that's OK? My friend is waiting in the other room.'

'Bloody hell, John. How did you know that I'd agree?'

'Because you're a –'

'A slut – yes, I know. Go on, then. Go and get your friend.'

As John left the room, I knocked back my drink and raised my gaze to the ceiling. How far would the slut go? I wondered. Were there no limits to her . . . to *my* decadence? Hearing voices coming from the hall, I realised that I'd forgotten about my quest to track down the other Ali. I was supposed to be looking for my twin sister, not fucking two old men. What the hell would my parents say if they discovered that their innocent little girl was a common prostitute? Alan believed that I was studying in my bedroom. What would he think if he discovered the shocking truth about the little girl next door?

'This is Ali,' John said as he led his friend into the room. 'Ali, this is Harry.'

'Hi,' I said softly, looking up at the second man. He was older than John, but he looked all right.

'It's a pleasure, Ali,' Harry said. 'What a beautiful little thing you are.'

'So,' John murmured, rubbing his chin and gazing at me. 'Er . . . where shall we start?'

'I suppose Harry would like to see me naked,' I said. 'After all, it's my body you –'

'If I might suggest something?' Harry cut in. 'May I undress you?'

I rose to my feet and smiled. 'Go ahead,' I said, thinking of the money I was earning. 'I'm all yours.'

I unbuttoned my blouse and he slipped it off my shoulders and stared longingly at my small bra. I'd thought that he'd have been eager to see my tits, but he ran his fingertips over the smooth flesh of my hips and stomach. Stroking my long blonde hair, he ran his hands over my naked arms and commented on my unblemished skin. He was admiring my youth, probably thinking back fifty-odd years to the days when he was young enough to get his hands on girls in their teens. In a way I felt sorry for him. I'd felt sorry for John because he was old and desperate for a young girl but now I was beginning to feel sorry for all old men.

'Such beauty,' he breathed, kneeling in front of me and tugging my short skirt down to my ankles. Stepping out of my skirt as he locked his stare to my red thong, I wondered what he'd say when he saw my hairless pussy slit. I didn't want to give him a heart attack, I thought, giggling inwardly. Maybe it was best that he was stripping me slowly. Too much too soon might kill him.

He stood, reached behind my back and unhooked my bra. John looked on as Harry released the straps and allowed the cups to fall away from my firm breasts. Harry focused on my elongated nipples and gasped, and I knew that he was pleased with his purchase. But I had more in store for both him and John. My hairless pussy was veiled only by my thong and I was as keen as the men were to unveil the most private part of my teenage body.

Harry knelt again before me and stared at my thong. He was deliberately teasing himself, I knew as he grinned and licked his lips. Leaning forward, he kissed the triangular patch of red silk and breathed in the scent of my pussy. His cock would be as hard as rock, I thought as he pressed his nose against the swell of my thong and breathed in my girl scent again. His hands reached behind me, clutching the rounded cheeks of my firm buttocks, and he finally looked up at me.

'You're an angel,' he whispered.

'Hardly,' I replied, with a giggle.

'It's been years since I've seen a naked teenage girl. And it's been decades since I've . . .'

'Get on with it, Harry,' John cut in. 'We'll be here all night at this rate.'

'You don't understand,' Harry retorted. 'Such rare beauty has to be handled with care, unveiled slowly and gently.'

John smiled at me. 'Did you shave?' he asked me.

88

'You'll have to wait and see,' I said impishly.

'No pussy hairs?' Harry gasped. 'To see a young girl with no pussy hairs would be . . .'

'Harry, we won't see anything unless you get on with it.'

'All right,' the other old man finally conceded. Releasing my thong, he pulled the material down slowly. 'Yes,' he gasped as the top of my crack came into view. 'Perfection, don't you agree? Now, slowly, slowly, down and down until . . . She's a sex goddess,' he gasped as my thong fell away and exposed the hairless cushions of my pussy lips. 'A sex goddess sent from heaven.'

Harry moved forward and pressed his mouth to my bald sex lips, kissing me there. His slow approach had heightened my arousal to the point where my vaginal milk was decanting freely from my tight slit. I'd have thought that he'd have almost torn my clothes off in his eagerness to get his hands on my teenage body, but he obviously had respect for the female form. Still, I was sure that he was a dirty old pervert at heart.

His fingers opened my sex valley wide and his tongue entered my wet hole. He sucked out my flowing juices as John moved in and squeezed the firm mounds of my young breasts. To have two men attending my feminine needs was heavenly. I breathed deeply as John sucked on each ripe nipple in turn and Harry tongued my hot vagina. My heart racing as Harry slurped at my vaginal hole and John bit gently on my erect nipples, I wondered whether other old men would pay me for the pleasure of my teenage body. I could earn a fortune, I thought happily. And derive immense sexual pleasure from my new job.

Harry finally stood upright and unbuckled his belt. John stepped back. As Harry dropped his trousers, I gazed in awe at his huge cock. I'd never seen one so big, and I was sure that I'd split open if he tried to push it into my young vagina. John too looked at Harry's cock in amazement and I reckoned that he was feeling inadequate. What the hell was I supposed to do with it? I wondered as Harry asked me to kneel down. I doubted that I'd get his ballooning knob into my mouth, let alone into my tight pussy.

Following Harry's instructions, I ran my tongue up and down his veined shaft and licked his scrotum. He gasped and shuddered and his cock twitched as I ran my tongue close to his purple knob, but he ordered me not to suck it. He was obviously enjoying my intimate attention and didn't want to shoot his spunk too soon. I spent several minutes licking his cock and kissing his balls, and I could hardly wait to take his bulbous globe into my sperm-thirsty mouth and suck hard. Sinking my teeth gently into his huge rod, nibbling the soft flesh of his scrotum, I felt my vaginal milk flowing and my clitoris swelling expectantly.

At last instructing me to suck his knob, Harry let out a rush of breath as I took his massive plum into my mouth and rolled my tongue over its velveteen surface. It was huge, bloating my mouth and stretching my red lips as I licked and sucked, and I wondered how much sperm he'd be able to produce. As I wrapped my fingers around his solid shaft, I also wondered whether he'd be able to manage more than one orgasm. To feel his magnificent cock stretching my small vagina open to capacity would be heavenly, I thought as I fondled his full balls and wanked his fleshy prick.

His body became rigid and his cock-shaft swelled in my hand before his knob exploded in orgasm and a gush of creamy liquid flooded my cheeks. Clutching my head, Harry rocked his hips and fucked my mouth as I breathed heavily through my nose and repeatedly swallowed hard. I thought that his knob was going to drive down my throat as he mouth-fucked me and my oral cavity overflowed. His sperm streamed down my chin and splattered my naked tits. My eyes were popping out of my head and I also thought that I was going to choke.

I sucked the remnants of sperm from Harry's deflating knob and I panted for breath as he finally slipped his cock out of my mouth and released my head. Coughing and spluttering, I gazed in awe as his horselike cock hung over his balls. It was massive, I thought again. There was no way he'd be able to force it into my small pussy. As Harry stepped aside and John stood in front of me with his cock standing to attention, I parted my sperm-glossed lips and took John's knob into my creamy-wet mouth.

John gasped as I licked his beautiful glans and wanked his rock-hard shaft. He was nowhere near as big as Harry, but I wasn't going to complain. Two cocks, two loads of fresh spunk ... and I was being paid for the pleasure. I'd have had to work at the store for several days to earn this sort of money, I reflected as I kneaded John's full balls. This was prostitution, although I didn't look at it that way. But it was also easy money and incredibly sexually satisfying. There was no way I was going to give up my new job, I thought happily.

Harry knelt behind me and pulled my hips up so that my naked buttocks jutted out, and I knew that he was ready to fuck me. As his huge knob ran up and down my juice-dripping vaginal slit I wondered how old men had such amazing staying power. Parting my knees wider, I squealed through my nose as he forced his bulbous knob into the tight entrance to my teenage vagina. He'd never do it, I thought anxiously, almost choking on John's knob as he rammed it to the back of my throat. Harry's shaft entered me, my vaginal muscles stretched to capacity, and I thought that the delicate flesh of my inner cunt lips would tear open as his ballooning knob finally pressed hard against my ripe cervix.

'She's a tight little beauty,' Harry breathed.

'She's perfect in every way,' John said.

'You're right there. Her body is perfect, and it's all ours.'

My lower stomach ballooned with every thrust of Harry's gigantic cock and I moaned through my nose as John pumped my bloated mouth full of creamy-smooth spunk. Swallowing hard as I wanked his shaft, I listened to the sound of flesh slapping flesh as Harry quickened his shafting rhythm. My naked body rocked back and forth with the double-ended fucking, my solid clitoris massaged by Harry's wet shaft, I knew that I was about to reach my orgasm as John's sperm-flow ceased. Gobbling and sucking, I sank my teeth into his deflating cock as he tried to pull away.

My pulsating clitoris erupted in orgasm as Harry's knob swelled and then flooded my contracting vagina with fresh spunk. I thought that I was taking the full length of his massive cock deep into my young body – I could feel his knob throbbing inside me as if it was embedded deep within my stomach while his spunk overflowed and sprayed my inner thighs. Never had I known anything like it. Slurping away on John's wilting cock as my inflamed vaginal throat swallowed Harry's cream, I knew that I'd reached the bottom of the pit of depravity as I revelled in the crude double fucking of my teenage body.

Dizzy with sex, I finally collapsed on the floor as Harry yanked his cock out of my spunked vagina with a loud sucking sound and John's penis left my mouth. Spunk was flowing in torrents from the gaping hole of my pussy, the taste of male cream lingered on my tongue . . . I'd been well and truly fucked senseless, but I knew that my beautiful ordeal was far from over as the men continued to talk about my naked body. They hadn't finished with me yet.

As they rolled me onto my back and spreadeagled my limbs, I closed my eyes and allowed them to squeeze the firm mounds of my young breasts and finger the sperm-drenched sheath of my inflamed vagina. They were insatiable, I thought, wondering what other crude sexual acts they were about to commit on my young body. I felt completely relaxed as they sucked on the sensitive teats of my nipples and fingered my aching cunt. I felt no shame, no embarrassment or guilt . . . only pure sexual bliss.

As they feasted on my naked body, I wondered what Alan was doing. Was he studying in his bedroom? Was he looking at the clock, wondering whether I'd call round to see him? I should never have got involved with him, I thought as several fingers opened my vaginal cavity to the extreme. If he could see me now, I thought as my outer sex lips were stretched wide apart and my erect clitoris was forced out from beneath its pinken hood. What would he think? What the hell would he say?

The two men may have been old, but they were very strong. As John lay on the floor, Harry lifted my naked body and plonked me on top of John on all fours as if I weighed nothing. I felt like a rag doll as I was positioned correctly with the gaping hole of my cunt hovering above John's solid cock – it had obviously revived swiftly after the blow job I'd just given it. Harry knelt behind me and parted the firm cheeks of my bottom as John forced his solid penis deep into my spunk-bubbling vagina, and I knew now what they planned to do to my teenage body.

'No,' I gasped as Harry's bulbous knob pressed hard against the tight ring of my anus.

'Relax,' John said, with a chuckle. 'You know that you love a good arse-fucking, so just loosen up.'

'It won't fit,' I said, staring into his dark eyes. 'Please – I'll tear open.'

'It'll fit,' Harry said, his knob pushing harder against the delicate flesh surrounding my tightly closed bottom-hole.

He was right, I thought as his knob slipped past my defeated anal sphincter muscles. I could feel his shaft stretching my rectum wide open as his prick journeyed along my restricted duct deep into the dank heat of my bowels. Even with John's rock-hard cock bloating my vaginal canal, my rectal duct managed to expand to accommodate Harry's huge shaft. I could hardly believe it as they rocked their hips and found their thrusting motions. My pelvic cavity inflating and deflating, I'd never have thought that I'd be able to take two cocks at once in my small sex holes. Harry was right: it did fit.

Two old men, two hard cocks in my holes . . . I'd plunged even deeper into the pit of depravity, and I knew that I'd never climb out. The worrying thing was that I didn't *want* to climb out. This was the real me, I realised as the two knobs rubbed together through the thin membrane dividing my sex sheaths. The nymphomaniac within me had surfaced and I knew that I'd never look back. Ali the slut had roused my inner desires. Now I wasn't playing the role of a slut, I *was* a slut. The truth sank in at long last and I also realised that Ali the prude had gone for ever. I was now going to have to play the role of Ali the innocent, which was no longer me. I could do it with ease, I decided as I listened to the squelching sounds of spunk and girl juice. As long as I didn't make any mistakes I could get away with it.

As the men gasped and my naked body rocked back and forth, I thought about my twin sister. When I finally met up with her I was going to have to play Ali the prude. I instinctively knew that a nightmare lay ahead. My parents would want to meet the other Ali, I might meet *her* parents and ... and our mutual friends would see us together and the truth would come out. I'd been playing the role of my twin, and the truth was bound to come out.

As Harry's spunk jetted from his throbbing knob and flooded my bowels, John released a deluge of sperm into the contracting sheath of my inflamed vagina. Two cocks were fucking me simultaneously, I mused again as my clitoris pulsated in the beginnings of orgasm. I was in my sexual heaven, I knew as my climax erupted and shook my teenage body to the core. The three-way coupling was the best sex I'd ever had, and I knew that I'd be entertaining the old men again. Maybe John had another friend, I thought in the grip of my debauchery. Three cocks fucking all three holes and filling my young body with fresh spunk? Sheer sexual ecstasy.

My orgasm finally faded as the men's cocks slipped out of my burning ducts. I rolled off John and lay on the floor beside him, panting for breath. I was exhausted, but I knew that the men hadn't finished with me yet. They were insatiable, I thought as they talked about swapping places and doing my arse and my cunt again. As they knelt either side of my head, I gazed at their flaccid cocks hanging over their balls. John grabbed a cushion from the sofa and placed it beneath my head, and I knew what they wanted me to do. I managed to take both their knobs into my mouth and sucked and gobbled, savouring the taste of sperm and vaginal milk as their shafts began to stiffen. Did my mother suck my father's cock? Did my father lick my mother's pussy? I found myself wondering. I couldn't imagine my parents having sex, let alone enjoying a mutual mouth-fucking.

I was eighteen years old, I thought as the knobs swelled and bloated my mouth. A young teenage girl, and I'd become a prostitute. The notion didn't bother me any more. Why *should* it bother me? It wasn't as if I was walking the streets looking for clients. I was working, having fantastic sex and earning money. And I was making two old men very happy. As I sucked and licked the bulbous knobs, I wondered how many old men looked at teenage girls and thought their wicked thoughts. It was a shame that more young girls didn't share their beautiful bodies with the older generation. It seemed that, once a man reached middle age, he had only memories of young girls. But I was doing my bit to help, I thought happily.

'Like it?' John asked me, looking down at my bulging eyes, my lips stretched tautly around the two knobs.

'Mmm,' I mumbled, breathing through my nose.

'Enjoying your double mouth-spunking?' Harry asked me, with a chuckle.

'Of course she is,' John said. 'Young Ali was made for fucking and spunking.'

'You're right there. Firm little titties, a hairless cunt and . . .'

Listening to them talking about my young body, I wondered whether Jackie would like to join me in my new business venture. She had no direction in life, she didn't know what she wanted . . . Why not join me and earn some real money? She was young and had a good body, and I was sure that my clients would love to have two naked girls to play with. She'd either jump at the chance or never speak to me again, I thought. She was a slut, but she might draw the line at prostitution.

96

My mouth bloated to the extreme, I almost choked as the men pumped out their spunk. I swallowed hard again and again, but I was on my back so my mouth flooded and the male cream ran down the sides of my face. I could feel the spunk flowing into my ears as the men shuddered and gasped. My hair would be matted, I knew as I drank the fresh cream, and I imagined my mother asking me what on earth I'd been up to. I needed two sets of clothes, I decided. I could sneak into the back garden and change in the shed, clean myself up and change into the innocent young girl they knew.

The knobs finally left my spunk-bubbling mouth. I sat up and coughed and spluttered as the men sat on the sofa. They were exhausted and couldn't manage another erection, I was sure as I gazed at their limp cocks. They'd certainly had their money's worth, I thought as I eyed the cash on the coffee table. One hundred pounds, I thought excitedly. I could buy some more clothes, make-up and ... I couldn't believe it when Harry asked me to finger myself and masturbate. He wanted to watch me writhe on the floor in the grip of an orgasm, but I was sure that I couldn't manage it.

'I've never seen a young girl bring herself off,' he said, chuckling as he grinned at me.

'Me neither,' John rejoined. 'Go on, Ali, give yourself a good seeing-to.'

'I ... I don't think I can,' I said quietly, lying back on the floor with my legs wide open. 'I'll try, but I don't think I can manage to come again.'

I reached beneath my thighs and drove two fingers into the sperm-slippery sheath of my vagina, massaging my sensitive clitoris with my free hand. Closing my eyes as I felt my clitoris swell, I thought that I might be able to manage one more orgasm. I should have brought my new vibrator with me,

I thought, wondering whether John had sent it to me. My clitoris responded beautifully to my intimate caress and my vaginal muscles tightened, gripping my thrusting fingers. I arched my back as my naked body shook uncontrollably.

I'd lost count of the number of orgasms that I'd had that day, but I knew that I was about to enjoy another one as my heart raced and my young womb contracted. I could hear the men whispering, sharing their dirty thoughts about my teenage body, as I cried out in the grip of a massive climax. Whimpering and writhing on the floor with my legs wide open and my gaping vaginal slit displayed, I felt my girl-milk gush from my fingered sex hole and splatter my inner thighs. The men cheered, praising me as I sustained my beautiful orgasm, and I knew that they'd want to visit me again and again.

My pussy felt as if it was on fire as I slowed my masturbating rhythm and quivered in the aftermath of my incredible orgasm. I couldn't take any more sex, I knew as I slipped my wet fingers out of my hot hole and panted for breath. I was awash with spunk, exhausted and sore, and I couldn't take any more. I protested as Harry rolled me over onto my stomach and stroked the smooth flesh of my firm buttocks. He spanked my naked bottom, chuckling wickedly as I tried to escape. John leaped off the sofa and pinned me down, allowing Harry to thrash my naked bum until my cheeks glowed.

'You're an angel,' Harry said, finally halting the gruelling spanking.

'I'm knackered,' I cried, at last escaping and leaping to my feet. 'You've worn me out.'

'Dress now,' John said, grabbing his trousers. 'You've earned your money, Ali. You're bloody amazing.'

'I don't like being spanked,' I replied, covering my sperm-dripping pussy with my flimsy thong.

'You need a good thrashing now and then,' Harry said as he dressed. 'Young girls need spanking.'

'And old men need ... I don't know what they need.'

'They need young girls like you, Ali.' He turned to John and grinned. 'Tomorrow evening all right with you?'

'Yes, if Ali can make it.'

'I can make it,' I said, grabbing the cash from the table. 'Have the money ready for me.'

'And *you* have your sweet little cunt ready for us.'

Showing me to the front door, John thanked me for allowing his friend to join us. I gave him my new mobile-phone number before leaving and suggested that I might entertain other friends of his. He smiled and said that he did indeed have another friend who would be very interested. Apparently he too was in his sixties and would love to get his hands on a horny teenage girl. And he had money. I told John to ring me and let me know how many men would be at his place the following evening. The more dirty old men, the better? I wasn't sure what I was letting myself in for as I said goodbye.

I cut through the park, hoping that I could get into the house without my parents seeing me. My hair was matted with sperm and I looked a real mess, a right slut. As I walked past the bench I thought again about hiding a set of clothes in the garden shed.

I suddenly remembered that I'd arranged to meet Ian in the park. I was in no state to entertain another man, I reflected as I walked briskly across the park. I didn't even know Ian and should never have given him a blow job, let alone arranged to see him again.

As I passed the woods edging the park I heard someone calling me. It was Ian, I was sure, but I didn't turn round to look. I didn't need twenty pounds, I thought as he called out again. I had earned more than enough cash for one day and I certainly didn't need any more. I didn't need another mouthful of spunk, either. I could hear him running, catching up with me, so I finally turned and faced him.

'Where are you going?' Ian asked me. 'We'd arranged to meet.'

'I didn't think you were going to turn up,' I said, offering him a slight smile. 'I'm sorry, Ian. It's late now and I have to get home so –'

'It's early,' he said, checking his watch. 'In fact, I'm ten minutes early.'

'All right,' I conceded, looking around the park. 'Just quickly, OK?'

'Let's go into the woods. It's too open here.'

'Behind that bush will do,' I said. The last thing I wanted to do was to go into the woods with him. 'You've got the money?'

He passed me the cash and followed me behind the bush where he dropped his trousers. I didn't want to do this, I thought, kneeling on the ground and grabbing Ian's solid cock by the base, but I couldn't let him down. Fully retracting his fleshy foreskin, I sucked his purple plum into my wet mouth and snaked my tongue over its silky-smooth surface. He breathed deeply, his body trembling as he clutched my head and rocked his hips slowly. It was only about nine o'clock, I thought as I wanked his rock-hard cock. The later I got home the better the chance of my parents being in bed. I was in no rush to get home. Besides, this was incredibly easy money despite what I'd thought earlier about not needing Ian's cash.

'Do you have a vibrator?' Ian asked me.

I slipped his swollen knob out of my mouth, looked up at him and frowned. 'No, I ... I don't,' I replied, wondering whether he'd followed me home the previous evening. 'Why do you ask?'

'I just wondered. I'd have thought that a girl like you –'

'I have no need for a vibrator,' I cut in.

As I sucked his purple knob into my hot mouth I felt sure that he'd discovered my address and sent me the vibrator. I should have been more careful, I reflected. Anyone could have followed me and discovered where I lived. The last thing I wanted was men calling at the house for sex. Maybe I should move out and get a flat, I mused as I licked Ian's knob and wanked his cock faster. I didn't want to have to move out but, if I was going to carry on working as a prostitute, I'd have no choice.

Ian's spunk gushed from his throbbing knob as he gasped and shuddered, and I gulped down his creamy offering. It had only taken a few minutes, I thought happily as my mouth overflowed and sperm splattered my blouse. In the past I'd have been delighted to have earned twenty pounds. Now I had so much cash that I wasn't really bothered. There again, five blow jobs every day would bring in some useful money.

Ian finally pulled his cock out of my spunk-flooded mouth and zipped up his trousers. Standing in front of him, I wiped my mouth on the back of my hand and brushed my long blonde hair back with my fingers. I thought it was odd that he hadn't wanted sex with me. He hadn't even wanted to look at my young body, let alone fuck me. Perhaps he'd thought that he couldn't afford it.

'Why did you ignore me earlier?' he asked me.

'I was walking and I didn't hear you.'

'No, I mean in the pub this evening. You were

101

sitting with a man and I smiled at you but you ignored me.'

'Oh, yes . . .' I stammered, realising that he must have seen the slut in the pub. 'Sorry, I was rather tied up.'

'A punter, was it?'

'Yes, yes, that's right.'

'You could at least have winked at me.'

I didn't need this, I thought as I walked away. 'I have to go now,' I called out.

'Tomorrow, same time?'

'Yes, yes – that's fine.'

While I was walking home I repeatedly turned round to make sure that I wasn't being followed. I should never have cut through the park, I thought, as I once more ran my fingers through my sperm-matted hair in an effort to tidy myself up. I wouldn't go to the pub again, and I wouldn't cut through the park, I decided. I had John and Harry, and another man turning up tomorrow evening, so I didn't need anyone else. When I reached my house my heart sank as I noticed that the lounge light was on.

'Where have you been?' Alan asked me as he approached. 'Your mum said that you'd gone out. I thought you were studying this evening?'

'An old friend rang me,' I lied as he looked me up and down. 'I went out with her for a drink and a chat about old times.'

'You said you'd see me, Ali. You said that, when you'd finished studying –'

'Alan, we didn't have a definite arrangement,' I interrupted, trying not to appear angry. 'Jenny rang just as I finished my work and wanted to meet up with me. I haven't seen her for several years.'

'Well, at least you're here now. That skirt . . . Why are you dressed like that? You look awful.'

'We . . . we walked back through the park and I tripped over.'

'Why wear a skirt that's so short it doesn't even cover –'

'I have to go, Alan. I have things to do, OK?'

'Your mum said that you'd been out for ages. She said that you hadn't done any studying.'

'She doesn't know what I do,' I retorted. 'I studied for a couple of hours and then . . . Look, I'm going in. I'll see you tomorrow.'

'Tomorrow evening?'

'Yes, I think so.'

'What time?'

'I don't know, Alan. I don't run my life to the clock.'

'Shall we meet at seven? I'll come to your house at seven and –'

'For fuck's sake, Alan,' I screamed. I'd finally lost my temper, which was unlike me.

'God, you're in a mood,' he complained. 'I thought we were supposed to be going out together?'

'Alan, I have tried to stay calm. Despite your persistence, I have tried to remain calm. I'm going in, OK?'

I walked up the path to my house, let myself in and breathed a sigh of relief as I closed the door quietly behind me. Alan was becoming a pain, I thought, as I crept up the stairs. Someone had sent me a vibrator, Ian had caught me in the park, and now Alan was pestering me. I didn't need this mess, I thought, closing my bedroom door behind me.

I heard someone coming up the stairs and I knew that I was in for a lecture. I was about to grab my dressing gown to cover my sluttish clothes, but my mother walked in and stared at me.

'Late again?' she said, looking me up and down. 'Why didn't you say hello when you came in?'

103

'I needed the loo,' I said, clutching my dressing gown.

'Ali, what's going on?'

'What do you mean?'

'This is the second night you've come in late. Why are you wearing that ridiculous skirt? It's so short that there's little point in wearing it.'

'It's the fashion, mum,' I sighed.

'What's that in your hair?' She took hold of a tuft of my matted hair and frowned. 'What on earth is it?'

'It's milk,' I lied. 'I was at a friend's and we were messing about in the kitchen and –'

'Ali, we need to talk,' she cut in. 'Someone came round asking for you this evening.'

'Alan, yes, he –'

'No, it wasn't Alan. It was a middle-aged man. He said that he wanted to make an appointment to see you.'

'Really?' I said softly, trying to conceal my horror. 'I wonder who he was?'

'He didn't say any more than that. I told him that you were out and he went away. Does it have something to do with you trying to trace your twin sister, if you have one?'

'Oh . . . oh, yes.' I sighed with relief. 'I've been trying to trace her and –'

'You should have told me, Ali. Have you discovered anything yet?'

'No, not yet. What did the man look like?'

'He was in his forties and had black hair. He was wearing a suit and tie. If I'd known what you were doing, I would have invited him in and . . . Mind you, he probably didn't want to say anything to me about it because he didn't know who I was.'

'He's from an agency. They try to put people in

touch with each other and ... well, I gave him my address.'

'He left his phone number,' she said, passing me a slip of paper.

'Oh ... er, right. Why didn't you tell me before?'

'I wanted to find out who he was first. You look tired, love. Why don't you have a shower and then go to bed?'

'Yes, I think I will. Thanks, mum.'

As she left my room and closed the door, I held my hand to my spinning head. Who the hell had called at the house? I wondered fearfully. Was it the man who'd sent me the vibrator? A middle-aged man in a suit and tie? Did he think that I was running a brothel? I grabbed my mobile phone from my bag and dialled the number. My hands trembling, my heart racing, I tried to calm down as I listened to the ringing tone.

'Hello,' a man said.

'You left your number,' I said.

'Is that Ali?' he asked me.

'Yes, it is.'

'I've been waiting for you to call. Did you use the vibrator?'

'I'm sorry? What are you talking about?'

'I sent you a package – didn't you get it?'

'Who are you? I think you've mixed me up with someone else.'

'There's no mix-up, Ali. I've been watching you.'

'Watching me? I'm sorry, but I have no idea what you're talking about.'

'Wearing that short skirt, fucking a young lad in the woods, sucking a man's cock in the park, meeting old men at that bungalow ...'

I hung up and dropped the phone into my bag before flopping onto my bed. I was shaking, my heart was banging hard against my chest, as I recalled his words . . . *sucking a man's cock in the park, meeting old men at that bungalow* . . . Who the hell was he? I wondered fearfully. More to the point, what did he want? John didn't know about the man in the park, and I'd only just met Harry. Was it Barry? Or Don, perhaps? No, they wouldn't play silly games like that. What if he called at my house again?

Six

God only knew what time I'd finally got to sleep, but I woke with a start and sat bolt upright in my bed. I'd had bad dreams, nightmares . . . There was a note on my bedside table. Mum had gone shopping – she'd set my alarm for eight o'clock so I wouldn't be late for work. I checked the time: ten to eight. My phone rang as I slipped out of bed. I grabbed my handbag from the floor and stared at my mobile. There was no number displayed.

'Hello,' I said softly.

'Ali, it's John.'

'Thank God. I mean, how are you?'

'Are you all right?'

'You woke me up.'

'Oh, sorry. I've contacted my other friend. There'll be three of us this evening, if that's all right with you?'

'Oh, er . . . yes, yes, that's fine.'

'Sorry to have woken you.'

'No, no . . . I have to get up now anyway. John, is there a back way to your bungalow? I don't really want to be seen visiting you all the time.'

'Yes, there's an alleyway running behind all the back gardens. Go into the alley from Gloucester Road and mine's the blue gate. I'll leave it unlocked for you.'

'OK, thanks. I'll see you this evening.'

'I'm looking forward to it.'

'Me too. Bye, John.'

My hands trembled as I placed my phone on the bedside table and I wished that I'd told John that I couldn't make it. But I couldn't let him down, I thought. He'd arranged things with his friends and . . . I'd make sure that no one followed me, I decided. If I sneaked along the alley no one would see me. Taking a deep breath, I pulled myself together. I had a shower and then dressed in my knee-length skirt and a white blouse and tried to eat some toast and marmalade.

I had no idea where I was going as I left the house. I didn't want my mother coming back to find that I wasn't at work, so I had to go out. Keeping well away from the park, I wandered across the common and sat on a bench. It was a beautiful day. The sun shining, the birds singing, I shouldn't have been plagued by worry, I thought dolefully. At eighteen years old I should have been enjoying life and having fun. What the hell was I going to do all day? I wondered. I had plenty of money with me, but nowhere to go.

'Hello,' I said, answering my phone when it rang unexpectedly.

'Morning, Ali,' a man breathed. 'Did you use the vibrator last night?'

'Who is this?' I snapped.

'It's me, your anonymous friend. After you'd called me last night I did the dial-back and got your number.'

'What do you want?'

'Just a chat.'

'I'm not in the mood for chatting. Please don't call me again or I'll –'

'I enjoyed watching you masturbate by the stream the other day. That hair-removing cream worked well, didn't it? I love a teenage girl with a hairless little pussy.'

'Leave me alone,' I said shakily. 'I don't know who you are and I don't *want* to know.'

'Meet me by the stream in half an hour and –'

I dropped the phone into my bag, held my hand to my head and sighed. What the hell was I going to do? I wondered anxiously. If I didn't meet him he'd probably turn up at my house again. There again, if I did meet him . . . I was sure that it wasn't any of the men I'd met recently. It must have been someone who'd seen me in the pub and followed me for some reason. They'd discovered that I was having sex with various men and realised that I was a prostitute. But why the mysterious phone call?

I left the common and walked to the park. I had to discover who this man was and what he wanted, and there was only one way to do that. I reached the park and hid behind some bushes rather than go into the woods and wait by the stream. I was bound to see the man, I thought as I looked around. He'd said half an hour, and I was a good twenty minutes early so I was safe enough.

After fifteen minutes, I began to think that the man must have already been in the woods. He was probably watching me, I mused as I headed for the trees. Thinking that he might have been an unsavoury character, I kept my eyes and ears open as I crept through the woods. I wanted to see him before he saw me so that I could sneak away if he looked weird or dangerous.

To my amazement, I saw a neighbour of mine walking his dog as I followed the narrow path through the trees. He didn't have black hair, as my mother had said, but I thought it odd that he was there. His name was Derek and he was in his mid-forties. He lived in the house opposite and was a good friend of my father's and I too knew him very well. Was he the one who'd seen me giving a man a blow job in the park? Had he followed me and seen me go into John's bungalow? I hid in the bushes and watched him for a few minutes and finally decided that he was my man.

'Hi,' I said as I joined him on the path.

'Hello, Ali,' he said, turning and facing me. 'What are you doing here?'

'Just walking,' I replied.

'Of course, you're not at university at the moment.'

'It's the summer holiday. Are you waiting for someone?'

'Waiting for someone?' Derek frowned, as if it was an odd question. I suppose it was odd. 'No, no. I'm just walking the dog,' he replied. 'I always come here.'

I reckoned that I'd made a mistake and wondered whether the other man was lurking somewhere nearby. 'Quite a few people walk in the woods,' I said. 'Have you seen anyone else here?'

'It's funny you should say that. I bumped into Simon about fifteen minutes ago.'

'Simon?' I echoed.

'Your next-door neighbour, the man from number twenty-five.'

'Oh, right. What was he doing here?'

'He just said that he couldn't stay and went off.'

'Oh, well,' I said, smiling at Derek. 'I'd better be going. Enjoy your walk.'

'Yes, I will. You take care, Ali.'

'I will. Bye.'

I left the woods, feeling totally confused. My mother knew Simon, so he couldn't have been the man who'd called at my house. The whole thing seemed very odd. Derek had been walking his dog, but what had Simon been doing in the woods? He was in his fifties, was married and had always seemed such a nice man. He certainly didn't seem the sort to follow me around and send me a vibrator. There again, John and Harry looked like perfectly normal old men.

As I walked home, I hoped that my mother would still be out. If she was there I'd say that I had a couple of hours off work. I wasn't going to knock on Simon's door, but I thought that he might come out if he saw me sunbathing in the back garden. He was always pottering in his garden so the chances were that he'd be around. When I got to my house I went up to my room and changed into my bikini. That would lure him out of his house, I thought as my phone rang.

Ignoring my phone, I went into the back garden and lay on the sunbed. It was a beautiful day and I should have been enjoying the sun, but my mind was in turmoil. How could I keep my two separate lives apart with someone following me around and phoning me? I wondered. If it was Simon, then he'd obviously had no qualms about meeting me in the woods. Perhaps he wanted sex in return for his silence?

'Hi, Ali,' he called over the fence as if on cue. 'Enjoying the weather?'

'Yes, I am,' I replied as I left the sunbed and walked over to the fence. 'I have some time off work so I thought I'd try to get a tan.'

'What sort of work do you do?' Simon asked me, looking down at the cleavage of my firm breasts.

'It's secretarial work. It's only part-time but the money is good.'

'An attractive girl like you should be able to earn a fortune,' he said, with a chuckle.

'I don't know how,' I replied.

'Don't you?'

'If I knew how, then I'd be doing it.' I was sure now that Simon was my man. Although he couldn't have been the one who'd called at my house. 'Tell me how I could earn a fortune.'

'I thought that you *were* earning a fortune, Ali. From what I've seen –'

'What do you mean?' I cut in.

'I saw you in the woods, Ali. I'm the one who sent you the vibrator.'

'*You* sent it?' I gasped, holding my hand to my mouth.

'I know your game, Ali. And I'd like a piece of the action.'

'Action? I don't know what you mean. Why on earth did you send me a . . .'

'I've seen you in the park, in the woods and at that bungalow. You're on the game, aren't you?'

'You're talking about my twin sister,' I said angrily. 'She's the prostitute, not me.'

'Twin sister?' Simon frowned and looked somewhat anxious. 'You don't have a twin sister.'

'That's where you're wrong. As you know, I'm adopted. I knew nothing about her until recently. If you want a piece of the action, as you put it, then you'd better see her.'

'But it was *you* in the woods.'

'We're identical twins, Simon. If my parents found out that you've sent me a vibrator . . . They know about my twin sister. They know that I've been tracking her down, but . . . I might show them the present you sent me.'

'No, no . . . look, I had no idea.'

'Who was the man that called at my house?'

'He's . . . he's a friend of mine. I thought you were . . . The idea was that he should make an appointment to see you. I've made a huge mistake, haven't I?'

'Yes, you have.'

'Hang on – do you have a mobile phone? I rang you . . . My friend gave his number to your mother. She must have given it to you, so how did your sister get it?'

'I gave it to her, Simon,' I replied. He was suspicious, I knew. 'I guessed that it was something to do with her, so I gave her the number. I also gave her the vibrator.'

'But I saw you . . . You have the same name. That's odd, isn't it?'

'Yes, it is. Several people have been mixing us up. It's impossible to tell us apart, and having the same name causes real problems.'

'Obviously. Look, I'm sorry.'

'It's all right, don't worry. Just don't tell my parents about my sister. They don't know that she's a prostitute and I don't want them finding out.'

'No, no – I won't say anything.'

'If you want to meet her that's your business. Just don't involve me.'

'I don't usually go with prostitutes,' Simon sighed. 'It's just that . . . well, my marriage isn't –'

'I don't want to know, Simon. All I'll say is that my sister is very expensive. If you want to meet her, then be prepared to pay.'

'Yes, yes, of course. She was very rude to me when I rang her.'

'She was annoyed because someone had called at my house. She doesn't want me involved in her business.'

'Oh, I see. OK, let's forget all about this. I'm sorry.'

'As you said, let's forget it. Now, I'm going to get a suntan.'

That shut him up, I thought happily as Simon scurried off into his house. I was lucky to have got away with it, I thought as I went up to my bedroom. Ali the slut was playing too close to home. There again, she was the perfect excuse for . . . What if Simon met the real slut? I thought as my mobile phone rang.

It was time I met the real slut, I knew as I answered the phone.

'Ali, my name's Simon,' he began. 'I made a mistake and –'

'Simon?' I interrupted him. 'I don't know you. What do you want?'

'I mixed you up with your sister. I made a huge mistake and . . .'

'Are you the one who rang me earlier?'

'Yes, I wanted to meet you.'

'It seemed to me that you were going to blackmail me.'

'No, no, I . . . I just wanted to meet you.'

'Meet me for what?'

'Well, sex.'

'All right,' I said softly. I was enjoying the game too much to say no. 'Fifty pounds for half an hour.'

'Yes, yes – that's fine.'

'Do you want me to come to you or would you rather meet somewhere else?'

'The woods, where you've been . . . The woods by the park. There's a stream.'

'Yes, I know it.'

'In about half an hour, if you're free?'

'I'll be there.'

As I hung up, I thought that I must have been mad. Simon had known me all my life, and I was sure that I'd never get away with playing my twin sister. Fifty pounds for half an hour was amazing, but it wasn't just the money. I was gripped by the game. Dangerous as it was, I was gripped by the excitement – and by the sex. Hoping that my mother wouldn't get back for a while, I changed into my slut clothes and applied my make-up. I gazed at my reflection in the dressing-table mirror and grinned. The transformation was amazing. I was now Ali the slut.

* * *

I took a change of clothes with me to the woods. Once I'd earned my money I'd wash in the stream, put my other garments on and become Ali the innocent once again. While walking to the park, I reminded myself that I didn't know Simon, that I'd never met him before. As long as I remembered that, I'd get away with it. The best thing was not to say too much, I thought as I followed the narrow path through the trees. Keep my mouth shut and I'd be all right.

'Hi,' I said when I found him by the stream. 'You must be Simon.'

'Yes, that's right. Look, I'm sorry about the mix-up.'

'Don't worry about it.'

'It's incredible. Apart from your clothes and make-up you could be Ali. Your sister, I mean.'

'You have half an hour, Simon. Do you want to spend it talking or . . .'

'No, no.' He passed me fifty pounds. 'Er . . . what do you normally do? I've never been with a . . . I don't know what happens.'

'Most older men like to undress me. They like to undress a teenage girl and look at her young body before they get down to business.'

'Yes, good idea.'

He stood in front of me, unbuttoned my blouse and gazed longingly at my bra. As he unhooked it and pulled the cups away from my firm breasts, I felt a pang of excitement course through my veins. It was strange to think that the man feeling the firmness of my small breasts was my next-door neighbour. Simon had watched me grow up, he knew my parents well . . . and yet he was stripping me and was about to have sex with me.

'I've often looked at your sister,' he murmured. 'I've

looked at her for years and thought about her young body and . . . and thought about fucking her.'

That was quite a revelation. 'You have me now,' I said. 'Forget about her.'

'I could be undressing her,' he said, with a chuckle. 'You must be identical in every way, so I could be feeling *her* little tits.'

I said nothing as Simon knelt on the ground and tugged my short skirt down. In fact, I found that the notion excited me. The next time he saw Ali the prude, he'd be thinking about her young body, her firm breasts and her pussy. He'd chat to her over the fence, and would imagine fucking her. The game had become a way of life, I thought as he removed my thong and let out a rush of breath. As he commented on the beauty of my hairless pussy, my tight little cunt-slit, I knew that I could never stop playing the game.

When . . . *if* I ever met the other Ali, I wouldn't tell her where I lived. I'd already thought that it might be best if we never met, if she never found out that I existed. John was bound to meet her in the pub at some point and he'd realise that she wasn't the girl he'd been fucking. I'd have some explaining to do. I might even have to tell him the truth. But I was sure that he'd understand. Besides, he wouldn't want to ruin our arrangement. It might be best if I told him the truth before he met the real slut, I reflected. It might stop a lot of problems arising in the future.

Simon breathed heavily as he pressed his mouth against my hairless pussy lips and slipped his tongue into my wet slit. I couldn't stop thinking that he was my next-door neighbour as he pushed his tongue into my tight vaginal hole and lapped up my flowing sex milk. I'd spoken to him over the fence less than an hour ago, and now he was licking and sucking between my legs. Wondering who his friend was that had called at my house, I decided to ask him.

'He wants you, too,' he said. He looked up at me, his pussy-wet face shining with sex juice.

'In that case, give him my phone number,' I said, kneading my naked breasts and pulling on my sensitive nipples. 'What's his name?'

'Jack – and he's got money.'

'I'm pleased to hear it.'

'He likes . . . we both like leather. Do you have any leather gear?'

'Yes,' I lied, making a mental note to go shopping. 'What sort of clothes?'

'Leather miniskirt, suspender belt and fishnet stockings, leather boots, leather top . . .'

'OK, no problem. Do you and your friend want to become regulars?'

'Oh, yes indeed. I can afford once a week if you can fit me in.'

'That's fine. You have my number, so ring me when you need to see me. Time's running out so you'd better get on with it.'

He stripped naked and asked me to get on the ground on all fours. I did as he wanted, jutting out my naked buttocks with my knees wide apart and my hairless pussy lips bulging between my slender thighs. He knelt behind me and ran his swollen knob up and down my well-creamed slit, lubricating his cock in readiness to penetrate my teenage vagina. As he drove the entire length of his solid cock deep into my sex-drenched quim, he talked about my sister, how he'd looked at her in the garden and imagined fucking her tight little cunt.

Grabbing my hips, Simon repeatedly drove his cock deep into my teenage pussy and said that he'd often managed to look up my sister's skirt and see her knickers. I'd had no idea that he'd looked at me with such dirty thoughts in his mind, and the notion really excited me. It might be fun if Ali the prude allowed him to glimpse her tight knickers now and then, I thought as my clitoris swelled against his thrusting shaft. Young Ali, in her sweet innocence, could drive Simon wild with her knicker flashing.

'God, you're so tight,' he gasped. His swinging balls slapped my hairless mons as he fucked me harder. 'I've dreamed about fucking you for years.'

'Dreamed about fucking my sister,' I corrected him.

'Yes, yes – that's what I meant.'

'Imagine that I'm her, if you want to.'

'Oh, I am,' he said, chuckling as he slapped my naked buttocks. 'The next time I see her, I'll be thinking that I fucked her in the woods. Since you're identical twins I know exactly what she has between her legs.'

'I don't suppose she shaves,' I said, giggling as I imagined him trying to look up Ali the prude's skirt.

Grunting, Simon increased his shafting rhythm and slapped my naked buttocks again. He was about to pump out his spunk, I realised as his cock swelled. His time was almost up and I thought it was a shame that I hadn't given him more than half an hour. But I had John and Harry to attend to that evening – and John's other friend. Three men, I mused as my clitoris began to pulsate. Three cocks, three loads of spunk, three mouths . . .

I cried out as my orgasm erupted within the pulsating nub of my clitoris. I shook violently as Simon's spunk filled me and he let out a low moan of pleasure. I imagined him thinking that I was Ali the innocent. I had a lot of fun ahead, I thought as my naked body rocked back and forth and my orgasm peaked. Gasping in the grip of my amazing climax as

Simon's spunk streamed down my inner thighs in rivers of milk, I realised that I was going to be fucked by four men in one day. I was a fully fledged slut, I thought. And I was earning a fortune.

'God, I needed that,' Simon gasped as he slid his deflating cock out of my spunked vagina. 'You were brilliant – thank you.'

'You were pretty good yourself,' I said softly, reclining on the ground and shuddering in the aftermath of my first orgasm of the day. 'You'll have to look out for my sister's knickers when she's in the garden.'

'Oh, I will,' he said excitedly as he dressed.

'She's so innocent and naive that it's unbelievable. If she flashes her knickers it will be perfectly innocent. She has no idea about sex or what men think when they look at young girls.'

'I'll get back now and see if she's in the garden. She was sunbathing in her bikini earlier. Anyway, thanks again. I'll ring you, OK?'

'Yes, you do that. And get your friend to ring me.'

'I will – thanks.'

As Simon walked away, I squatted in the stream and washed the spunk away from my sex-slimed slit and my inner thighs. It had been a good day so far, I thought as the water cooled my outer cunt lips. I'd earned fifty pounds and I still had three more men to entertain that evening. I washed the make-up off my face, grabbed Ali the prude's clothes from my bag and got dressed. I had a lot to do, I thought as I walked along the path to the park. I had to buy some leather clothes, fishnet stockings . . . But first, I wanted to go into the back garden and give Simon a glimpse of my tight knickers.

Luckily, my mother was still out when I got home. My skirt's hem was just below the knee, but I knew that

I'd be able to show off my knickers if I sat on a patio chair with my skirt hoisted up a little. Simon was there, hovering in his garden, watching, waiting. I thought that he hadn't seen me as he slipped behind a bush, but then I realised that he was spying at me through the leaves. I reclined on my chair and pulled my skirt up. It was a hot day, and he'd think that I was behaving perfectly innocently as I parted my thighs and displayed the bulging crotch of my tight knickers.

I was tempted to pull my knickers to one side and masturbate, but I was supposed to be Ali the prude. Besides, Simon would see that I had no pubic hair and would become suspicious. I was quite happy to show him my knickers, especially as he'd be imagining himself fucking me. After ten minutes, he emerged from his hide and showed himself. I lowered my skirt as he smiled at me and commented on the weather. I left my chair and joined him by the fence. He didn't mention my sister, but he did ask me whether I had a boyfriend.

'I'm not interested in boys,' I replied. 'I'm too busy studying.'

'You've never had a boyfriend?' he persisted.

'Never.'

'So you're a . . . well, I'm sure the day will come when you'll meet a nice young man.'

'Maybe I'll meet someone after I've finished at university. I don't have the time or the inclination at the moment.'

'No, well . . . I'm sorry about earlier, Ali.'

'Don't worry. Lots of people have confused me with my sister.'

'You must think me terrible – because I want a prostitute.'

'I don't think anything, Simon. It's entirely up to you.'

'Yes, of course. Tell me . . . I know you don't have a boyfriend but . . . Would you be interested in an older man? Would you be looking for someone your own age or someone older?'

'I'm not looking for anyone,' I said, forcing a giggle. 'If I *was* looking, then it would definitely be for someone older.'

'How much older?'

'Well, probably someone who's middle-aged. If I was looking, that is.'

'I've always liked younger girls. When I was in my thirties . . .'

As Simon went on about young girls I wondered whether to take the game further and allow him to get to know Ali the prude intimately. The trouble was that I had no pubic hair. He was bound to think it odd that a naive virgin of eighteen should shave her pussy. It was too risky, I decided. Although it would be fun for the prude to play around with Simon, I had to keep the two sisters well apart. Luckily, at this point my doorbell rang, which gave me a good excuse to cut off the conversation before it went too far. I'd allow Simon to see my knickers again, I thought, dashing through the hall. Maybe I'd excite him with a glimpse of my nipples later.

'Hi, Jackie,' I said as I opened the door.

'Have you been in hiding?' she asked me as she followed me into the kitchen. 'Whenever I phone your mum says that you're out.'

'Sorry, I've been pretty busy lately. She hasn't said that you've called. Anyway, how are you?'

'I'm fine. I thought you were avoiding me for some reason.'

'Why would I do that?'

'I saw you yesterday and you ignored me.'

'Yesterday? Where was that?'

'I was walking back from town and I saw you going into a house in ... what's that road opposite the church?'

'Harvey Road?'

'Yes, that's it. I called out to you but –'

'That was my twin sister,' I cut in.

'Twin sister? You haven't got a sister.'

I poured two cups of coffee and told Jackie about the other Ali. I didn't mention that she was a prostitute, but I did say that I'd been trying to track her down. Unfortunately, Jackie didn't know which house Ali had gone into as she'd been too far away. But she did say which side of the road it was and that it was roughly in the middle of the street. I wondered whether I should go and have a look, but I wasn't sure that it was a good idea. Did I want to meet my twin sister or not? I was having fun enjoying sex and earning money. The last thing I wanted to do was to ruin my new and exciting life.

'Have you ever thought about prostitution?' I asked Jackie. She almost spilled her coffee as she stared wide-eyed at me. 'I only wondered,' I added, wishing now that I hadn't mentioned it.

'What a funny question,' she said, frowning at me. 'Have *you* ever thought about it?'

'Yes, I have,' I blurted out. 'I don't like university, I don't want to be a nurse ...'

'You want to become a *prostitute*?'

'Why not?'

Jackie brushed her long black hair away from her pretty face and grinned at me. 'Tell me the truth, Ali,' she said, with a giggle. 'Are you on the game?'

'I ... well, there was one man. I was short of money and ...'

'God,' she breathed, shaking her head. 'You, of all people.'

122

'I've shocked you, haven't I?'

'No, not really.' Jackie paused and locked her dark-eyed gaze with mine. 'OK, you've been honest with me so I'll be honest with you. There was this man ... It was a couple of months ago. I'd been clubbing and this man had been chatting me up all evening. He seemed OK so I let him walk me home. It's a long story but he wanted sex with me. I said no and he offered me twenty pounds to wank him.'

'And did you?' I asked her expectantly.

'I'd spent a lot of money in the club and ... yes, I wanked him for twenty pounds.'

'OK,' I said, grinning at her. 'I'll tell you more. I have two clients.'

'*What?*' Jackie gasped, holding her hand to her mouth.

'Two men in their sixties.'

'In their *sixties?*' she echoed.

'They pay me one hundred pounds for an hour or so.'

'Fucking hell, Ali,' she cried. 'How long has this been going on? I mean, how often do you see them? What do you have to do? Do they fuck you or –'

'Calm down,' I interrupted her. 'I do everything with them. I'm seeing them this evening.'

'God, I can't believe that you ...'

'Although I haven't met my twin sister yet I know that she's a prostitute. I've been playing the role of my sister, stealing her clients and earning a hell of a lot of money.'

'You must be loaded.'

'I am. And you could be, too.'

'What?'

'Come on, Jackie. You know very well that you're a bit of a slut.'

'I might be a slut but I'm not a ...'

'You charged a man twenty pounds for a wank.'

'Well, yes, but . . .'

'It was easy money, wasn't it?'

'Yes, but I didn't have to take my knickers off. And he wasn't some old pervert in his sixties.'

'What does age matter? You think about it while I make another coffee.'

I was really keen to get Jackie involved in my illicit business. She was extremely attractive, with a bloody good body, and she'd be a great asset. We could work together, I mused as I poured the coffee. Two eighteen-year-old girls working together . . . We could earn a small fortune. I realised that my life was going way off track, not that I'd been going in any particular direction, but I found the prospect of working with Jackie extremely exciting. I also realised that Ali the slut was taking over my life, but I thought that I could turn back at any time and lead a normal life. Once I'd earned enough money to get my own flat and buy a car . . . The future was looking good, I thought.

'It's one thing fucking lads of my own age,' Jackie said. 'But two old men . . . that's a different matter altogether.'

'Why?' I asked her. 'They have cocks, just like teenage lads. The difference is that they'll part with a hell of a lot of cash.'

'I suppose so,' she sighed, obviously coming round to the idea. 'But you and I would see each other naked.' Jackie grimaced and shook her head. 'I shouldn't have said that. It sounds stupid.'

'It *is* stupid,' I replied, laughing as she toyed with her coffee cup. 'We've both got tits, we've both got pussies . . . I don't suppose they're very different. Shall I phone my clients and say that I'll have another girl with me tonight?'

'No . . . I mean . . . we'd have to share the money. Or would they pay double?'

'I'll ring and find out.'

I took my phone from my handbag, called John and put the idea to him. He was all for it, and he said that he'd pay double. I realised that I could have given Jackie less than half the cash, seeing as I was the boss, but I didn't want to rip her off. I slipped my phone back into my bag, gazed at her and smiled. Jackie looked anxious as her eyes darted between her coffee cup and me, but I reckoned that I'd won her over. She asked me what time we'd meet and where, so I told her to wait at the end of the alleyway in Gloucester Road.

'Be there at seven,' I said. 'We'll go in through the back gate.'

'What shall I wear?' she asked me.

'I was supposed to be wearing a leather miniskirt and boots, plus some other kinky stuff, but I haven't been shopping yet. Wear a miniskirt – that'll be fine.'

'I'm not sure about this,' Jackie said softly. 'I mean . . . is it just a fuck, or what?'

'Well, it's more than that,' I admitted. 'A blow job and –'

'A man in his sixties?' she cut in. 'I don't think . . .'

'Jackie, just come along this evening and give it a try. If you don't feel comfortable or you don't want to do it, then leave.'

'Actually, now that dad has left, mum is short of money. If I could help her out . . . I'll get one hundred pounds?'

'More, I think.'

'More? Why?'

'There might be a third man there. One hundred and fifty, Jackie.'

'Fucking hell.'

'Just think, if we earn that sort of money a couple of times a week, or more, we'll be loaded. It beats working at the store.'

'Yes, yes, of course. It's just that –'

'I don't look at it as prostitution. I mean, I know it *is*, but . . . the way I look at it is that I'm keeping some old men happy and they're paying me. There's nothing wrong with that.'

Jackie finished her coffee and left the table. 'OK, I'll be there at seven,' she said.

'That's great. We're in business, Jackie. We're going to be rich.'

'I'll be able to buy a car and . . . Mum was in tears this morning. The bills are coming in and it seems that dad isn't going to help her out. OK, I'd better go. See you at seven.'

I saw her out, closed the front door and punched the air with my fist. It would be nice to have a business partner, I thought. A partner in crime? I checked the time and decided to go into town to buy some leather gear. I'd have to change my clothes in the woods before I went to John's, I reckoned. I'd also have to make sure that I wasn't followed. This was the beginning of a new chapter in my life, I thought as I grabbed a wad of cash from my bedroom. I was building up my clients, I had money, now I had Jackie with me . . . Things were looking good.

Seven

I was wearing a red leather miniskirt with a matching top and leather boots when I reached the alleyway at seven o'clock. Jackie was waiting for me, hiding in the bushes like a thief in the night. Dressed in a tiny miniskirt and a crop-top, she looked stunning. She also looked extremely anxious. At least she'd turned up, which had obviously taken courage. But she still had time to change her mind.

'Are you OK?' I asked her as we walked along the alley.

'No, not really,' she breathed. 'The idea of old men fucking me –'

'A cock is a cock, Jackie,' I cut in. 'Don't think about their ages, just think about the money you'll be earning. When we leave the bungalow later you'll have one hundred and fifty pounds in cash.'

'I really do need some money,' she sighed. 'I like your leather skirt and top. Are they new?'

'You need a regular income, and that's what you'll get. I bought these clothes with the money I'd earned. You'll be able to buy things, Jackie. You'll be able to buy anything you want.'

'God, I'm about to become a prostitute.'

'Don't look at it that way. We're out for some fun, just as if we were going clubbing or . . .'

'It's hardly the same, Ali.'

'I know. Just relax and enjoy the evening.'

As I led Jackie through the gate to John's back garden, I imagined her taking her clothes off and standing naked in the lounge. I'd never seen another girl naked, and I wondered what her young body was like. She wouldn't have shaved her pussy, I thought as I tapped on the back door. What would she think when she saw my hairless slit? How would she feel when I watched her getting fucked? She still had time to change her mind.

John invited us into the lounge where Harry was waiting with another man. All three men looked Jackie up and down, their eyes widening as they admired her young body. John made the introductions and then poured two large gins with tonic for Jackie and me. The third man, Keith, was a real good-looker. Although he was in his late sixties, he'd kept in shape and showed a perfect set of white teeth as he smiled at me. Things were going to be fine, I thought as Harry said that he was keen to take a look at Jackie's naked body and suggested that he should strip her.

Jackie glanced at me as Harry unbuttoned her top. I flashed her a reassuring smile as I sat on the sofa, hoping that she wouldn't back out. She seemed to be all right as Harry slipped her top off and unhooked her bra. John and Keith waited expectantly for the firm mounds of her teenage breasts to come into view, and I too was eager to take a look at her young body. The cups fell away and her pointed breasts were exposed – I thought how long her erect nipples were. She had a beautiful body, and I could hardly wait to see her pussy as Harry knelt down in front of her.

Jackie glanced at me again as Harry tugged her short skirt down and revealed her tight knickers. They were white cotton with a damp patch on the crotch, and they hugged her sex lips beautifully. She had an amazing figure, and I realised that I'd never even seen her in a bikini, let alone naked. Harry finally pulled her knickers down and gazed longingly at the well-trimmed pubic curls veiling her sex slit. I'd never had lesbian tendencies, but for a while I couldn't drag my stare away from the full lips of her young pussy. I finally tore my gaze away from Jackie's naked body. I didn't want arousals in the depths of my mind, I didn't want any lesbian thoughts erupting.

Jackie was finally told to kneel on all fours and rest her head on the armchair cushion, and I knew that she was about to earn her money. The men were ignoring me but my turn would come before long. Jackie was the new girl and they obviously wanted to try her out before pumping my own three holes full of fresh spunk. Harry knelt behind Jackie and stroked the smooth flesh of her naked bottom while the other men stripped off. Harry was to be the first to have her. He parted the rounded cheeks of her bottom, exposing her tight brown hole as the others looked on appreciatively, and I wondered whether he was going to force his huge cock into her bum.

I could see the girl's swollen pussy lips bulging between her slender thighs and I knew that was how I'd looked when I'd been ordered to get on all fours. I'd never seen my pussy from behind and hadn't realised that the lips protruded so much – and so alluringly. Jackie's outer lips were like miniature balloons, puffing up either side of her tight crack. I focused on the petals of her inner lips as they protruded from her pink sex valley and I felt my clitoris swell. Harry moved in and licked her tight anal entrance, and I sensed my stomach somersaulting and my young womb contracting as Jackie let out a gasp.

Trying again to clear my mind of lesbian thoughts as the men discussed Jackie's naked body, I watched Harry drive two fingers into the girl's vagina. Her outer lips stretched around his fingers, her juices squelching as he kneaded her inner flesh. I felt my own vaginal muscles tighten and my juices of desire seep between my swelling sex lips. I couldn't see Jackie's face, but I could hear her whimpers as Harry repeatedly thrust his fingers deep into her wet sheath. Hoping that she was enjoying the crude attention, I gazed wide-eyed as Harry slipped his fingers out of her teenage pussy and unzipped his trousers. This was it, I thought. This was Jackie's first fuck for cash.

Jackie said nothing as Harry rammed his solid shaft deep into her young cunt, and I wondered what she was thinking. She must have recalled my saying that a cock was a cock, I thought as he grabbed her shapely hips and repeatedly thrust the entire length of his rock-hard penis deep into her trembling body. Age didn't matter, I reflected as she gasped and writhed. Besides, we were being paid well for our services.

Harry threw his head back and let out a low moan of pleasure as he pumped out his spunk, and I felt pleased that Jackie had satisfied her first client. My clitoris swelled as I watched his sex-slimed cock repeatedly withdraw and thrust back into her young body and I realised how desperate I was myself for a crude vaginal shafting. I'd changed beyond belief, I mused as Harry finally slipped his deflating penis out of the girl's spunked pussy and moved aside for the next man. Jackie had also changed, I thought as spunk flowed from her gaping vaginal entrance.

'She's bloody tight,' Harry said as John positioned himself behind the girl.

'Tight and hot,' John breathed, sliding the full

length of his solid penis deep into her spunk-bubbling pussy.

Harry looked at me and grinned. 'I think Keith should strip you,' he said, eyeing my leather miniskirt. 'We don't want to leave you out of the fun.'

'OK,' I said, standing up as Keith walked towards me.

Keith unbuttoned my leather top and wasted no time in yanking my bra off and exposing the firm mounds of my young breasts. Jackie was gasping and writhing with her second fucking, but she managed to turn her head and gaze at my teenage tits. She smiled at me as Keith knelt in front of me and tugged my skirt down, and I knew that she'd settled into her new job. We were a team, I thought happily as Keith yanked my knickers down and stroked the hairless lips of my dripping pussy. And we were going to earn a fortune.

The feel of Keith's tongue running up and down my vaginal crack drove me wild. I parted my sex lips wide to give him access to my wet hole, my solid clitoris. He lapped like a dog, drinking the hot milk from my cunt as John announced that he was coming and pumped Jackie's young quim full of spunk. We were doing well, I thought as Jackie cried out in what must have been a massive orgasm. Her naked body shook wildly and her cries of pleasure resounded around the room – she was obviously enjoying her new job.

'Suck the spunk out of her cunt,' John ordered me as he slipped his limp cock out of Jackie's creamy vagina.

'No . . .' I sighed softly. 'I –'

'Come on,' Keith said impatiently. 'We want some lesbian action.'

'But I thought . . .' Catching Jackie's wide-eyed stare, I wondered what she was thinking.

'Yes, lesbian action,' Harry chipped in. 'Suck the spunk out of her tight cunt.'

I knelt behind Jackie and squeezed my eyes shut as I tentatively licked her yawning vaginal crack. The men cheered as I lapped up the blend of spunk and pussy juice flowing from her open hole. I hadn't expected this, I thought anxiously. And I was sure that Jackie hadn't dreamed that we'd be asked to perform lesbian acts for our paying clients. Would they demand that she lick my pussy? I wondered, slipping my tongue deep into her hot vagina. Should we have charged more for a lesbian sex show? Still, I reckoned that the men were paying us enough as it was. I had no idea what the going rate was, but as far as I was concerned we were earning more than enough.

Jackie began to tremble and writhe as I licked the wet flesh of her inner lips and swept my tongue over the sensitive tip of her solid clitoris. She was enjoying it, I reckoned. And I had to admit that I loved the taste of her pussy milk blended with fresh sperm. But I wasn't a lesbian, I reminded myself. I was simply doing my job and pleasing our clients. My life had changed dramatically since I'd discovered Ali the slut. Never in a million years would I have thought that I'd be licking my best friend's pussy. There again, never would I have thought that we'd be working together as prostitutes.

Swivelling her hips, jutting her naked bum out and giving me better access to her rock-hard clitoris, Jackie began to gasp and squirm as I sucked and mouthed between her spunk-drenched pussy lips. She really was enjoying my intimate attention, I thought as I sucked her clitoris into my hot mouth and snaked my tongue around the solid protrusion. Had Jackie always harboured lesbian thoughts? I wondered. Realising that she was going to reach her climax, I licked and sucked

132

for all I was worth as the men gathered round and whispered crude comments.

The lesbian act felt so natural, which worried me. A cock was a cock, I thought. But what I was doing didn't involve the men. This was a blatant act of lesbianism. I loved the taste of the girl's cunt juice, the scent of her black pubic curls, but I wasn't a lesbian. This was purely business, I reminded myself again as Jackie whimpered. I was licking Jackie's cunt for money, doing it for our clients. The feel of her swollen pussy lips on either side of my mouth, her solid clitoris pulsating within my wet mouth ... this was purely business.

Jackie reached her orgasm and uttered a cry of pleasure. Her vaginal milk spewed from her open sex hole and flooded my face, her rock-hard clitoris pulsated beneath my sweeping tongue, and she shook violently as I worked between her slender thighs to sustain her climax. My own juices of arousal streamed from my vaginal entrance and ran down my inner thighs as I gasped through a mouthful of vaginal flesh. Then one of the men knelt behind me and thrust his cock deep into the tight sheath of my neglected cunt.

The men cheered again as my naked body rocked back and forth and I sucked and mouthed on Jackie's orgasming clitoris. Never had I known such debased sex, never had I dreamed of indulging in an illicit three-way coupling, let alone realised that I'd derive such pleasure from the debauched act. Swinging balls battering my hairless mons, a swollen knob pummelling my ripe cervix, a hard shaft massaging the sensitive tip of my erect clitoris, I knew that I'd soon be writhing in orgasm as I sucked the hot sex milk from Jackie's gaping vaginal hole. Moving back to her pulsating clitoris and sustaining her pleasure, I licked and sucked fervently, and I wondered whether I'd woken latent lesbian desires lurking deep within my mind. I wasn't a lesbian, I told myself for the umpteenth time.

My contracting vagina swallowed a deluge of fresh spunk before I moved again to Jackie's gaping sex hole and sucked out her hot milk as her orgasm faded. My own climax erupted within the solid nub of my clitoris and I breathed heavily through my nose as I drank from the girl's teenage body. This was incredible sex, I thought as the man behind me repeatedly rammed his spunking knob deep into the tight sheath of my fiery cunt. Was I now hooked on lesbian sex?

The cock finally slid out of my burning vaginal shaft as I moved away from Jackie's trembling body and wiped my mouth on the back of my hand. This would be Jackie's real test, I knew as we were ordered to swap places. Resting my head on the armchair cushion, I jutted my naked buttocks out as she knelt behind me. John told her to lick my pussy, and I thought that she was going to refuse. She hesitated, mumbling something as John ordered her to suck the spunk out of my cunt. I was as eager to feel her tongue between my sperm-dripping sex lips as the men were to watch the lesbian act, but I reckoned that Jackie couldn't bring herself to do it.

To my surprise, she began to lap up the sperm dripping from the swollen pads of my outer lips. The feel of another girl's tongue between my naked thighs was heavenly, and a pang of excitement coursed through my veins as Jackie's hot breath warmed my flesh. Wondering whether she liked the look and feel of my hairless pussy, I thought I might suggest to her that she should shave her pubic curls. To suck on her smooth pussy lips, to slip my tongue into her hairless crack would be – I was thinking like a lesbian, I realised. I was confused by my feelings, by my attraction to another girl. I had to pull myself together and quash my alien desires.

I could feel Jackie's long black hair tickling my inner thighs as she tongued my sex hole. Her tongue repeatedly darted into my dripping pussy sheath, her hot breath blowing against my most intimate flesh, I and swivelled my hips as she'd done to align the solid protrusion of my expectant clitoris with her hot mouth. She sucked and licked my pleasure button, sending ripples of pure sexual ecstasy deep into my contracting womb. I knew that, for the first time in my young life, I was about to come in another girl's mouth.

Jackie eased a finger deep into my rectal duct as my orgasm erupted within my pulsating clit-bud. My mind was blown away and my anal-sphincter muscles rhythmically contracted. I whimpered uncontrollably as my naked body shook violently. In my sexual delirium I could hear one of the men talking, saying something about Jackie's tight cunt, and I knew that she was being fucked from behind as she sucked my orgasm from my spasming clitoris. This was real sex, I mused in the grip of my earth-shuddering climax. Cold, hard, crude sex.

My orgasm began to recede as I rested my head on the cushion, gasping for breath as Jackie sucked out the remnants of my sex cream from my inflamed vaginal duct. I needed to recover after my amazing orgasm, and I was pleased to leave the chair as John said that he wanted to take my place. Settling on the floor and watching him sit with his knees either side of Jackie's head and his erect cock hovering before her flushed face, I caught her wide-eyed stare as she looked at me. I smiled and nodded as she grabbed John's cock shaft and pulled back his fleshy foreskin. She seemed happy enough, I thought as she returned my smile. We were a team, partners in sex.

Lowering her head, Jackie sucked John's purple knob into her pretty mouth and closed her eyes. Her naked body rocked as Keith fucked her from behind and she moaned softly through her nose as she took half the length of John's rock-hard penis into her mouth. I reached beneath her young body and squeezed the firm mounds of her pert breasts, toying with her erect nipples as she slurped and gobbled on John's cock. No one had told me to touch her, to knead the hardness of her breasts and pinch and twist her succulent nipples. Was it instinctive? I wondered as I stroked her naked bottom and cupped her breast in my hand. Was the lesbian in me surfacing from the dark depths of my mind?

I ran my hand over the firm flesh of Jackie's rounded bottom, slipped a finger between her buttocks and teased the eye of her anus. Her young body quivered as I drove my finger deep into the dank heat of her rectum and once more pulled and twisted her erect milk teat. I could feel Keith's swollen knob through the thin membrane dividing her vagina and her rectum, the veined shaft of his cock as he fucked her. Easing a second finger into her tight anal sheath as Keith let out a gasp, I massaged his knob through the thin wall of skin to bring out his spunk.

Jackie's mouth overflowed as John breathed heavily and pumped out his male cream. She was shaking uncontrollably and moaning through her nose, and I knew that she'd reached her own mind-blowing orgasm. I kneaded the firm globes of her tits, simultaneously massaging deep inside her rectal duct and adding to the pleasure she was receiving from the two spunking cocks shafting each end of her naked body.

It was strange to think that Jackie had been my best friend since our schooldays. We'd gone to each other's birthday parties, spent the school holidays together and shared everything. Now we were sharing our naked bodies with three old men and being paid for sex. I'd wondered recently what my parents would say if they were to discover that I was a prostitute. Jackie's parents were strict Victorian types and I knew that they'd throw her out and disown her if they discovered the shocking truth about their teenage daughter. We were playing a dangerous game, but no one would ever discover our illicit business.

Jackie rolled onto the floor and lay on her back as the cocks left her holes. Panting for breath, her eyes rolling, she looked dazed in the aftermath of her coming. But the men hadn't finished with her yet. I sat beside her on the floor and watched the spunk oozing from the gaping hole of her vagina. The men were discussing their next crude act, so I took advantage of the pause and positioned myself between Jackie's splayed thighs, parted the sperm-drenched lips of her pussy and slipped my tongue into her hot vaginal entrance.

She squirmed and whimpered as I licked the pink funnel of flesh surrounding her sex hole. My tongue darted into her tight sheath, bringing out the cocktail of sperm and girl-milk, and I filled my mouth with the creamy blend. The taste was heavenly, and I drank from Jackie's young body until I'd sucked her dry. Moving up to the solid bulb of her exposed clitoris, I licked the sensitive tip. She gasped, squirming again as I sucked and mouthed on her come-bud. Reaching up and squeezing the firm mounds of her small breasts, I tweaked her ripe nipples and took her closer to her climax as the men watched.

I couldn't get enough of Jackie's beautiful pussy. Sucking, licking, mouthing, tonguing . . . I sustained her amazing climax until she begged me to stop. She was shaking wildly and gasping for breath as she rolled about on the floor. On her stomach, with her legs parted and the swollen lips of her vagina ballooning between her thighs, she flopped like a rag doll as Harry grabbed her hips and pulled her onto all fours. His cock was huge and rock-hard, and I knew what he intended to do as he parted the firm cheeks of her bottom and exposed her anal hole.

Jackie cried out, protesting wildly as Harry pressed his huge knob hard against the tight ring of her anus. I moved closer, watching as her anus finally yielded and stretched wide open to accommodate Harry's knob. His solid shaft entered her tight rectum, sinking deep into the very core of her squirming body, and he impaled her completely on his massive cock. I was amazed as he grabbed her hips and rolled back, pulling her with him until he was lying on his back and she was full-length on top of him.

Jackie's legs were open wide and I could see clearly the brown ring of her anus stretched tautly around the root of Harry's cock. Her vaginal entrance had been laid bare, gaping wide, and I focused on John's purple knob as he settled between her legs and rammed his bulging glans deep into her young body. Keith positioned his knees either side of her head and drove his swollen knob deep into her pretty mouth as Harry held her tight. Three cocks, I thought enviously as the squelching sounds of crude sex resounded around the room. Even I hadn't had three cocks simultaneously fucking my wet holes.

I stood in front of Keith and peeled the wet lips of my pussy wide open to offer my gaping sex hole to his mouth. His cock was still embedded deep within Jackie's mouth as he slipped his tongue into my dripping vagina and lapped up my flowing cunt milk. The five-way coupling was amazing. Three men and two girls fucking and sucking and licking ... I imagined a fourth man thrusting his knob into my mouth as Keith licked my solid clitoris, and a fifth man fucking my tight rectal duct.

There was no limit to the depths of my decadence now. I was a fully fledged whore, a prostitute and a filthy slut. But I was enjoying every minute of my new-found life – and I was earning a small fortune. As Jackie moaned through her nose, I realised that she was nearing another massive climax. My clitoris responded beneath Keith's sweeping tongue, pulsating in the beginnings of orgasm, and I wondered whether the men would have had enough sex once they'd finished with Jackie's naked body.

My climax exploded within my solid clitoris and shook my young body to the core as the men pumped spunk into Jackie's three holes. The smell of sex hung heavy in the air, which resounded with the sound of naked flesh meeting flesh, and I let out a cry of pleasure as my orgasm peaked. My body shook, my legs sagged, and I knew that I couldn't take much more. Jackie's young body was awash with male cream, and I had no doubt that she was totally exhausted. We'd earned our money, I thought as my vaginal milk splattered Keith's face and my climax finally began to recede.

Standing above the naked bodies that were writhing on the floor, I knew that the evening's session of crude sex was now over. I grabbed my clothes, dressed, and announced the end of the sex games. I told Jackie to get ready to leave. The men stayed on the floor, exhausted from their fucking, obviously satisfied after their time with two teenage girls. John frowned at me and I wondered what the problem was as he climbed to his feet and nodded towards the lounge door. He led me into the hall and closed the door behind us.

'You did well,' he said, passing me a wad of notes. 'But I think we need to have a chat.'

'What about?' I asked him, counting the money. 'You're happy with Jackie, aren't you?'

'Yes, yes, of course. I went into the pub earlier. I was talking to Ali.'

'Ali? But –'

'What's going on?'

'Nothing's going on.' This was it, I thought. I'd been exposed as a fraud. 'I don't know what you mean.'

'You told me that you had a twin sister.'

'That's right. And you've just said that you met her in the pub earlier.'

'You made out that you were the Ali I'd known for a few months. You made out that you were the Ali I met in the pub this evening.'

'No, I . . .'

'You're *not* the Ali I've known for several months, are you? You're the sister.'

'Yes, I'm the twin sister,' I sighed. 'We've never met and she doesn't know that I exist. It's a long story, John.'

'She knows that you exist now because I told her.'

'Oh, right. What did she say?'

'She wasn't at all happy. Other people have confused you with her. Or, I should say, they've confused her with you. Why on earth did you make out that you were her?'

'I didn't, John,' I replied. 'People kept mistaking me for her and I tried to put them right. By the time I'd met you in the pub I'd given up trying to explain.'

'She told me that you'd posed as her and had some porn photos taken.'

'Yes, that's right. I was trying to track her down and . . . I just sort of ended up being her. John, this doesn't affect our arrangement. Forget about my sister. I'm the one who's here with you, I'm the one you're paying and –'

'You're right, this doesn't affect us at all. But she's not happy.'

'I can't help it if people mix us up. It's as much her problem as mine.'

'I know, but people now think that she's into porn.'

'From what I've heard, she's a right little slut. I suppose I'd better meet her and sort this out. What did you tell her about me?'

'Nothing, because I don't know anything about you.'

'Didn't you give her my phone number?'

'No, I thought it best not to. This has nothing to do with me, Ali. I just thought that I'd better mention it.'

'I've made a mess of things,' I sighed.

'No, you haven't. The chances are that you'll never bump into her. Keep away from the pub, and I doubt that you'll ever –'

'I'd already thought about that,' I cut in. 'To be honest, I don't want to meet her. If I keep out of her way . . . Anyway, have you enjoyed this evening?'

'It's been a great evening, Ali.' John smiled at me and kissed my cheek. 'Jackie is amazing – I hope we see her again.'

'I'm sure you will, John.' As Jackie joined us in the hall, I passed her half the cash. 'We'll go out the back way,' I said.

'I'll ring you,' John said, following us into the kitchen. 'Be good.'

'We'll try,' I called as I walked across the lawn to the back gate.

Dusk was falling as I walked along the alleyway with Jackie. I suggested that we should go back to my house for a chat, but I had to go to the woods first and change into my ordinary clothes. Jackie wouldn't stop chatting, talking about the things she was going to buy with her money and asking me whether I had any other clients. On reaching the woods, I took my bag from beneath the bushes and changed my clothes as she rambled on about earning a thousand pounds every week.

'I doubt it,' I replied, giggling. 'We don't want to wear our pussies out. So, you're happy with your new job?'

'Wow, yes,' Jackie said softly as we left the woods. 'I didn't like having a cock up my arse, though. Actually, I suppose it was quite nice, once the first shock was over.'

'You had three cocks stuck in you at one stage.'

'I've never come so much in all my life,' she said, laughing as we neared my house. 'Three cocks, spunk everywhere . . . God, it was amazing. *And* we got paid for it.'

I led her through the front door and was thankful to find a note on the hall table saying that my parents had gone out for the evening and wouldn't be home until late. The way Jackie was dressed it was just as well, I thought as we went up to my bedroom. Her skirt was so short that it wasn't worth wearing, and we both looked as though we'd been fucked all night long. Jackie sat on my bed and gazed at me, and I knew that we needed to talk about our feelings for each other. I looked at her short skirt, her naked thighs, and my clitoris swelled and my vaginal muscles tightened.

'So,' I sighed, wondering what to say. 'You were OK with the lesbian stuff?'

'At first I was horrified,' she confessed. 'But, then . . . it was beautiful, Ali. It was absolutely beautiful. Have you done that before? I mean, have you been with a girl before?'

'No, I haven't,' I replied, wishing that I could drag my stare away from her naked legs.

'Did you like it?'

'I tried to look at it as part of our business arrangement,' I said as matter-of-factly as I could. 'It was purely to please our clients.'

'You *tried* to look at it that way? So you *did* enjoy it?'

'Well, I . . .'

'That was my first time with a girl, and I felt that . . . what I mean is . . . would you do it again?'

'For our clients' sake, yes.' I so much wanted to take Jackie in my arms and kiss her, but I felt that I had to fight my inner desires. 'We're in business, Jackie. The lesbian stuff is part of our business.'

'You remember how we used to have sleepovers? I was wondering . . . would it be OK if I stayed the night?'

'Yes,' I said, trying not to appear too eager. 'I'm sure my mum won't mind.'

'I need a shower, if that's OK?'

'You have a shower and I'll get some drinks. Dad won't mind if I nick some of his gin.'

'We could shower together,' Jackie persisted.

'There's no room for both of us,' I said, forcing a giggle.

As Jackie went into the bathroom, I knew that we were going to have sex that night. She obviously wanted it and I . . . I wanted sex with *her*. If my mind had calmed and allowed me to relax, I would have gone into the shower with her. But the battle between right and wrong in my mind was still raging. I was a heterosexual teenage girl, not a lesbian. I went down to the kitchen and poured two large gins, to which I added a little tonic. I needed a drink, I thought. My hands trembled as the doorbell rang. Thinking that my parents had forgotten to take a key, I hid the drinks in the dining room and dashed through the hall.

143

'I saw you get home,' Alan said as I opened the door. 'I thought we were going to –'

'Sorry,' I interrupted. 'My friend's here and we're . . . we're going to do some studying.'

'You've been out all evening, Ali. I saw you leave the house earlier and you've been out all this time. Where did you go?'

'I've been out for a drink with Jackie.'

'I thought we were going to see each other?'

'We will – when I get time. Alan, I have other friends and I also have studying to do.'

'Other boyfriends, you mean?'

'I have many friends, Alan. I can't stay in all the time – I need to get out and meet people.'

'How about tomorrow evening? We could go to the pub or something.'

'Yes, maybe. I'll let you know, OK?'

I closed the door before he could answer, grabbed the drinks and went up to my room. The last thing I needed was Alan pestering me, and I knew that I should have told him that anything between us was over. As I paced my bedroom floor, I also realised that I had to sort my life out. I was lurching from one direction to another with no real aim. I was playing games with the man next door, leading Alan on and . . . My stomach somersaulted and my womb fluttered as I heard the bathroom door open. I waited expectantly for Jackie to appear.

'That's better,' she said, walking into my room with a towel wrapped around her naked body. She closed the door and smiled at me. 'Are you going for a shower?' she asked.

'In a minute,' I replied, sipping my gin. 'There's a drink there for you,' I said, pointing to the dressing table.

'I hope your dad won't mind,' she said, her dark eyes locked to mine. 'But I . . . I borrowed his razor.'

She allowed the towel to fall away from her young body and crumple around her ankles. Then she stood in front of me and displayed her bald pussy lips. I held my hand to my mouth and let out a rush of breath as I focused on Jackie's hairless mons, her naked sex crack. Her inner lips protruded from her tight slit and she looked beautiful. Doing my best not to give in to my desires and drop to my knees and kiss her there, I sat on the edge of my bed and sipped my drink.

'Well?' she said. 'What do you think?'

'I . . . I think it's nice,' I replied.

'Is that all?'

'Well, *very* nice. Jackie, I . . .'

'Kiss me there,' she said. 'Kiss my smooth pussy and lick me.'

Jackie jutted her hips forward and offered her hairless slit to my mouth. After knocking back my drink, I placed the glass on the bedside table and kissed the smoothness of her swollen outer lips. I reached behind her naked body and I clutched the firm orbs of her buttocks, pulling her towards me. My face pressed hard against the smooth flesh of her vulva as I slipped my tongue into her sex valley and tasted her hot milk. I'd known that we'd have sex and I'd tried to fight my inner desires, but I was weak in my arousal.

I ran my tongue up and down Jackie's creamy slit, wondering where our relationship would go from here. We were the best of friends, and now we were working together successfully, but I'd never imagined that we'd become lesbian lovers. Rick had mentioned Ali's lesbian friend, Amy, and I realised that I was becoming more like the Ali slut with every passing day. Since Ali had reared her head, I'd become a prostitute and was now a lesbian as well.

'That's heavenly,' Jackie breathed, clinging to my head as I licked deep inside her wet slit. 'Don't stop.'

145

'We really shouldn't be doing this,' I said stupidly. 'We're not lesbians, are we?'

'I don't care what we are – just don't stop.'

Jackie peeled her hairless cunt lips apart and exposed the wet petals of her inner labia, the solid bulb of her sensitive clitoris, and begged me again not to stop. The taste of her sex juices were driving me wild as I sucked her clitoris into my hot mouth and ran my tongue over the small protrusion. She gasped and trembled and I clutched her rounded buttocks harder, digging my fingernails into her firm flesh. I sucked and mouthed fervently on her teenage clitoris, wanting her to reach her climax and shudder in the grip of a massive orgasm and pump out her hot milk. I wanted to pleasure my . . . my lesbian lover.

Jackie leaned over me, clutching my head harder and whimpering as her orgasm shook her naked body. Her vaginal milk gushed, splattering my chin as I licked and sucked on her climaxing clitoris. I thrust two fingers into her tight sex sheath and I breathed in the scent of her teenage pussy as I sustained her shuddering orgasm. I'd never felt so physically close to anyone as I tongued her pulsating clit and kneaded the inner flesh of her young vagina. My own clit-bud called for attention as my knickers filled with my pussy milk. Still, I hoped that my parents would be back before Jackie started to attend my feminine needs. Although I'd have loved to take her into my bed and writhe around in lesbian passion with her, it was too risky. If my mother caught us entwined in lesbian love . . . no, it was *far* too risky.

'No more,' Jackie finally managed to gasp. 'Ali . . . please, no more.'

'Did you like it?' I asked her as I slipped my wet fingers out of her hot hole.

'That was the . . . the best orgasm I've ever had,' she

146

sighed, collapsing onto the bed. 'God, I've never known anything like it.'

'We're not lesbians,' I murmured, eyeing the swell of Jackie's outer cunt lips rising alluringly either side of her gaping sex valley.

'So you keep saying,' she retorted, with a giggle.

'What I mean is . . .' My words tailed off as I heard the front door close and I leaped off the bed. 'Get dressed,' I ordered Jackie. 'That'll be my mum and dad.'

'I was hoping to love you,' she said as she grabbed her clothes and dressed hurriedly.

'And I was hoping . . . I'll go down and tell mum that you're here. She won't mind you sleeping over, so we can love again later.'

I left my bedroom, closed the door behind me and waited on the landing. I must have looked a mess, I thought as I ran my fingers through my blonde hair and straightened my clothes. My clitoris was solid in arousal, my knickers were soaked with my juices of lust – I hoped that my parents would go straight to bed and leave me to love Jackie. Whenever I'd had a friend stay over, mum had put a sleeping bag on the floor in my bedroom. Once my parents were asleep, Jackie could sneak into my bed and we'd love and . . . What had I become? I wondered as I went downstairs. A prostitute, a lesbian – from Ali the prude to . . . What had I turned into?

Eight

Jackie and I had, after all, been exhausted the previous evening – too worn out to make love to each other – and had gone straight to sleep in our own beds. I was woken at seven by my mother. She was going shopping with my father and would be out of the house for at least an hour. I couldn't believe my luck as she closed the bedroom door behind her. Jackie was still sleeping, so I waited until I heard the front door close before I woke her. Stirring, she pushed the sleeping bag down and exposed the firm mounds of her teenage breasts as she stretched her arms. Her nipples were erect, elongated, and I licked my lips as I imagined sucking on her ripe milk teats.

She slipped beneath my quilt and snuggled up to me, pressing her naked body against mine in the warmth of my bed. We were facing each other, our firm breasts pressed together as our lips met in a passionate kiss. I felt my stomach somersault as our tongues met and our saliva mingled. My clitoris was solid in arousal, my lesbian milk seeping between the swollen lips of my hairless pussy, and I wondered whether I was in love.

'When are we working again?' Jackie asked me as our lips separated. 'Do you have any other clients?'

'No . . . well, there *is* a man I meet in the park now and then, but I don't think I'll bother with him again.

148

Apart from the three old men, I don't have any other clients. I suppose we could find some.'

'We'll have a lot of free evenings so we might as well work.'

'Oh, there's the man next door,' I said, remembering Simon as I ran my hands over the rounded cheeks of Jackie's bottom.

'Next door? God, that's a bit close to home.'

'It's much *too* close to home, Jackie. I'm going to have to be careful because if my parents find out what I'm up to . . . well, it doesn't bear thinking about.'

'If *my* mum found out, she'd throw me out of the house. But they won't find out. It's our secret, Ali.'

'Yes, it is,' I murmured as she slipped beneath the quilt. 'It's our secret.'

I rolled onto my back as Jackie kissed the gentle rise of my stomach, parted my legs and breathed deeply. I could feel her hot breath against my pussy lips as she moved down and licked my opening crack. My mind drifted as she sucked on each outer lip in turn and I wondered whether I'd ever meet my twin sister. Now she knew that I existed she might come looking for me, I mused. I began to think that I'd have some explaining to do. But then I thought that the confusion, the mix-up, was as much down to her as it was to me. People had mistaken me for her, and her for me, so I didn't have to explain anything.

Jackie parted my thighs wide, settled between my legs and repeatedly ran her wet tongue up and down the full length of my yawning slit. I tried not to think of the other Ali. My parents would be home in less than an hour, and I wanted to enjoy Jackie's intimate attention, the delights of her young body. Her long black hair tickled my inner thighs, my lower stomach, as she parted the swollen lips of my vulva and slipped her tongue deep into my creamy-wet sex sheath. I

149

could feel her probing inside me, lapping up my juice and drinking from my trembling body.

My mind drifted back to my twin sister again, to her lesbian lover, Amy, and I wondered whether we'd been born lesbians. Was it purely coincidence that we both enjoyed sex with other girls? Or was it in our blood? I'd known plenty of pretty girls at school, and yet I'd never thought about them in a sexual way. I'd been with girls in the changing rooms after playing netball, but had never given a thought to their young bodies. Had I recently become a lesbian, or had I always been a lesbian? I was bisexual, I concluded as Jackie sucked my erect clitoris into her hot mouth and eased two fingers deep into my contracting vagina.

'I love your cunt,' she breathed. 'I love your cunt, your tits, your whole body. You're beautiful, Ali.'

'So are you,' I murmured. Did she love me? 'Let's do sixty-nine.'

Jackie moved on top of me with the shaved slit of her vulva over my face. Once again she licked and sucked my solid clitoris. I reciprocated, licking between the fleshy lips of her vagina and tasting her teenage love juice. We breathed heavily in our lesbian loving, our naked bodies entwined in lust, trembling uncontrollably as we mouthed and sucked between each other's naked thighs. Pressing my lips to the pink funnel of flesh surrounding Jackie's vaginal entrance, I sucked out her hot milk, drinking from her tight sex sheath as she drank from mine.

I thought about our time with the three old men and recalled a huge cock sliding in and out of her young vagina, the sperm oozing from her bloated hole and streaming down her inner thighs. I pictured two cocks driving deep into the tight holes between her splayed thighs, the inner lips of her pussy hugging one shaft and her tight anal ring rolling back and forth along the other. We were good together, I mused dreamily as I neared my orgasm. We were a team, and we were going to earn a fortune.

Jackie gasped through a mouthful of my vaginal flesh as her orgasm erupted within her solid clitoris and her sex milk spewed over my face. I moaned through my nose, shuddering as my clitoris burst into orgasm beneath her sweeping tongue. The slurping and whimpering sounds of lesbian sex resounded around my bedroom as we clung to each other and writhed in our mutual ecstasy as our climaxes rocked our naked bodies. I could feel my womb rhythmically contracting, my rock-hard clitoris pulsating, as I rode the crest of my lesbian-induced orgasm, and I knew that Jackie and I would always be together.

'No more,' she gasped, finally rolling off my naked body and panting for breath as she lay beside me. 'God, I can't take any more.'

'You were amazing,' I murmured, turning my head and smiling at her. Our pussy-wet lips met in a passionate kiss and I wondered again whether I was in love with her. 'Jackie ...' I began, wondering what to say. 'I –'

'Let's get a flat together,' she cut in excitedly. 'With the money we earn, we could easily afford a flat.'

'Leave home?' I said, sitting upright. 'Well, I ... I don't know.'

'Why not? We'll have more than enough money, and we'll be able to work from home and ...'

'I don't think we should have clients calling round, Jackie. We wouldn't want anyone to know our address so it would be best if we visited them.'

'Yes, good point. Let's start looking for a flat today.'

'Hang on, hang on. We'll need some money behind us first. Maybe, after a few weeks when we have a lot of cash, we'll get a flat.'

'We need more clients,' Jackie said as she leaped off the bed and grabbed her clothes. 'I'm going out to find some.'

'Where from?' I asked her, frowning as I slipped into my dressing gown. 'You can't go up to people in the street and –'

'No, no. If I go to the pub at lunchtime, dressed like this in my miniskirt, men are bound to come up to me.'

'We need to plan this, Jackie,' I sighed. 'If you did find a man, he'd want your phone number. You wouldn't want to give him your mobile number, would you?'

'No, I suppose not.'

'I've bought a new mobile phone, just for business use. If it rings, I know that it'll be a client and not a friend. Also, I've bought new clothes which are just for business. I'm trying to separate my two lives. Ali the slut, and Ali the innocent. The slut wears make-up and –'

'Yes, I see what you mean,' she interrupted. 'OK, I'll buy a new mobile and some clothes. But how do we find more clients?'

'Leave that to me,' I said, writing my new phone number down and passing her the piece of paper. 'I'll have a word with John, and there are one or two other men I could approach.'

'OK, I'll go into town now and do some shopping.' She opened the bedroom door, turned, and smiled at me. 'I'll see you later, Ali.'

'I'll ring you, OK?'

'OK.'

After I'd had a shower, I dressed as Ali the innocent in a knee-length skirt and a demure blouse and made myself some toast and coffee. My parents were due home and, since I was supposed to be at work, I decided to tell them that I had a couple of hours off. I

152

munched my toast and wondered where to find more clients. I doubted whether John had any more friends available and, besides, it would be nice to entertain some younger men, I decided. I wandered out into the garden with my coffee and thought about Jackie's idea of getting a flat. My parents wouldn't be at all pleased, especially when they discovered that I wasn't going back to university. But it was my life, and I had to live it the way I wanted to.

'Hello,' Simon called as he leaned over the fence.

'Oh, hi,' I said. 'It's a nice day again.'

'Yes, it is. I might go for a walk in the woods later.'

'I have to work, I'm afraid,' I lied, trying to change the subject.

'Have you seen your sister lately?' he asked me, with a glint in his eyes.

'No, we don't have much to do with each other. I'm always busy and she –'

'Keeps pretty busy too, I would imagine.'

'I have no idea.'

'I'll have to ring her,' Simon said, grinning at me.

'Yes, do that. Well, I must get back to work.'

'I'll ring her now and –'

I walked back into the kitchen and closed the door before he could say anything else. I realised that he could never meet Jackie. He'd recognise her immediately as my friend, which would ruin the game. I heard my phone ringing and dashed upstairs to my bedroom. It was Simon, asking me to meet him in the woods that afternoon. I needed the money but, as Jackie had said, it was playing too close to home.

'I've just been chatting to your sister in the garden,' he said. 'I suppose there's no chance of bringing her along to the woods?'

'No,' I said firmly. 'And *I* can't make it either – I'm afraid I'm busy this afternoon.'

'Oh, that's a shame. Jack, the friend I told you about, wants to meet you.'

'Did you give him my number?'

'Yes, so he should be contacting you soon. Ali, I was wondering . . . I'd like to play a little game with you.'

'What sort of game?'

'Would you dress like your sister and . . . I'll meet you at the end of her garden – when everyone's out, of course – and you pretend to be her.'

'That won't be easy,' I replied, realising that actually it would be an exciting game. 'I don't go to the house and I haven't met her mother yet so . . .'

'I know that, but when they're all out . . .'

'I'll think about it, Simon.'

'I'm free this afternoon.'

'I haven't been to the house before so it won't be easy. Besides, I have no idea when they go out together, if at all.'

'I'll find out from your sister and I'll ring you later.'

'OK,' I sighed. 'But it'll be dangerous so . . . It'll cost you, Simon.'

'You charged me fifty last time. I can't afford –'

'As I said, it'll be dangerous. One hundred, up front.'

'All right, one hundred.'

I dropped my phone into my bag and imagined hanging about at the end of the garden as Ali the innocent and . . . Too close to home, I thought again. Besides, I was bound to confuse myself by playing Ali the slut who was playing Ali the innocent. Although it was far too risky, the idea had grabbed me – excitement was welling in my young womb. Ali the innocent fucked in the bushes by the man next door . . . The ultimate deception, the ultimate exhilaration. But my parents would have to be out and then Ali the slut

154

would have to explain to Simon how she'd got into the house. It would never work.

As it happened, my parents went out after lunch. I'd told them that I had to get back to work and I'd see them that evening. One hundred pounds, I thought as they drove off. But how was I going to play the game? The slut would have to get into the house to borrow her sister's clothes, which would be impossible unless she broke in. I was sure that it would never work, but I had to give it a try.

Although I was playing the innocent sister, I changed my hairstyle and applied the smallest amount of lipstick. I couldn't wear the same clothes so I found a skirt that I hadn't worn for a long time and donned a baggy T-shirt. This really was risky, I thought as I wandered out into the back garden. I was jeopardising my business and I was sure that Jackie would think I was mad if she discovered what I'd done. I must have been crazy, I reflected as I waited on the patio. Simon hadn't phoned, so I wasn't even sure that he was at home.

'Hello again,' he called over the fence. 'I thought you were going back to work?'

'Dad wants me to water the tomatoes,' I said, walking across the lawn. 'Then I must get back to work.'

My hands trembling, my heart racing, I hid behind the shed where only bushes divided our gardens. I didn't even know whether Simon had realised that I was supposed to be Ali the slut, and I had a job remembering which sister I was playing. I heard a rustling in the bushes and knew that he was there. I lifted my skirt, slipped my hand down the front of my knickers and massaged the swell of my pussy lips. Who was I supposed to be? I wondered as the bushes rustled again. I'd thought that the game would be exciting, but now I was in two minds. Deciding to call it off as Simon emerged from the bushes, I played myself, Ali the innocent.

'What are you doing?' I gasped, lowering my skirt as he grinned at me.

'Are your parents out?' he asked, winking at me.

'Yes, they ... they went out,' I stammered.

'You were playing with your pussy, weren't you?' he said.

'No, I ... I have to water the plants.'

'You're a sweet little thing, Ali. I've watched you for a long time, thinking, imagining, picturing ...' Thrusting his hand up my skirt, Simon pressed his fingertips into the soft material of my knickers. 'Beautiful,' he said as I stepped back and held my hand to my mouth.

'Please,' I cried, a look of horror in my wide eyes. 'What are you –'

'Playing with your pussy behind the shed?' he cut in, a cruel smirk on his face. 'You wouldn't want me to tell your parents, would you?'

'No, no, I was just –'

'Take your T-shirt off,' he ordered me. 'If you don't, I'll tell your parents what you were doing behind the shed.'

As I pulled my T-shirt over my head, I wondered again which sister I was supposed to be. I thought it might be fun to allow him to fuck me and then have him believe that I really *was* the innocent sister. I'd thought that I must have been crazy to believe that I could get away with this. But Simon must have been *really* mad to believe that I was my own sister. Were identical twins truly identical? I wondered as he gazed at my bra. Mannerisms, the voice ... were they identical in *every* way?

I protested as Simon ordered me to remove my bra. I reached behind my back, then hesitated. I said that I had to get back to work, that my parents would be home at any time . . . He grinned and again ordered me to remove my bra. Unhooking the garment, allowing the cups to fall away from my teenage breasts, I hung my head as if in shame. He reached out, stroking my ripe nipples with the back of his hand and remarking on the beauty of my small tits.

'Now take your skirt off,' he told me.

'I . . . I have to go to work,' I stammered.

'You *are* at work,' Simon quipped, kneeling in front of me. 'Take your skirt off, Ali. I want to see your wet knickers.'

I unfastened my skirt and watched his eyes widen as it fell down my legs and crumpled around my ankles. He gazed longingly at my white cotton knickers, licking his lips as he ordered me to pull them down and show him my cunt. Complying, I knew that I couldn't play the role of Ali the innocent as my pussy was hairless. He stroked my lips, running a finger up and down the length of my sex slit and licking his lips.

'You've shaved,' Simon muttered, leaning forward and kissing the fleshy swell of my naked lips. 'Why did you do that?'

'I . . . I've always shaved,' I said shakily.

'I knew that you were a naughty little girl, Ali. Have you ever been fucked?'

'No, no, I . . .'

'You mean to say that no huge knob has ever slipped between those sweet little pussy lips and fucked you?'

'Please – I have to go to work.'

'There's plenty of time. I just want to look at you first.'

Licking my sex slit before reaching behind my naked body and clutching my firm buttocks, Simon pushed his tongue into my vaginal hole and sucked out my hot milk. Maybe I wasn't crazy, I reflected as my clitoris swelled and my womb contracted. One hundred pounds for a quick fuck behind the garden shed was easy money that I wouldn't have to share with Jackie. Although I was in business with the girl, I thought it might be a good idea to have one or two private clients. Especially if all I had to do with Simon was meet him at the end of the garden occasionally.

Following his orders, I turned round and leaned against the shed. Standing with my feet wide apart and my naked buttocks jutting out, I breathed heavily as he ran his tongue up and down my anal crease. My clothes strewn over the grass, my next-door neighbour's tongue teasing the delicate brown tissue encircling my tight bottom-hole, I couldn't help think – yet again – how much I'd changed since Ali the slut had arrived on the scene. From an innocent and extremely naive prude, I'd been transformed into a filthy little whore. But, no matter what I labelled myself, I was earning real money.

'Bend over and touch your toes,' Simon ordered me.

'I must go to work,' I whimpered.

'Do it, or I'll tell your parents that I've seen you masturbating with a cucumber.'

I heard Simon's trouser zip rasping down as I touched my toes. Looking up between my naked thighs as he dropped his trousers, I watched as he grabbed his solid cock by the root and pressed his purple knob between the well-salivated lips of my vagina. Another fuck, another wad of cash, I thought happily as he drove the entire length of his fleshy rod deep into my tightening sex sheath. Another rock-hard cock, another load of fresh spunk . . . This was my life now.

'Slut,' Simon breathed as he grabbed my hips and repeatedly battered my ripe cervix with his swollen knob. 'Dirty, filthy little whore. You love it, don't you? Tell me how much you like being fucked.'

'I . . . I like it,' I stammered as my naked body rocked back and forth.

'Beg me to fuck your little cunt harder.'

'Please, fuck me harder.'

'Your little cunt,' he insisted. 'Beg me to fuck your little cunt harder.'

'Please, fuck my little cunt harder.'

Simon was loving the game – I knew this as I watched his swinging balls pummelling my hairless mons. His sex-slimed shaft repeatedly emerging from and driving back into my tight duct, my inner lips rolling back and forth along his veined shaft – he gasped and increased his fucking rhythm. He was about to pump out his spunk, I thought as my clitoris began to pulsate against his thrusting cock shaft. His lower belly slapped the rounded cheeks of my naked buttocks while the squelching of my vaginal juices mingled with his gasps and he finally flooded my contracting sex sheath with his male cream.

My orgasm erupted and my erect clitoris pulsated wildly. I whimpered and trembled as my young body flopped back and forth like a shaken rag doll. My blonde hair hung like a curtain of gold silk, trailing over the grass, and I closed my eyes as my vaginal cavern overflowed and streams of creamy spunk coursed down my inner thighs. I could feel Simon's cock-head driving deep into my spasming cunt, as if his knob was pummelling my stomach while he fucked me. My orgasm shook me to the core. Another hundred pounds, I thought happily as his sperm-flow stemmed and his cock finally began to deflate.

'I'll be fucking you again,' Simon said, tugging his trousers up as I stood upright and faced him. 'That sweet little cunt of yours needs to be shafted regularly.'

'No,' I murmured, grabbing my clothes. 'I . . . I have to go now.'

As he tossed a wad of notes onto the ground, Simon grinned at me. 'I'll ring you,' he said. 'Keep your cunt shaved for me.'

As he disappeared back into the bushes, I dressed hurriedly and grabbed the cash. Too close to home? I asked myself as I headed back to my house. I closed the back door behind me and I went upstairs to take a shower. Too close to home or not, the money for ten minutes of crude sex behind the shed was amazing. I sat on my bed and gazed at the pile of cash that I'd earned since I'd ventured into prostitution. If I carried on like this I'd be able to *buy* a flat, I mused. There'd be no need to rent a place.

My phone rang. I hid the money behind the wardrobe and took the call.

'Is that Ali?' a female voice asked me.

'Yes, it is.'

'My name's also Ali.'

'Oh, er . . . Hi,' I stammered as my heart banged hard against my chest.

'I've been hearing things about you.'

'Yes, I . . . I've heard things about you, too.'

'I've seen the photographs that Don took of you.'

'Oh?'

'You might look like me, but I'm not your sister.'

'But –'

'I don't have a sister. And I don't like you pushing yourself into my life.'

'No, I wasn't . . . People mixed us up and I –'

'I've heard that you've changed your hair colour and

160

your clothes to look like me and I don't like it. Just keep out of my life, OK?'

'Can we meet?' I asked her. 'Please, if we could just meet and –'

'I told you, I don't have a sister.'

'Please, Ali . . .'

I flopped onto my bed as she hung up and I wondered who had given her my mobile number. It must have been John, I decided. Simon didn't know the girl, so it must have been John. Ringing the dial-back number, I wasn't surprised to find that she'd blocked her number. Would I ever get to meet her? I wondered. Did I *want* to meet her? At least she'd made contact, even if it was only to tell me to keep out of her life. Still, I was beginning to feel annoyed. I should have told *her* to keep out of *my* life, I thought angrily. Who the hell did she think she was?

Although I felt that I was making a big mistake, I went to the pub that evening. I sat on a bar stool wearing my miniskirt, a flimsy crop-top and my leather boots. As I flashed my knickers and sipped a gin and tonic, I looked like Ali the slut. I *was* Ali the slut. If the other Ali came in, if she had a problem with me, then it was down to her to sort it out. I couldn't help it if I had a twin sister who looked like me. It wasn't my fault that I'd been mistaken for another girl. I wasn't going to hide, I decided, downing my drink and ordering another one.

'You look good,' Simon said as he walked up to the bar and grinned at me.

'What the hell are *you* doing here?' I asked him.

'Like most people, I've come here for a drink. You did well this afternoon, Ali. You looked just like –'

'What are you talking about?' I cut in, deciding to confuse him.

161

'When I saw you earlier, you looked just like –'

'You must have seen my sister,' I said. 'I hope you weren't rude to her.'

'But . . . I thought . . .' he stammered.

'I've decided not to play the part of my sister,' I said. 'It would be too risky.'

'Oh, er . . . right.' Simon ordered a pint of lager and fiddled with a beer mat. 'Well then, I saw your sister this afternoon.'

'Oh? What was she up to?'

'Nothing, nothing. She was just sitting in the garden.'

'I don't see much of her,' I sighed. 'We might be identical sisters, but we're nothing like each other. She's a virgin, did I tell you?'

'Yes, yes – you did mention it.'

'The last time I saw her, she said that she wanted to be more like me.'

'Really?'

'I happened to mention that I shaved my pussy and she said that she'd do the same. God knows why she wants to do that because she'll never be like me.'

'Oh, right. So, are you meeting anyone this evening?'

'Yes,' I lied. 'So it might be best if you made yourself scarce.'

He downed his beer and placed the glass back on the bar. 'Well, I'll ring you some time.'

'OK.'

'Er . . . bye, then.'

As Simon left the pub, I almost burst out laughing. He must have been totally stupid to believe that he'd fucked Ali the innocent behind the shed. Didn't he realise that he'd been conned? He must have realised that there was only one Ali. The trouble was, there really were two Alis, and the other one might walk into the pub at any time. I'd confront her, I decided. I wouldn't take any nonsense from her, and I certainly wouldn't allow her to threaten me.

As I fiddled with my long blonde hair I wondered what Simon would say the next time he saw Ali the prude in the garden. He'd blackmailed her, I reflected. He'd threatened to tell her parents that she'd been masturbating in the garden. He'd used blackmail to fuck her, and now he was probably worrying himself silly. His problem was that his cock ruled his head. If he was so stupid as to believe that Ali the prude would have succumbed to blackmail and allowed him to fuck her ... Maybe she would, though? I thought. If she believed that her parents would think she was a slut if they discovered that she masturbated, perhaps she would give in to blackmail.

'I'm surprised to see you here,' Barry said as he leaned on the bar beside me.

'Why's that?' I asked him.

'After the row we had last night ... I thought you'd gone back to Birmingham.'

'I'm here, Barry. So I can't be in Birmingham, can I?'

'Look, Ali ... I didn't mean what I said about your sister. OK, so I fucked her. But I only did that because you'd left me. I mean, I'm not going to remain celibate just because you don't want me.'

'The things you said ...' I began, trying not to put my foot in it.

'OK, OK – so I said that she was better than you. I was only joking. Besides, I haven't seen her since.'

'Perhaps she thought you were no good in bed.'

'I don't know,' Barry sighed. 'I wish I hadn't told you about it. I only mentioned it because you said that she was trying to take your place.'

'Yes, well . . . She is, isn't she? I mean, she's fucked you and –'

'That's all she's done, Ali. Anyway, I don't know why you're so bothered about her. OK, so she looks identical to you. So what?'

'I don't have a sister, Barry. Whoever this girl is . . .'

'You said yourself that it was quite possible. You said that you'd never met your mother, so you could have a twin.' He ordered himself a drink and sat on the stool beside me. 'Want one?' he asked me.

'Gin and tonic,' I said, wondering whether the slut would have added the word 'please'.

'And all that stuff about Don,' Barry continued. 'If this girl wants to do porn shots, then why should that bother you?'

'Because people will think it's me, Barry. I don't like the idea.'

'You've never bothered about what people might think. I know you're on the game, so there's no point in denying it.'

'What's that got to do with it?'

'One minute you're making out that you don't like the idea of porn, and then you charge men for sex. I don't think you know *what* you want, Ali.'

'What do you think I should do about this girl, then?' I asked him, trying to glean more information.

'I think you should either meet her, or forget about her. After what you were saying last night . . . Are you going to find a flat here, or go to Birmingham?'

'I don't know yet,' I sighed. 'I don't know what to do. If the other Ali came in here now, what do you think I should say to her?'

'God knows,' he replied, with a chuckle. 'It would be amazing to see you both standing side by side.'

'Confusing, more like. You know me well enough, Barry. What do you reckon I'd do?'

'I reckon you'd be pleased to meet her. As you said last night, it's not her fault that you look like each other. She might be blaming you for the confusion.'

As he sipped his beer, I wondered whether the other Ali would walk into the pub. I'd be in trouble if she did, I thought anxiously. Barry thought that I was the slut, his ex-girlfriend, and if she walked in . . . At least I'd learned something about my twin. According to Barry, she'd said that it was possible that she had a sister. But I still wasn't sure whether or not I wanted to meet her. Maybe I should never have been the prude, I thought. Maybe Ali the innocent should have been a second slut. I was confusing myself, I knew.

Barry finished his drink. 'I'd better go,' he sighed. 'I'll see you around sometime.'

'Yes, I'm sure you will,' I said, wondering whether to smile at him.

'You know where I am if you want me.'

As I watched him leave the pub I felt sorry for him. With his dark hair and deep-set eyes, he was good-looking. He was also good in bed, I remembered. But I didn't want Ali the prude to get involved with him. She'd already been to his flat and . . . It was best to keep Ali the prude at home for a while, I decided. The pub was empty and I thought it might be best if I went home. There was no point in sitting there alone all evening, but I reckoned I'd have one more drink before I left.

After an hour – and another three drinks – I was feeling somewhat tipsy. I needed some excitement and thought about going home through the park in the hope that my blow-job man might be there waiting for me. I also wondered whether to ring Jackie and get her to come to the pub. I began to feel despondent because I didn't know what to do. I'd had so much excitement and sex recently that I felt as if I was coming down from a high. Was I hooked on crude sex? I wondered.

'Well, if it's not little Ali,' a man said as he wandered into the pub and joined me at the bar.

'Oh, hi,' I said, wondering who the hell he was. In his thirties and with blond hair, he wasn't bad-looking but he wasn't my type. 'How are you doing?' I asked him.

'I'm doing fine,' he replied.

'The usual, Mick?' the barman asked.

'Oh, go on, then.'

'So, Mick,' I said. 'What have you been up to?'

'Oh, this and that. By the way, the flat is free.'

'The flat?' I echoed.

'My flat, Ali. The one I let out.'

'Oh yes, of course.'

'The people moved out yesterday so it's yours – if you want it?'

'Well, I . . .'

'I know you haven't seen it yet. But if you're still looking for a place it's yours.'

'How much?'

'Five hundred a month. You'd have to find someone to share with. If you can't afford it, I mean.'

'Yes, I have a friend who might . . . Where is the flat?'

'Barnham Road, number five. It's furnished, but feel free to chuck stuff out and move your own gear in,' Mick said.

'Could you take me there now?' I asked him before knocking back my drink.

'Well, I suppose so. I don't want to be too long, though. I'm meeting a girl in here later.'

'Barnham Road isn't far,' I persisted.

'Look after that,' Mick said to the barman, pointing to his beer. 'I'll be back in five.'

I followed him out of the pub, knowing that I was going to have to be careful. If the other Ali discovered that I was renting Mick's flat ... I didn't even know Mick, I thought as we turned the corner into Barnham Road. I didn't know what his relationship with Ali was or anything else about him. I went after him through the front door of a Victorian house and waited in the hallway while he picked up some letters and fumbled for a key. He opened the door to the ground-floor flat and ushered me inside.

'This is it,' Mick said, leading me into the lounge and switching on the light. 'There are two bedrooms, a kitchen, bathroom and toilet, and this is the lounge. Oh, and the back garden is yours. The people upstairs have the front garden.'

'It's really nice,' I said quietly, looking around the large room. 'The thing is . . .'

'Don't worry about a deposit, Ali. Just give me a month's rent up front.'

'No, it's not that.' I sat down on the sofa. I knew that I had to be honest with Mick. 'I'm not Ali,' I blurted out.

'How many drinks have you had?' he asked me, laughing as he joined me on the sofa. 'So who are you? Mary? Jane?'

'No, no . . . just listen to me.'

I told him everything. From Ali the prude to Ali the slut, from my being on the game with Jackie to my not wanting to meet the other Ali ... I told Mick everything, and he said nothing until I'd finished. I thought that I'd blown it as he left the sofa and paced the lounge floor. Holding his hand to his head, he looked at me and opened his mouth now and then as if he was about to say something. Then he shook his head and stood in front of me. I smiled and twisted my long blonde hair nervously around my fingers as he

167

gazed down at me. Finally I could take no more and broke the silence.

'Well?' I said. 'Say something.'

'Fuck me,' Mick muttered. 'Identical twins? I can't believe how alike you both are.'

'Believe it or not, it's true.'

'OK, well . . . Do you want the flat or not?'

'Yes, if you don't mind letting it to a stranger.'

'I don't feel that you're a stranger, Ali. This is incredible. Right, so . . . As you said, you don't want the other Ali to know that you're here. That's not a problem. There's no need for me to tell anyone who's renting the place. If you're on the game with your friend . . . that's nothing to do with me. Er . . . have you got five hundred?'

'Not quite, but I will have in a day or so.'

'OK, that's fine. When do you want to move in? I suppose you'll want to show your friend first?'

'No, no, she'll be fine with the flat. I should have the money by –'

'Here's the key,' Mick said. 'You move in when you like and I'll be round at the weekend for the cash.'

'Great,' I said, taking the key. 'Wow, I can hardly believe it.'

'Neither can I,' he murmured. 'You and Ali are so alike, it's weird. Anyway, she won't know anything about this. I'd better show you round.'

As I followed Mick to the kitchen I couldn't believe my luck. I hoped that Jackie would be up for it and wondered what I was going to say to my parents. I'd have to lie to them, but I was becoming used to that. The bedrooms were lovely, and I knew that I'd made the right decision as Mick talked about the electricity and gas meters. It was a lot of money to find each month, but Jackie and I would be earning ten times that amount between us.

I finally left the flat and decided to go home. Mick had a girl to meet and I wanted to talk to my parents and phone Jackie. This was meant to be, I reflected as Mick returned to the pub and I walked home. Jackie had suggested getting a flat, I'd met Mick and told him the truth . . . This was meant to be. All I had to do now was talk to my parents. And I didn't think that would be easy.

Nine

I'd talked to my parents for two hours and had got to bed late. They'd questioned me, and I'd lied. I'd said that the flat belonged to a friend and the rent was only two hundred a month. I hadn't had the courage to tell them that I was leaving university so I said that I'd be going back at the end of the summer holiday. At first they'd seemed suspicious and upset, but I thought that they were basically all right with the idea.

Dad had gone to work and mum was out when I finally crawled out of bed. This was going to be an interesting day, I thought as I stepped into the shower. I washed my hair, and my cunt, in readiness to sell my young body for sex. My cunt, I thought. My cunt was a commodity, something to be sold to earn me money. I laughed as I stepped out of the shower and dried myself. I could sell my cunt time and time again, and yet it would still be mine. I was just hiring it out, I mused happily.

I got dressed in a knee-length skirt and discreet blouse and thought that I'd better ring Jackie. She was keener than ever about the flat and wanted to meet me there within half an hour. I agreed, and told her to bring money with her. We needed five hundred pounds within two days, so we were going to have to work hard – fuck hard. Jackie said that she'd go shopping and stock up on food. She also said that she'd found a new client, and that she'd tell me about it later.

I arrived at the flat in a taxi to find Jackie waiting on the doorstep surrounded by carrier bags of food and drink. The taxi driver dumped my things on the path, and I knew that we had a lot of work ahead of us. My clothes alone would take an age to put away, but I had all day. Jackie was wearing just jeans and a T-shirt, but she still looked incredibly sexual. We kissed before going into the flat, and I knew that we'd be christening our new home before the day was out. As I showed her round the place, she talked about her mum. What with her father moving out and then Jackie leaving home, her mother wasn't happy. Birds have to fly the nest at some stage, I thought, hoping that my mother was going to be all right. After we put the food away in the kitchen we got round to talking about money and pooled our cash. We had over four hundred pounds between us.

'We're going to have to work,' I said as Jackie made two cups of coffee.

'I have a new client,' she said proudly. 'He's in his early twenties and he's loaded.'

'That sounds good,' I said, smiling at her as she placed a coffee on the table in front of me. 'When does he want to see us?'

'He's going to phone. I gave him your number, seeing as it's the business number. His name's Terry.'

'Well, let's hope he calls soon. Where did you meet him?'

'In the street.'

'Jackie, you . . . you didn't just go up to a stranger in the street?'

'He came up to me. I was standing on a corner and he –'

'That's soliciting,' I cut in. 'You *are* naughty.'

'I wasn't looking for a client. He must have assumed that I . . . anyway, he said that he'd phone.'

'Well, let's just hope that he's all right. I'd better put my things away. What about your stuff? Why didn't you bring it round?'

'My mum's dropping my things round later. Oh, do you have a key?'

'I only have one but I'll get another cut. So, Jackie, it was only yesterday that you suggested we get a flat and here we are.'

'It's a lovely place. I can't believe how lucky we are.'

We talked about the flat and the things we'd need and decided which of the bedrooms each of us would have. I knew that we'd be sharing a bed more often than not, but we'd need our own rooms. I didn't want our clients calling at the flat, and Jackie agreed, but that was going to create problems. Visiting John and his friends would be fine, but not all clients would welcome us at their homes – especially if they were married.

It felt strange being in my own flat with Jackie. It wasn't at all like home but I was sure that we'd be fine after a few weeks. I'd miss my bedroom, I thought as Jackie took a bottle of cleaner from the cupboard and sprayed the worktops. I'd also miss my mother, not least because she washed and ironed and cooked . . . But the way Jackie was polishing the sink and cleaning the cupboard doors, I hoped that she was into housework. It certainly looked that way.

'Are you any good at cooking?' I asked her as she loaded the dishwasher with just about everything in sight.

'Good enough,' she replied. 'I suppose you want the kitchen to be my domain?'

'Well, it would be nice. I'm not really into –'

'I know you're not, Ali,' she cut in, with a giggle. 'I remember that time you made a birthday cake for your

172

mum. God, what a mess you made of it. The cake ended up in the bin and the kitchen looked like a bomb had hit it.'

'That's settled, then,' I said happily. 'I'll run the business, work out the money and pay the bills and stuff. Obviously, we'll only take cash from the clients. We'll pool the money and I'll deal with the finances.'

'That's sounds good to me, especially as I'm useless with money. Ali, I don't think we should tell anyone that we live here. Our friends, I mean.'

'I agree. The last thing we want is a stream of visitors. This is our home, our lust nest.'

'Our *love* nest?' she asked softly, locking her dark-eyed gaze to mine.

'Yes, yes – our love nest.'

Jackie's mother dropped her things off and Jackie and I spent the day organising the flat. We finally flopped onto the sofa with a bottle of wine. Raising our glasses, we toasted our new home – and our new business venture. Jackie suggested that we should go to the pub, but I declined. The last thing I wanted was to bump into Barry or one of the other men, not to mention Ali the slut. Jackie was right, we needed to find some new clients. But not in our local pub.

'Hello,' I said, answering my mobile.

'Is that Ali?' a male voice asked.

'Yes.'

'Jackie gave me your number. My name's Terry.'

'Ah, yes, she did mention you. How can we help you?'

'I would have thought that was obvious,' Terry said, with a chuckle. 'Seriously, she said that you'd give me your price list, if I can call it that?'

'OK, so what are you looking for? Anything in particular?'

'Just a wank,' he replied unashamedly.

'Is that all?'

'To begin with, yes. I'm short of money, but at the end of the month . . . Are you free this evening?'

'Yes, we're both free. Where would you like us to meet you?'

'Can't I come round to you?'

'No, we don't work from home. We'll meet you in the park by Lenox Road in, say, half an hour?'

'Yes, that's fine. But . . . how much?'

'As you're short of cash at the moment, I'll make it thirty.'

'Oh, er . . .'

'Is that all right?'

'It's a bit more than I'd expected.'

'I can't drop the price any lower,' I sighed, winking at Jackie. 'Two girls, four hands . . . we do a good job, Terry.'

'I'm sure you do. OK, that's fine. So, you'll both be there?'

'Yes. Cash up front, of course.'

'Right, I'll be there.'

I looked at Jackie and grinned. Thirty pounds wasn't a great deal of money, but it would all add up. Besides, it would only take ten minutes or so. Jackie seemed happy enough and, as she pointed out, thirty pounds covered half the shopping she'd bought. We changed before leaving the flat because I thought we'd look better in miniskirts than in jeans. Chatting excitedly about our new business venture, we headed for the park. The sun was still shining as we reached our destination and I began to wonder what we were going to do during the winter months. I didn't fancy the prospect of getting laid in the snow.

Jackie pointed Terry out as he walked towards us across the grass. He looked younger than I'd imagined him, and I wondered why he didn't have a girlfriend. His hair was dark and he was wearing blue jeans and a T-shirt and he wasn't unattractive, so why did he have to pay for a wank? He must have had his reasons, I reckoned as Jackie introduced us. We led him into the woods and found a nice spot behind some bushes where he passed me the cash. Easy money, I thought happily as he unbuckled his belt and dropped his jeans.

'Nice,' Jackie breathed, kneeling in front of him and stroking the solid shaft of his cock.

'Will you become a regular?' I asked him, joining Jackie on the ground.

'Well, when I can afford it,' Terry replied. 'I don't have a girlfriend so . . . I work all hours and it's not easy.'

'I understand,' I said, looking up and smiling at him. 'That's what we're here for. Don't worry, we'll look after you.'

Terry gasped as I cupped his heavy balls and Jackie moved his fleshy foreskin slowly back and forth over his swollen glans. We wanted to give him his money's worth so we took it slowly. He was good-looking and his cock was pretty big, and I thought that he'd be a nice catch for some girl or other. But, whatever his reasons, he had come to us for satisfaction. As I kneaded his full balls and Jackie rubbed her thumb over the smooth surface of his purple knob, I thought how sad it was that he had to pay for a wank. There again, it was just as well.

'How much extra for a blow job?' he asked us.

'Well . . .' Jackie began. She looked at me and winked. 'What do you think?'

'Give us another ten,' I said. Although I was tempted to do it for the same price, I was in business to make money and wasn't going to do him any favours. 'Two mouths for forty pounds is cheap,' I added.

175

'OK,' he said, bending over and tugging out a note from his jeans pocket.

I took the money and ran my wet tongue up and down his rock-hard shaft as Jackie licked his rolling balls. He gasped again, thinking – I hoped – that his money had been well spent. I had no idea what other prostitutes charged and I was basically playing it by ear. Once we were up and running properly with a list of regular clients, I'd know what I could get away with. I was running a business, and there was no way I was going to cut my prices.

Terry looked down and watched as Jackie and I kissed each other with his swollen knob sandwiched between our wet lips. As our tongues snaked over the velveteen surface of his knob, meeting now and then as we licked and slurped, our stares locked and we both knew that we wanted each other. It was amazing to think that we were being paid for pleasuring ourselves and I thought it was unfair that men had to resort to prostitutes. If a girl wanted sex, all she had to do was go to the pub and find a young man. Unfair though it was, I wasn't complaining.

'I'm coming,' Terry announced as Jackie and I licked and sucked his bulbous knob and wanked his solid shaft.

'We'll both drink your spunk,' I whispered huskily.

'We'll suck out your spunk and swallow it all,' Jackie said, her crude words adding to his pleasure.

His beautiful knob once more sandwiched between our full lips, his spunk jetting, we sucked and slurped and swallowed hard as he let out a low moan of pleasure. His cream splattered my face and dribbled down my chin as Jackie and I engulfed his throbbing knob in our hot mouths and he mumbled his crude words about giving teenage girls a facial. We sucked and drank until he crumpled and his knob began to deflate, and then we kissed and licked the cream from each other's faces.

'You two are amazing,' Terry said as he tugged his jeans up. His words drifted over my head as I kissed Jackie and probed her spermed mouth with my tongue. I felt my clitoris swell and my juices of lesbian desire flow into the tight crotch of my knickers. 'Are you lesbians?' he asked us. We finally stood up, wiped our mouths on the backs of our hands and smiled at him.

'Was that all right for you?' Jackie asked him.

'It was amazing,' Terry said, grinning. 'Are you lesbians?' he asked again.

'We can be anything you want us to be,' I replied.

'You mean, you'd do a real lesbian show for me?'

'Of course.'

'How much? I mean, not now but . . . how much?'

'Wait until the end of the month when you get your money,' Jackie said. 'You have our number, so ring us when you get paid.'

'Yes, yes, I will. Right, well . . . thanks very much. I'll ring you, OK?'

'OK,' I said, smiling at him.

We waited until Terry had gone before we headed home. Jackie chatted about the money we'd earned and repeatedly asked me how much we should charge for a lesbian show. But I was more interested in making sure that we weren't being followed. Jackie was even newer to the game than I was and obviously didn't worry about being followed. I had a bit more experience, I thought, looking over my shoulder every now and then.

'It's this way,' she said as we reached the end of our road. 'Where are you going?'

'Round the block,' I replied. 'I thought I saw someone following us. It was probably nothing, but we

177

can't be too careful. I don't think we should go straight home.'

'Oh, right. I know you don't want to go to the pub, but . . . how about going to that wine bar in the High Street?'

'Good idea,' I said. 'You're probably thinking that I'm paranoid, but . . .'

'No, not at all. I mean, anyone could follow us and find out where we live.'

There were only half a dozen people in the wine bar, which pleased me. Hoping that Ali the slut didn't use the place, I ordered two spritzers and led Jackie to a secluded corner table. She sipped her drink, smiled at me and said that I was the boss. She was right, I thought happily. One of us had to run the business and deal with the finances, and I preferred it to be me. Jackie had always been hopeless with money and, seeing as she was brilliant in the kitchen, we made a good team.

'What are you doing?' she asked me as I took a pen and paper from my handbag.

'Our accounts,' I replied. 'I'm writing down everything we earn, and everything we spend.'

'Even the drinks?'

'Yes, even the drinks. Don't forget that we have rent to pay. There's the shopping, toiletries, clothes . . .'

'Tampons,' she added with a giggle.

'Trust you to think of that.'

'Anal lubricant.'

'Anal . . . you *are* a naughty girl. That reminds me, we need an internet connection.'

'What for?'

'We both have computers so we might as well be on the internet.'

'We could have our own website,' Jackie suggested excitedly. 'Girls in the woods, dot com.'

'Don't be silly, Jackie. Actually, you might have an idea there. Once we have real money coming in, I'll give it some thought.'

'I'm not just a pretty face.'

'You're pretty all over,' I said softly. 'Especially between your . . . well, you're pretty all over.'

'This will be our first night in our new home. Are you coming in my bed or shall I come in yours?'

'As long as we come, I don't care which bed we're in,' I quipped. 'I have a vibrator in my room. Perhaps we should try it out?'

'Wow, yes. Let's go home now and –'

'Hang on,' I cut in as I grabbed my ringing phone from my bag. 'Hello, Ali speaking.'

'Ali, it's Jack.'

'Jack? Oh, you're Simon's friend.'

'Yes, that's right. Can you fit me in this evening?'

'Er . . . actually, I've finished for the day. I'm free tomorrow evening if –'

'No, I can't make it tomorrow evening. I suppose I only wanted to meet you, take a look at you and find out what you offer. Is there somewhere I could meet you, just for a few minutes?'

'I'm in the wine bar in the High Street,' I said, winking at Jackie. 'You're welcome to come along and buy my friend and me a drink.'

'Oh, you're not alone?'

'My *girl*friend – we work together.'

'Oh, right. Well, I'll be there in ten minutes. Er . . . how will I recognise you?'

'Just look for two stunning teenage girls sitting together at a table.'

'Who was that?' Jackie asked me as I dropped my phone back into my bag.

179

'His name's Jack – he's a potential client. He wants to take a look at us and find out what we offer.'

'That's great. At this rate we'll be booked up every day of the week. Perhaps we could wank him off under the table?'

'I'll wank *you* off under the table in a minute, you naughty girl.'

'I wish you would, Ali. I'm so wet and . . .'

'Look, we have to be businesslike when he arrives. No giggling or messing about.'

'Yes, boss,' Jackie said, knocking back her drink.

'There's ten pounds. Go and buy two more spritzers. And bring me the change.'

As I watched her walk up to the bar I knew that we were going to work well together. She'd always been the fun-loving type, but she also had her serious side and I was sure that we'd live together in harmony. She was extremely attractive and . . . My stomach somersaulted as I pictured the hairless lips of her young pussy and I wondered again whether I was in love. I couldn't be in love with another girl, I tried to convince myself. It just wasn't possible, was it? What the hell would my parents say if they discovered that I was a prostitute living with her lesbian lover?

'Is that him?' Jackie asked as she returned to our table with the drinks.

'I think so,' I whispered as a middle-aged man approached.

'Ali?' he said, looking first at Jackie and then at me.

'I'm Ali,' I said.

'I'm Jack – pleased to meet you. I see you've got drinks.'

'We'll have two spritzers, please,' I said. 'This is Jackie, my friend.'

'Hi, Jackie. Er . . . OK, two spritzers coming up.'

'We've already got drinks,' Jackie whispered as the man went to the bar.

'If he's buying, we'll have another one. What do you think of him?'

Jackie grinned. 'If he's got money, then he's OK.'

'Leave this to me,' I said. 'OK, here he comes. Only speak if you're spoken to.'

'Yes, boss.'

'I'm looking for some fun once a week,' Jack said as he placed our drinks on the table and took a seat.

'Aren't you drinking?' I asked him.

'No, I'm not staying. I'd like to see what's on offer before we talk money. I'd like to see what you have between your legs.'

'And I like to see cash before I show you what I've got,' I returned. 'Look, we're both eighteen years old so what we've got is pretty obvious.'

'Just a glimpse?' Jack persisted.

I glanced around the bar to make sure that no one was looking. 'Jackie, show him,' I ordered her.

'What?' she gasped, glancing around the bar herself. 'You mean, show him my –'

'Just do it, Jackie.'

Jackie eased her miniskirt up and pulled the front of her knickers down to display her hairless sex slit to Jack. He nodded approvingly, mumbling something about shaved pussies as he adjusted the bulge in his trousers. Making sure again that no one was watching, Jackie lifted her T-shirt and yanked her bra clear of her firm breasts. Jack nodded approvingly once more and then asked me to show him what I'd got.

'I've got the same as Jackie,' I said. 'So, do you approve?'

'Very much,' he said quietly, grinning at me.

'One hundred pounds for half an hour,' I enlightened him.

'That's for full sex?'

'Yes.'

'That's not a bad price for two girls.'

'That's for one girl. If you want both of us, it's one hundred and fifty.'

He frowned, his stare darting between Jackie and me. 'Will that include everything? I mean, oral and . . .'

'Everything, but not anal.'

'Anal is my fetish,' he said, raising his eyebrows. 'I must have anal.'

'Two hundred.'

'I'll have to think about it,' Jack said as he left the table. 'It's a hell of a lot of money for half an hour.'

'And, between us, we're a hell of a lot of girl,' I countered. 'Ring me, OK?'

'OK, I'll think about it. I really don't think I can pay that much, but I'll think about it.'

Jackie waited until he'd left the bar before grimacing at me. 'You've just lost us a client,' she said. 'Two hundred quid for half an hour? You must be crazy. No one would pay that for –'

'We're not cheap sluts, Jackie. We're sluts, but we're not cheap.'

'I know, but . . .'

'I'm the boss, so trust me.'

'OK, if you say so. At least I got a drink for showing him my tits and pussy. Why didn't you show him yours?'

'I don't pull my knickers down in seedy bars,' I said, giggling as she frowned at me again. 'I'm a refined young lady.'

'So what does that make me?'

'My employee.'

'I'm not sure that I like this,' Jackie murmured.

'Have a lager, then,' I quipped.

'No, I mean . . .'

'I know what you meant, Jackie.'

'Anyway, this isn't a seedy bar.'

'It is now that you've flashed your body in public. Seriously, Jackie, leave the business side of things to me.'

'I don't want to be your employee.'

'You're not, you silly girl. We're working together, OK? We're equal, except that you'll do as I tell you. If I tell you to pull your knickers down in a bar and show your pussy to a man, then you'll do it.'

'You're the boss.'

'Exactly.'

'I still say that you've lost us a client.'

'Shut up, or I'll spank your bare bottom.'

'Promise?' Jackie said, giggling as she left the table. 'I need the loo – I'll be back in a minute.'

We were getting on well, I thought as I downed my drink. She was fun to be with, and she had a perfect body. I wasn't going to say anything to her, but I reckoned that she was right about Jack. I'd probably just lost us a client. But I didn't want to become a cheap prostitute. Giving a man a blow job in the woods for forty pounds wasn't the way a high-class pro would behave, but we had to start somewhere. And I didn't intend to carry on the way we'd started.

Turning my thoughts to Simon as I sipped my drink, I wondered whether his friend Jack would tell him that he'd met Jackie and me in the pub. I couldn't allow Simon to meet Jackie because he'd recognise her as my friend, so I had to be careful. The best thing to do would be to meet Simon in the woods whenever he needed me. He was bound to hear that Ali the prude had left home, so there'd be no more dangerous episodes at the end of the garden.

Things were working out well, I thought happily, except I was still concerned about the winter months.

Where would we meet our clients? I didn't want to have to use our flat as a brothel, but I couldn't see that we were going to have a choice. I also had my parents to worry about. When they discovered that I'd left university they'd go mad. As it was, I'd lied to them about my job as a secretary. They were bound to want to see the flat once I'd settled in and ... It was early days, I reflected. I had several bridges to cross, but not for a while.

'Ali speaking,' I said, answering my phone as it rang suddenly.

'I don't know what your game is,' the slut said. 'But I don't like it.'

'And I don't like *your* game,' I countered.

'I'm not playing games. Why the hell are you pretending to be me?'

'I'm not pretending to be anyone, Ali. To be honest, I've had enough of people mixing us up.'

'From what I've heard, you're making out that you're me.'

'Why would I do that? Look, I don't even know you. We've never met or –'

'What's your real name?' she cut in.

'Ali, which is short for Alison. What's *your* real name?'

'Ali, which is short for Alice,' she enlightened me. 'And we are *not* sisters.'

'In that case, we must be each other's doubles. Why don't we meet somewhere for a chat?'

'No, I ... I don't want to,' she muttered.

'Come on, Alice. If we really are identical in looks, it would be fascinating to meet.'

As she hung up, I reckoned that she would agree to meet me at some stage. Maybe the notion frightened her? Meeting someone who looked identical would be quite daunting. But I was sure that she was faltering and the time would come when intrigue got the better of her. I'd keep this to myself, I decided as Jackie neared the table. There was no need to involve her.

'I've had an idea,' she said as she retook her seat opposite me.

'Oh, dear,' I murmured, grinning at her. 'Go on.'

'I've been thinking about the flat and taking clients back.'

'Great minds think alike.'

'What?'

'Nothing. Go on.'

'We can't take them home, right? So how about renting a bedsit somewhere?'

'A bedsit?' I echoed, frowning at her.

'Just a single room with a bed where we can meet our clients.'

'That's not a bad idea, Jackie. You're not just a pretty face, are you? OK, your job is to find a place. It needs to be close to our flat, and cheap. Don't go signing anything until I've seen the place, OK?'

'Who's that girl over there?' Jackie asked me, looking at the bar.

'I have no idea,' I replied, glancing at an attractive teenager who had long blonde hair. 'Why do you ask?'

'She's been looking at you for ages. I just wondered whether you knew her.'

'No, I don't. There's one way to find out,' I said, grabbing our empty glasses. 'Same again?'

'Mmm, please.'

I said nothing as I stood by the girl and ordered the drinks, but I could feel her staring at me. Was this something to do with Ali the slut? I wondered, taking my purse from my bag. If she'd thought that I was the slut, she'd have said something. But she just looked at me, scrutinised me. As I paid for the drinks and slipped my purse into my bag, I turned and faced her.

'How are you?' she asked me.

'I'm fine,' I replied. 'I'm sorry, but I don't think we've met before.'

'You're Ali, aren't you?'

'Yes, that's right. And you are?'

'I'm Amy.'

My stomach sank. I knew that she was the slut's lesbian friend. 'Do I know you?' I asked, frowning at her.

'I'm Ali's friend. The other Ali, I mean.'

'Oh, I see.' Unsure what to say, I took the drinks from the bar. 'I have to get back to my friend,' I murmured.

'Wait, don't go yet. The likeness is incredible. I've been watching you for a while and . . . It's amazing.'

'It also causes problems,' I said, forcing a smile. 'People mix us up and . . . well, it causes problems.'

'Yes, Ali's told me about it. Do you think that she's your sister?'

'I have no idea. It is possible but . . . She won't agree to meet me, so I doubt that I'll ever find out. She rang me this evening but –'

'She's worried,' Amy cut in. 'Her family history is a mess. Her mother was a whore – *is* a whore, I should say – and she never knew her father. She thinks that, if you are her sister, she'll discover things that she'd rather not know.'

'So her mother might be my mother?'

'Yes, that's right.'

'Where does she live, Amy? I need to talk to her.'

'I can't tell you that. She asked me to find you so I've been going around the bars and pubs looking for you.'

'And now that you've found me?'

'She wanted me to meet you and find out what sort of person you are, what you're like.'

186

'What will you tell her, then?'

'That you seem nice enough.'

'So, where to from here?'

'I don't know,' Amy sighed. 'I didn't want to get caught up in all this. I've told her to meet you but she won't. Hadn't you better get back to your friend?'

'Yes, I suppose so. Look, can we meet again?'

'Is she more than a friend? The girl you're with, I mean.'

'No . . . I mean, yes, she is. I know about you and Ali. I mean, I know that you're a . . .'

'A lesbian? It's all right – it's not a secret.'

'Right, well . . . I'd better get back.'

'I'd like to talk to you, when you're alone and you have more time. What are you doing later this evening?'

'Well, I . . . nothing, I suppose.'

'Can you come back here later?'

'Er . . . I'll try.'

'OK, I'll be here until they close.'

'Yes, well . . . I'll see what I can do.'

As I walked back to the table I felt my stomach somersault. Although Jackie and I had a lesbian relationship, I'd never met a self-admitted lesbian before. I found Amy extremely attractive, sensual and . . . She had full red lips and dark, sparkling eyes. God, I thought as I sat opposite Jackie. What the hell was I thinking? Jackie frowned and asked me who the girl was, so I had to explain. She listened intently, sipping her drink now and then without taking her eyes off me. When I came to the end of my revelation, Jackie suggested that she should go home, giving me time to talk to Amy.

'I'll wait for you at the flat,' she said. 'You've got to sort this thing out with the other Ali, so give me the key and I'll see you later.'

'OK,' I murmured, gazing across the bar at Amy. 'You're right, I have got to sort this out.'

'I don't know whether it's a good idea to leave you alone with an attractive young girl,' Jackie said, giggling as I slid the key across the table. 'You might run off with her and have sex.'

'Don't be silly,' I retorted. 'It's you I want, and you know it.'

'She might become a client,' Jackie said, her dark eyes sparkling with mischief. 'We could have lesbian clients as well as men.'

'Well, yes – I suppose we could. I hadn't thought of that.'

She knocked back what was left of her drink and stood up. 'Don't be too long,' she said, smiling at me. 'I'll be waiting for you.'

'I won't be long, I promise.'

As Jackie left the bar, I felt my hands trembling and my heart racing. Amy was so incredibly attractive and young and slim and . . . I reminded myself that I was supposed to be finding out about the other Ali as I watched Amy order two drinks. She was going to join me, I knew as she turned and smiled at me. She was wearing a turquoise miniskirt and a white blouse, and she looked stunning. Her small breasts were clearly outlined by the thin material of her blouse and I found myself wondering whether she'd shaved her young pussy.

'OK to talk?' she asked, placing the drinks on the table.

'Yes, of course,' I replied. 'Thanks for the drink.'

'You got rid of her, then? Your friend, I mean.'

'She's gone back to . . . She has things to do.'

Sitting next to me, Amy gazed into my eyes. 'You're sweet,' she murmured huskily. 'You're just like Ali, but . . . I can tell the difference.'

'I'm glad someone can,' I said, with a chuckle. 'Other people I've met ... well, there's been one mix-up after another.'

'There is a subtle difference. Your lips are slightly fuller than Ali's. And your eyes are wider.'

'Right, well ... Tell me all about Ali.'

'She has beautiful round tits and her pussy is divine.'

'No, I mean ... what's she like as a person? Where did you meet her and how long have you known her?'

'I've known her for a year or so. We met in a pub and ... we've had some wonderful times together, sexy times. The trouble with Ali is that she flits about from here to there. I never know where she is or when I'll see her again.'

'I've heard that from other people. So, is she living nearby? In Harvey Road, for example?'

'How do you know about Harvey Road?'

'I've been doing my homework, trying to find out where she lives.'

'She doesn't live in Harvey Road – she has a friend there. She doesn't have her own place at the moment. She was thinking about moving to Birmingham, but I don't think she knows what she wants.'

'Is she a ... I don't know how to put this. Does she work for herself?'

'She's on the game, if that's what you mean?'

'Yes, that is what I meant.'

'Although I've known her for a year or more, I don't really know anything about her. I've never met her mother, I don't know many of her friends ... Actually, she doesn't go in for friends. She has one or two, but that's about all. She's a mysterious girl.'

'Perhaps I should just forget about her,' I sighed.

'Yes, that might be a good idea,' Amy said softly, placing her hand on my naked knee.

I began to tremble as Amy slipped her hand between my thighs. I wanted to stop her but my heart raced and my stomach somersaulted at the prospect of enjoying her young body. The fragrance of her perfume, the feel of her fingertips pressing into the swell of my knickers . . . I had no power to resist her advances as she massaged my fleshy pussy lips through the tight material of my knickers. No one could see what she was doing beneath the table, so I parted my thighs and gave her better access to the most private part of my young body.

Pulling the wet crotch of my knickers to one side, Amy slipped two fingers deep into the heat of my tight pussy and massaged my creamy-wet inner flesh. I gasped, my gaze darting around the bar as my clitoris swelled and my juices of lesbian desire flowed over her hand. Using her thumb, Amy massaged the solid bulb of my sensitive clitoris, taking me dangerously close to my desperately needed climax. I couldn't come in the bar, I thought anxiously. People were around – someone might see me and –

'No,' I whispered. 'No, Amy, not in here.'

'Why not?' she asked me, kissing my cheek.

'Because . . .'

'Just relax and let it come.'

I couldn't relax, but I knew that I was going to come anyway. I thought about Jackie as my orgasm neared. She'd be waiting in the flat for me, looking forward to going to bed and loving me and . . . I tried to feel guilty, but I couldn't. I breathed in Amy's perfume again and my womb fluttered. Her hair was blonde and shone like silk, her lips were full and succulent, her probing fingers were soft and feminine . . . My orgasm exploded within the pulsating bud of my clitoris as I hung my head and stifled my whimpers of ecstasy.

'Come,' Amy whispered in my ear. 'Keep coming for me.'

'Don't stop,' I gasped, my young body trembling uncontrollably.

She didn't stop, and my orgasm rolled on and on. My flushed face veiled by my long blonde hair, my breathing fast and shallow, I gripped the sides of my chair as my pleasure peaked again and shook me to the core. I could feel the wetness of my knickers against my skin, and I knew that the back of my skirt was soaking up my lesbian milk. What would Jackie say? I'd have to change my skirt and knickers. Would she be suspicious? Although we shared our bodies with men, I'd never cheated on her like this. I'd fucked Simon, but that was different. Now I was with another girl, a self-confessed lesbian, and I was cheating on Jackie.

I wanted Amy to feel my firm breasts and toy with my erect nipples, I wanted to reciprocate and slide my fingers into her young vagina and take her to an amazing orgasm. But there were other people in the bar. People were drinking and chatting, totally unaware that I was in the grip of a lesbian-induced orgasm. I wanted to take Amy to my bed and love her.

'Stop now,' I whispered as my orgasm began to fade. 'Amy, please . . .'

She slipped her wet fingers out of my sated vagina, pulled my knickers across and concealed the swollen lips of my dripping pussy. 'Was that nice?' she asked me.

'God, yes,' I breathed softly. 'That was heavenly.'

'I'm pleased that you're bald down there,' Amy said, her dark eyes sparkling lustfully. 'I love licking and eating bald pussy.'

Her words excited me and I looked down at her naked thighs, resting my hand on her leg as she sucked my pussy milk from her fingers. She parted her thighs, offering me access to the sexual centre of her young body. My fingers pressed into the warmth of her knickers and I pulled the crotch to one side and slid my fingers into her young vagina. She was so tight, hot and wet, and I knew that I'd be seeing her again. A little guilt seeped into my mind as I massaged her erect clitoris with my thumb and I realised that I wasn't in love with Jackie. We were business partners, flatmates, sex partners. We weren't lovers.

Amy came quickly, her clitoris pulsating beneath my thumb and her sex milk flowing over my fingers as I sustained her lesbian pleasure. I wanted to squeeze the firmness of her pert young breasts and suck on her milk teats, but . . .

When I noticed the barman looking our way I massaged Amy's clitoris more slowly, bringing out the last of her pleasure as she stifled her gasps of lesbian pleasure. I'd have to arrange to meet her somewhere, I decided, finally retrieving my pussy-wet fingers and sitting upright.

'You're beautiful,' Amy whispered, adjusting her skirt and brushing her long blonde hair away from her sex-flushed face. 'I want you, Ali. I want all of you.'

'I know,' I murmured. 'And . . . and I want you.'

'Come back to my place with me.'

'No, I . . . I can't,' I stammered. I took a pen and paper from my bag and wrote down my phone number. 'Ring me,' I said, passing her the piece of paper. 'Ring me tomorrow and . . . and we'll meet.'

'You know what I want to do to you, don't you?' Amy asked quietly. 'I want to suck out your pussy juice. I want to suck your clitoris into my mouth and –'

'Amy, stop it,' I cut in, giggling as she licked her full lips and grinned at me. 'My knickers are soaking wet as it is.'

'Take them off,' she whispered. 'I want to taste them.'

'Tomorrow,' I said firmly. 'I must go now.'

'Go home to your girlfriend?'

'Yes, no, I mean . . . We share a flat but . . .'

'It's all right – you don't have to explain.'

I finished my drink and stood up. 'Tomorrow, OK?'

'I'll dream of you tonight,' Amy said.

'Ring me tomorrow, Amy.'

'I'll dream about licking you and drinking your pussy juices and –'

'Tomorrow,' I repeated.

I left the bar, breathed in the warm evening air and headed home. My knickers were soaked and I could feel my vaginal milk running down my inner thighs. I'd go straight to the bathroom and wash away the evidence of lesbian sex, I decided as I reached the flat. I'd go to bed with Jackie and we'd have sex, and I'd imagine that it was Amy licking me. I was making a mess of my life, I knew as I rang the doorbell. I was losing my direction in life yet again.

Ten

Jackie had been quiet when I'd got back to the flat the previous evening. I'd told her what Amy had said about the other Ali, but she didn't seem interested. Whether or not she'd been suspicious, had thought that Amy and I had got up to something, I wasn't sure. She'd said that she was tired and, much to my disappointment, we'd slept in our own rooms.

Although I was up early, Jackie was already in the kitchen making breakfast. She poured me a cup of coffee and seemed all right, but I felt that there was something wrong. I didn't like mind games and decided not to ask her what the problem was. If something was bothering her then she'd have to tell me about it.

'Breakfast smells good,' I said, sitting at the table. 'Eggs and bacon – my favourite.'

'And fried bread and grilled tomatoes and mushrooms,' she said. 'I hope you're hungry?'

'Starved,' I replied. 'So, what shall we do today?'

'You're the boss, so you tell me.'

'We need money to pay the rent,' I sighed.

'We might have had Jack, that man in the pub, as a client. But you're the boss.'

'As I said last night, Jackie: we're sluts, but we're not cheap sluts.'

194

'And, as you said just now, we need money to pay the rent.'

Jackie chatted as we enjoyed out breakfast, but I still felt that something was wrong. I helped her to clear the kitchen and do the washing-up and then we sat in the lounge and talked about the business. I was hoping that John and his friends would need our services before Mick came round to collect the rent. I also wondered whether Simon would phone and ask me to meet him in the woods. One thing was certain: if we were going to survive, we'd need more clients. As I seemed to be doing all the talking, I finally asked Jackie what the problem was.

'Last night,' she began. 'I . . . I was followed home.'

'Who followed you?' I asked her. 'A man or . . .'

'Your twin sister,' she told me. 'I thought it was you at first. She looked identical to you, but she had different clothes on.'

'So she knows now that you live here?'

'Yes, I'm afraid so. I'm sorry, Ali. I should have made sure that –'

'Don't worry about it,' I cut in. 'Why didn't you tell me last night?'

'I thought you'd go mad. You'd been saying that we have to be careful about being followed and . . . well, I thought you'd go mad.'

'I think the other Ali might want to meet me at some stage. So is that why you were quiet last night?'

'Yes, it is.'

'You *are* silly, Jackie. To be honest, I'm not worried about my sister any more. If she discovers that I live here, then so what? There's not much she can do about it, is there?'

'No, I suppose not.'

'From what Amy told me, my sister might be moving to Birmingham. The only thing that's bothered

195

me is people mixing us up. If she moves away –' My mobile rang. Answering it, I was surprised to hear Jack. 'Good morning,' I said, winking at Jackie.

'I've been thinking about your proposition,' Jack said. 'I've decided to go for it.'

'A wise decision,' I replied. 'You won't be disappointed, I can assure you.'

'So, are you both free this morning?'

'As it happens, we've just had a cancellation.'

'That's great. Would you meet me in the church?'

'The church?' I echoed, thinking that I must have misheard him.

'The church in Green Lane. I'm the vicar there.'

'Oh, er . . . yes, of course. What time?'

'Now, if that's OK with you? I have the cash with me – two hundred pounds.'

'We'll leave straight away, Jack.'

'Good. Oh, er . . . I'll want anal sex.'

'No problem. Like I said, two hundred gets you anal.'

'OK – I'll see you soon.' Jack rang off.

I grinned at Jackie. 'We're in business,' I said. 'Two hundred, in cash.'

'I was wrong, then?' she asked.

'You certainly were. OK, let's go. We have to meet him at the church. He's a vicar.'

'A vicar?' she gasped, holding her hand to her pretty mouth.

'Vicars have cocks, Jackie,' I replied, giggling.

'I know but . . . I mean, he's supposed to be a man of God.'

'Perhaps God told him to fuck prostitutes. Come on, we have work to do.'

'God's work?'

'The work of the Devil, more like. That's a thought. We could call ourselves the Devil's Daughters.'

* * *

I felt my heart leap as Jackie and I left the flat. Two hundred pounds, I mused happily. The first month's rent was covered, which was a relief, and we had another month before the rent was due again. Things were going to work out well, I thought as we reached the church. If the vicar could afford to see us once a week, his money alone would cover the rent and the food. I wasn't bothered about my slut sister. My only problem was Amy. She was beautiful, and I wanted her. But I already had Jackie.

'Hi,' the vicar said as he ushered us into the church and locked the doors. He passed me a wad of notes and grinned. 'I'd like you to bend over the altar,' he said, adjusting his cock through his cassock. 'Both of you, with your feet wide apart.'

OK,' I replied as I stuffed the cash into my handbag. 'We're all yours for the next half-hour.'

'I must repent,' Jack sighed. 'I'm a sinner and . . . I have to offer your bodies to God by way of a sacrifice.'

Jackie and I looked at each other and tried not to giggle as we walked down the aisle. As I leaned over the altar I breathed in the musky smell of the church. The air in the old building was cold, and I shuddered as I wondered whether ghosts were lurking. I'd gone to church regularly when I was younger, but I'd never dreamed that one day I'd be leaning over the altar with a vicar behind me and . . . A sacrifice? I wondered what that might mean as I gazed at the huge candles adorning the altar. What did he intend to do to us?

We were both wearing miniskirts, and I pictured the view that the vicar must have had as he knelt behind us. He lifted my skirt up and pressed his face into the groove between my firm buttocks. He breathed in. Then he moved to Jackie and inhaled the scent of her young bottom through the thin material of her tight knickers. Were all vicars like this? I wondered. Were they all sad perverts? It didn't matter what the vicar was, I decided. He'd paid two hundred pounds for the pleasure of our teenage bodies, so as far as I was concerned he could play his sacrifice games and satisfy his lust for young girls.

After yanking my knickers down and exposing the firm cheeks of my bum, Jack the vicar moved to Jackie and did the same to her. Then he parted my naked buttocks, stretching my cheeks open wide and licking the delicate tissue surrounding my tight bottom-hole. He licked and slurped for several minutes, tasting me there before moving to Jackie and licking the tight hole of her anus too.

His saliva cooled quickly in the cold air and ran down my inner thighs, and I shivered. There was a strange atmosphere in the church – it was eerie, as if unseen eyes were watching me, and I began to wonder whether this was a good idea. By offering my young body to the perverted vicar, I was desecrating a holy place. But I'd been paid and I had a job to do. Besides, half an hour wasn't long and I'd soon be back outside in the sunshine.

As the vicar walked round to the other side of the altar and bound my wrists together with rope, I wondered whether I should protest. He pulled on the rope, stretching my arms across the altar before securing the end. Then he did the same to Jackie, binding her wrists together and pulling her arms across the altar before he stood behind us once again. He hadn't mentioned bondage when we'd agreed on the price, but I thought that it was probably all right.

'I offer you the flesh of these whores,' Jack bellowed, his voice echoing around the church. 'I offer you, oh master, the defiled flesh of these young girls.'

Jackie and I looked at each other, frowning as the vicar began chanting and again offered our young bodies to his unseen master. His time was running out, I mused. There again, with our wrists bound he could keep us there for as long as he liked. I watched him take a huge candle from the altar and knew what he was about to do as he knelt behind Jackie. Grimacing, she whimpered as he forced the candle deep into her teenage vagina. Then he took another candle, parted the fleshy lips of my pussy and pushed the waxen phallus deep into my sex sheath too.

I'd never had my young vaginal opening stretched so far, and I thought that I was going to split apart as the vicar pushed the candle fully home. My clitoris forced out from beneath its protective hood, the delicate petals of my inner lips stretched tautly around the wax shaft, it felt as though the candle had sunk deep into my contracting womb. He'd said that he'd wanted anal sex, but there was no way he'd be able to push his cock into the restricted sheath of my rectum.

I reminded the vicar that his time was running out as he bound my right foot to Jackie's left foot with rope, but he said nothing. After licking my bottom-hole again he eased a finger deep into the tight duct of my rectum and massaged my hot inner flesh. He was in control now that we were tied over the altar, and I felt a little apprehensive. Reaching across to Jackie with his free hand, he pushed a finger deep into her tight anal duct and began his crude double thrusting. We were his victims now.

My vaginal muscles tightened, gripping the huge candle, and I began to tremble as my clitoris swelled and my sex milk flowed. Jackie was gasping, her eyes rolling as she quivered. I imagined the view that the vicar had of our stretched pussy lips, the huge candles emerging from our teenage pussies, as he fingered the hot sheaths of our rectums. He began chanting again, his low voice resounding around the church as he called again on his master to take our young bodies.

Jack finally slipped his fingers out of our bottoms, lifted his cassock and pressed the head of his cock hard against my tight anus. Clutching my hips, he moved forward, his solid shaft entering me slowly, forcing my rectal duct wide open as I whimpered and gasped. My sex holes bloated, stretched to capacity, I thought again that I was going to split open as he rammed his rock-hard cock fully home.

'You're so tight and hot,' he breathed, withdrawing his solid shaft before driving his knob deep into my tethered body again. 'A slut like you should have her arse fucked every day. You're dirty-cunted little bitches. Filthy, common little whores like you two should . . .'

My young body jolted with the crude shafting of my inflamed bottom-hole as Jack uttered his words of debased sex. I felt my aching vaginal muscles tighten again around the huge candle. Jackie winked at me as the vicar called us vulgar little schoolgirls. We were certainly earning our money, I thought, smiling back at her. I didn't like the idea of being bound with rope over the altar, but we were earning two hundred pounds.

The vicar's spunk jetted from his throbbing knob and lubricated my anal sheath as his gasps of debauched pleasure resounded around the church. He held my hips tighter and rammed his solid cock deep into my tight arse with a vengeance. I could feel his unholy seed oozing from my bloated anus and running in rivers down my inner thighs as his lower belly repeatedly slapped my naked buttocks.

Finally he yanked his deflating cock out of my aching rectal duct, knelt behind Jackie and licked the brown ring of her anus. I could hear him slurping, breathing heavily as he savoured the taste of her teenage bottom. His attention was now focused on Jackie so I had some time to rest after the crude anal fucking he'd just given me. I also had time to think about the future. Amy would phone at some stage and I'd have to go out to meet her. I'd also have to lie to Jackie. The strange thing was that, although we were both having sex with men, there was no jealousy between us. Maybe Jackie wouldn't be jealous if she discovered that I had something going with Amy.

I wondered how I'd feel if I discovered that Jackie was going out to meet another teenage girl to have lesbian sex with her. I recalled her comments about having lesbian clients as well as men. Were there girls who'd pay for lesbian sex? I asked myself. Older women might be interested in having sex with two teenage girls. My head resting on the altar as I heard Jackie gasp, I knew that the vicar had forced his huge cock into her tight bum. Her eyes bulged and she bit her lip as the anal shafting began – her young body jolted with every thrust of the vicar's cock.

I was sure that Jack the vicar would become a regular client. Now I turned my thoughts to my twin sister. How well was she doing as a prostitute? I wondered. Did she just give the odd blow job to men she'd met in bars for ten pounds, or was she running a successful business? It would have been interesting if I'd set up in business with her, I thought. The vicar would love the idea of fucking twin sisters.

Jackie cried out as the vicar rammed his solid cock into her bottom-hole with such force that she flopped back and forth like a rag doll. His sperm was pumping deep into her hot bowels, I knew as he let out a long low moan of pleasure. His half-hour must have been up, I thought as he called Jackie a filthy arse-slut. Would he go back to the vicarage and write his Sunday sermon once he'd finished with us? Perhaps we should go to church on Sunday, sit amongst the congregation and grin and wink at him as he talked about the sanctity of marriage, I thought in my wickedness.

'Tight-arsed little slut,' Jack gasped as he finally withdrew his spent cock from Jackie's rectal duct. 'You're both filthy little slags.'

'Your time is up,' I said, turning my head and looking at him. 'You've had your half-hour, so –'

'I have five minutes left,' the vicar interrupted, untying the rope binding our ankles. He moved around the altar and released my hands. 'Kneel behind the slut and suck my spunk out of her arse,' he ordered me.

The huge candle came out of my aching vagina with a loud sucking sound as I took my position behind Jackie and I let out a sigh of relief. I could feel my pussy milk streaming from my gaping vaginal entrance as I parted Jackie's firm buttocks and pressed my red lips hard against her sperm-oozing anal hole. I sucked out the vicar's cream and breathed in the scent of Jackie's anal crease as she let out a rush of breath.

The aphrodisiacal taste of Jackie's rectum blended with fresh sperm was delicious – I sucked fervently and swallowed hard repeatedly. I pushed my tongue into her tight hole, licked the dank walls of her rectal duct and breathed in her heady scent again. The intimate lesbian act sent my arousal soaring – and my clitoris swelled and my juices of desire flowed freely from my yawning vaginal hole. Slurping and sucking, I swallowed the creamy liquid and drained Jackie's rectal duct. Hoping that the vicar would order her to suck the spunk from my anal hole, I followed his fresh instructions and clambered to my feet.

I should have charged the vicar more for a lesbian show but I'd have been pushing my luck, I reckoned. Two hundred pounds was enough, I thought happily as he untied the rope binding Jackie's wrists. Following Jack's orders, I leaned over the table as Jackie knelt behind me, closing my eyes as she parted the firm cheeks of my naked buttocks. I felt her hot breath in my anal crease, and then her wet tongue as she lapped at my brown hole.

Her tongue probed deep into my rectal tube, lapping up the vicar's spunk, and she stretched my firm buttocks wide apart to gain better access to my most private hole. My young body trembled as my yearning clitoris inflated and I had to remind myself that I was at work. What an amazing way to earn money, I reflected as Jackie sucked the vicar's spunk out of my rectal sheath. I'd moved into a nice flat with my best friend, I was earning a fortune ... But I had problems.

My parents would want to see the flat, I'd lied to them about university and my secretarial job, I had the other Ali to worry about ... and now Amy wanted sex with me. I didn't want Jackie to become a problem, I mused as she slurped and sucked at my anal hole. If she discovered that I was seeing Amy she might become jealous, possessive, and I didn't want to have to deal with that. We lived and worked together, but I needed my own space, my own life.

As Jackie sucked my rectal tube dry, I decided that it was time to leave the church. We'd earned our money and the vicar had had his fun, and he'd had the use of our young bodies for more than half an hour. I was enjoying Jackie's tongue licking deep inside my rectum, but this was supposed to be business, not pleasure. Besides, we'd have plenty of time for lesbian sex once we were back at the flat.

'Your time is up, vicar,' I said, hauling myself upright as Jackie sat back on her heels. 'You've had more than half an hour.'

'I'd like you to come here once a week,' Jack said. 'Both of you – if that's all right?'

'That's fine,' I replied as I adjusted my clothes. As Jackie sorted herself out, I grabbed my handbag, brushed my tousled blonde hair away from my face and grinned at the vicar. 'You're happy with our services, then?'

'I'm very happy. I have several fetishes and . . . I don't suppose you could give me an hour in future?'

'All right,' I conceded. 'As you'll be a regular, two hundred for an hour each week.'

'Excellent,' the perverted priest said, beaming. 'Same time next week, then?'

'Same time next week,' I confirmed as I took Jackie's hand and followed Jack along the aisle to the church doors.

Out in the sunlight, I breathed in the warm air as we walked along the street. I loved the summer, I mused as Jackie chatted excitedly about the money we'd earned. I wondered where we'd meet our clients during the winter months and decided that renting a bedsit wasn't such a good idea, after all. Apart from having to find the rent, we'd be going back and forth to meet clients. The vicar had his church and John and his friends had the bungalow, but we were bound to have other clients who'd want to come to our flat.

'This could be a client,' I said as my phone rang.

'More money,' Jackie trilled.

'Ali speaking,' I said softly.

'It's me,' Amy said. 'How are you?'

'Oh, er . . .' I smiled at Jackie and moved away from her. 'I'm fine,' I said softly.

'Can we meet somewhere?'

'Yes, that would be nice,' I replied.

'Are you with your girlfriend?'

'Yes, that's right.'

'OK, I understand. Where shall we meet? Would you like to come round to my place?'

'No, no . . . the woods by the park. By the stream.'

'I'll go there now.'

'OK – thanks for ringing.'

Jackie looked at me with expectation reflected in her dark eyes as I slipped my phone into my handbag. I smiled and told her that it was our landlord just making sure that I was happy with the flat. How was I going to get away and meet Amy in the park? I wondered. I stopped and held my hand to my mouth as an idea came to me.

'God,' I said. 'I've just remembered that I told my mum I'd go and see her this morning.'

'Why were you telling the landlord about the woods by the park?' Jackie asked me.

'He said that he might have a client for us,' I lied. 'He wondered where we could meet him.'

'Oh, I see. So are you going to your mum's now?'

'Yes, I'll have to. You go back to the flat and I'll see you there later. Here, take my key. We'll get another one cut later.'

'I'll get one cut on my way back.'

'Good idea,' I said, passing her a ten-pound note. 'That should be enough to pay for it. OK, I won't be too long.'

As I walked away I felt guilty about lying to Jackie. I should have told her the truth, I thought as I headed for the park. Now that I'd lied to her I'd have to keep on lying. I should have been honest and said that I was meeting Amy. After all, it was my life and Jackie and I weren't an item or . . . This was another mess in the making, I realised as I crossed the park to the woods.

* * *

205

After my visit to the church with the vicar and Jackie, my pussy was aching and my knickers were very wet. I knew that Amy would want to lick me, push her tongue into my teenage vagina and suck out my juice. As I followed the narrow path through the trees I felt my clitoris swell and my young womb contract at the prospect of lesbian sex. But I still felt guilty about Jackie.

As I approached the stream, I noticed Amy dropping stones into the water. I hid behind a bush so that I could spy on her. She was wearing knee-length black boots with a red miniskirt and a white T-shirt. Her long blonde hair shone in the sunlight, her full red lips pouted – she looked stunning. My heart raced as I gazed at her slender thighs and imagined her succulent pussy lips, her tightly closed sex crack. I emerged from my hide, walked over to her and smiled.

'Hi,' she said softly, lowering her eyes and gazing at the cleavage revealed by my partially open blouse. 'Was your girlfriend OK about you going out?'

'Yes, she . . . she's fine,' I replied. 'It's not serious or anything. We just . . . well, it's not serious.'

'Ali's moving to Birmingham,' Amy informed me. 'The other Ali, I mean. She's going tomorrow.'

'Oh, right.'

'She's had enough of everything. She never did like this town.'

'Has she had enough of my being around?'

'That's part of it, yes. She has friends in Birmingham and . . . there's nothing here for her, so she's moving.'

'So I never will get to meet her.'

'She wants to meet you before she goes.'

'Really?' I said. 'When? I mean, where?'

'She's going to phone you. Do you want to meet her?'

'I don't know,' I murmured. I sat down beside the stream. 'I really don't know.'

Amy settled beside me on the grass, stroked my long blonde hair and kissed my cheek. The fragrance of her perfume filled my nostrils and I felt a quiver run through my womb. She was so sensual, I thought as I lay back on the grass and closed my eyes. I could feel her hands wandering over the firm mounds of my pert breasts as she leaned over and pressed her full lips to mine. She kissed me passionately, ran her hand down over my stomach and tugged up my short skirt. Her fingertips pressed into the wet material of my bulging knickers and she massaged me there. I breathed heavily, my young body trembling as Amy pressed her fingertips harder into the groove of my pussy and rubbed my solid clitoris. She hadn't pulled my wet knickers aside because she was teasing me, I thought dreamily. She was going to make me wait for the pleasure of her fingers deep inside my tightening vagina.

After opening my blouse and lifting my bra clear of my firm breasts, Amy sucked my erect nipple into her hot mouth and snaked her tongue over its sensitive tip. Finally she moved my knickers aside, massaged the hairless flesh of my swollen outer lips and ran her fingertip up and down my opening valley of desire. My juices of lesbian lust streamed from my neglected vaginal sheath and flowed down to the inflamed ring of my anus – I recalled the vicar's huge cock fucking me there.

My life centred around sex now, I thought as Amy sucked my other milk teat into her wet mouth and sank her teeth gently into the areola. Before I'd discovered the other Ali I'd never really given a thought to sex, let alone sex with another girl. Now I was moving from one sexual encounter to another.

Anal sex with a vicar while I was bent over the altar, I mused. Had God been watching me?

Amy pulled my knickers down and slipped them off over my feet along with my shoes – I knew that she was going to lick me as she parted my legs wide. She settled between my splayed thighs, peeled the fleshy lips of my pussy wide apart and teased the tip of my sensitive clitoris with her wet tongue. I gasped, writhing on the grass as she repeatedly ran her tongue up and down my yawning sex crack. I could hear her tongue licking, slurping as she lapped up my flowing sex milk. She knew exactly how to please another girl, I thought happily as her tongue entered my vaginal duct. Being a girl, she knew what a girl wanted.

'You're the most beautiful girl I've ever been with,' Amy breathed softly. 'You taste heavenly.'

'How many girls have you been with?' I asked her.

'Five. I've had sex with five girls. You're number six, Ali. And you're the best ever.'

'What was my sister like?'

'The same as you in looks, but nowhere near as sensual. She liked rough sex, not gentle, loving sex the way you do. Would you like to come now?'

'Yes, yes – I need to,' I replied shakily.

'OK, relax and I'll take you to heaven.'

Amy suckled my erect clitoris into her pretty mouth, drove at least two fingers deep into my vaginal sheath and massaged my creamy-wet inner flesh. The sensations were fantastic, sending ripples of sex right through my pelvis and deep into my contracting womb. Amy was an expert, I thought dreamily. Her long blonde hair tickled my inner thighs and my lower stomach as she licked and sucked between the splayed lips of my pussy. I knew that I was about to reach my orgasm.

My clitoris pulsating, my womb rhythmically contracting, my vaginal muscles tightened and gripped

Amy's thrusting fingers as my climax erupted and shook my young body to its core. I writhed on the grass beneath the summer sun, lost in my lesbian passion as Amy sustained my powerful orgasm with her tongue and fingers. Amy had said that she'd take me to heaven, and she'd kept her promise. My cries of sexual satisfaction resounded through the trees and I felt that I'd given not only my body to Amy but my soul. We were as one, locked in our lesbian devotion, and I knew that we'd never be parted. I didn't know what the future held but, as I began to drift down from my amazing climax, I knew that I couldn't live without Amy.

As my new lesbian lover slipped her fingers out of the fiery sheath of my pussy and lapped up my orgasmic juices, I thought about Jackie. She'd be waiting at the flat, wondering how long I'd be. Never in a million years would I have dreamed that I'd be cheating on a lesbian lover with another girl. Had anyone told me that I'd be writhing in orgasm with a girl sucking my clitoris and fingering my tight pussy, I'd have thought they were crazy. To have *two* lesbian lovers was unbelievable.

'Good girl,' Amy said as her grinning face appeared above my hairless vulva. 'I'll take you to heaven every day, Ali. Come and live with me, move in with me and –'

'I can't,' I said softly, propping myself up on my elbows as Amy licked her pussy-wet lips. 'I'll see you every day, but I can't live with you.'

'Are you in love with that other girl?' she asked me.

'Yes, no, I mean . . . I don't know *what* I mean. I don't think that I know what love is.'

'*I* know what it is, Ali. And I've found it. You're an angel, and I won't ever let you go.'

'We can see each other every day, Amy. We'll see each other as often as we can, but –'

'I need to come,' she cut in as she slipped her knickers off. 'Make me come, Ali.'

Amy knelt astride my head as I lay on the grass, lowered her young body and pressed her hairless cunt lips against my mouth. I breathed in the heady scent of her teenage pussy, slipped my tongue into her wet slit and tasted her juices of arousal as she gasped and writhed. Her milk flowed in torrents into my mouth as I drove my tongue deep into her hot hole. I could feel the hardness of her erect clitoris pressing against my nose, and I knew that her arousal was running dangerously high.

Whimpering as she gyrated her hips and ground her open sex flesh hard against my face, Amy aligned the tight ring of her anus with my mouth. I pushed my tongue into the dank heat of her hole and savoured the bitter-sweet taste of her rectal duct. As I licked and sucked in my sexual delirium I breathed in repeatedly through my nose. The intoxicating perfume of Amy's anal crease blew my mind: I arched my back as she leaned over my young body, pushed her tongue into my gaping vaginal hole and sucked out my fresh cunt milk.

Believing again that we were as one as our entwined bodies writhed in lesbian passion, I moved my attention back to Amy's vaginal hole and sucked out her creamy juices. I took her ripe clitoris into my wet mouth and swept my tongue over its sensitive tip, feeling my vaginal muscles contract as she sucked my own solid clit-bud into her hot mouth. Locked in lust, I knew that we were going to reach our climaxes together as our young bodies trembled and our milk of desire flowed.

Oblivious to my surroundings, I moaned through my nose as my orgasm erupted within the solid bulb of my come-button and Amy reached her climax. Writh-

210

ing on the grass, breathing heavily as we clung to each other, we sucked and licked and sustained our incredible orgasms. I was drunk on sex, my mind blown away on clouds of lesbian passion, and I hoped that I'd never come down from my sexual heaven. Shaking wildly as I rode the crest of my ecstasy, I drove a finger deep into Amy's anal hole and massaged her hot inner flesh. She reciprocated, pushing a finger deep into my rectum and teasing the sleeping nerve endings there as she sucked my orgasm from my pulsating clitoris.

Sucking and fingering and squirming, we finally began to drift down from our lesbian-induced pleasure. Never had I known anything like it. Amy rolled off my trembling body and lay on the grass beside me. I was shaking violently in the aftermath of my best orgasm ever. I finally opened my eyes and gazed at the sunlight streaming through the trees high above me. My body calmed and I felt relaxed as never before as my heartbeat slowed and I breathed deeply.

'Are you all right?' Amy finally asked me.

'God, yes,' I replied, turning my head and smiling at her. 'Are *you*?'

'I'm better than ever, Ali. I want you again.'

'No, I . . . I have to go now,' I said, hauling myself up and grabbing my knickers. 'Phone me, OK?'

'I must see you again today.'

'I have things to do and –'

'Please,' she persisted. 'I need you.'

'All right,' I sighed. I slipped my knickers on and concealed my sex-dripping vaginal slit. 'Ring me later and we'll meet here.'

'This evening?'

'I'm not sure what I'll be doing but . . . Ring me later this afternoon. Now, I really must go.'

'OK,' Amy said, her pretty face beaming as she looked up at me. 'I'll stay here for a while and rest.'

I left her on the grass and followed the narrow path through the trees to the park. My knickers were filled with my hot cunt milk and I couldn't stop thinking about Amy. She was beautiful, and I wanted to go back to the park and love her again. Trying to take control of my inner desires, I breathed deeply and did my best to compose myself. But I was still shaking as I neared the flat, and I knew that Jackie would be suspicious.

'Your mum has been round,' Jackie said accusingly, opening the front door to me. 'I thought you'd gone round to –'

'That's great,' I cut in. 'I'd said that I'd go and see her, so she comes here instead.'

'So where have you been?'

'I waited ages for her to get back and then gave up.'

'She said that you hadn't arranged to go there this morning.'

'It was her idea, for God's sake. She must be losing her memory.'

'You look flushed, Ali,' she persisted. 'Where have you been?'

'It's bloody hot out there,' I sighed as I walked into the lounge and flopped onto the sofa. 'I'm on fire. What did my mum say about the flat?'

'She liked it. But she was disappointed because you weren't here.'

'I'll ring her later. Did you get a key cut?'

'Yes, I did. Ali, have you been to see Amy?'

'Amy? Why would I go and see her? I don't even know where she lives.'

'That phone call you had earlier, when we were outside the church . . . was it Amy?'

'I told you, Jackie, it was the landlord. Why all these questions?'

'I don't know – I'm sorry.'

'What if I had been to see Amy? So what?'

'I know that you like her and she's a lesbian so . . .'

'Yes, I do like her and she is a lesbian. I want to see her again to find out more about my sister.'

'Do you want sex with her?'

'I haven't thought about it, Jackie. What if I do have sex with her? How will that affect us? I mean, we fuck men all the time so –'

'Yes, but that's business. You know what I mean, Ali. I thought that we were . . .'

'Look, this isn't going to work if you're going to be suspicious every time I go out. Amy said that she'll ring me when she's spoken to my sister, so I might go and meet her somewhere. I don't want a load of questions, Jackie. What we have here is good, so don't spoil it.'

'I'm sorry,' she sighed. 'It's just that I can't bear to think of you with another girl.'

'Go and make some coffee,' I ordered her. 'And don't be so silly.'

As Jackie left the room I shook my head in despair. I'd had no idea that she was going to be like this. I thought that she might be suspicious, but to fire accusing questions at me like that . . . I'd been firm with her, I thought. I wasn't going to put up with any nonsense from her. As much as I liked her and wanted her I had my own life to lead. Amy had come on strong, I thought. Going on about needing to see me again and insisting that I meet her . . . I was going to have to be firm with her, too.

It was strange to think that teenage girls were falling in love with me and wanting to have sex with me. The doorbell rang and I hoped that my mother hadn't come back. Perhaps it was Jackie's parents, I thought. No one else knew where we lived, apart from the landlord and . . . I walked through the hall, opened the

213

door and stared at Alan, my jaw dropping. What the hell did he want? I wondered, frowning at him. How had he found out where I was living?

'Hi,' he said. 'Your mum told me where to find you.'

'Oh, right,' I breathed. 'I'm . . . I'm a little busy at the moment.'

'Hi,' Jackie said, obviously recognising Alan as my neighbour as she joined me. 'Come in and take a look at our new flat.'

'Thanks,' Alan said and walked past me into the hall.

'I'll make another coffee,' Jackie said, returning to the kitchen.

I led Alan into the lounge and smiled at him. 'I'm about to go out,' I sighed. 'I'm afraid you won't be able to stay for long.'

'I haven't seen you for ages,' he whined. 'Why didn't you tell me that you'd moved out?'

'It all happened so quickly, Alan. Look, I don't want you coming round here. I know that sounds rude but –'

'Have you got someone else, then?'

'Alan, we're not going out together or anything.'

'I thought we were.'

'No – what we did in the woods was fun, but that's all it was.'

'Oh, I see. You *have* found someone else, then?'

'No, I haven't. I don't want to be tied down to anyone.'

'OK, so what about having sex with me?'

'Sex?' Jackie echoed as she brought the coffees in. 'Have we got a new client?'

'A new client?' Alan said, frowning at me.

'She was joking,' I said as I turned and glared at Jackie.

'That's a shame,' Alan murmured. 'I know a man who's looking for a prostitute.'

'What?' I gasped. 'How come you know a man who —'

'It's my friend's dad. His wife ran off and he's always going on about finding a prostitute. At first I thought he was joking, but he's serious. He's got loads of money.'

'I might be able to help him,' Jackie said. 'I know a girl who would see him.'

'Really? Give me her number and I'll get him to call her.'

Jackie wrote down my mobile number and passed it to Alan as I sipped my coffee. Alan, of all people, I thought. As long as he didn't discover that we were on the game, I was happy enough to entertain his friend's dad. *He's got loads of money*. Recalling his words, I winked at Jackie. We really were in business, I thought happily. Perhaps Alan's visit was a good thing after all.

'Maybe I should phone this girl,' he said. 'I don't have a girlfriend so —'

'You haven't got any money,' I cut in.

'Yes, I have.'

'It would cost you a fortune.'

'How much?' he asked me.

'I don't know, do I? But I reckon a girl would charge fifty pounds for sex.'

Alan downed his coffee and smiled at me. 'I can afford that,' he said. 'I might ring this girl and ask her about it.'

'*I*'d have sex with you for fifty pounds,' Jackie said, giggling.

'So would I,' I said. 'It would help to pay the rent.'

'Really?' Alan breathed. 'Are you serious?'

'We're not prostitutes but . . . yes, why not?'

'Wow, that's great. When can I come round, then?'

'Tomorrow morning,' Jackie replied. 'We're out tonight, but tomorrow morning will be fine.'

'I'll be here,' Alan said, grinning at me. 'Wow, that's great.'

'Get here at nine,' I said. I took his empty coffee cup and ushered him into the hall. 'And bring the money with you.'

I returned to the lounge after I'd seen him out and burst out laughing. I couldn't believe that Alan was going to be paying to fuck us, and neither could Jackie. With Alan as a new customer and, possibly, his friend's dad to be added to our client list, the future was looking great. But I couldn't stop thinking about Amy. She was going to ring me and arrange to meet me for sex, and my sister wanted to meet me too. I still had problems, but the future looked good, I thought again.

Eleven

I'd waited up until midnight but Amy hadn't phoned me. Jackie had been asleep by the time I'd joined her beneath the quilt, and I'd felt despondent and frustrated. I'd wanted to meet Amy again, I'd wanted sex with Jackie ... I woke up alone in the bed and heard Jackie moving about in the kitchen. Ali the slut was going to Birmingham today, I thought as I leaped out of bed and had a shower. Why hadn't she phoned me? Today was our last chance to meet.

I didn't feel like seeing Alan and wished that we hadn't arranged for him to come round. With Amy continually on my mind, the last thing I wanted was sex with Alan. But he was a client now, I reminded myself as I dressed in a miniskirt and skimpy crop-top. He wanted to pay for the use of my pussy, and business had to come first.

I was about to go down to the kitchen to find Jackie when my mobile phone rang. It was John: he wanted Jackie and me to go to his bungalow that evening. Apparently his friends were eager for another session of crude sex and they had their cash ready. I agreed, and the minute I dropped my phone back into my handbag it rang again. This time it was Amy. She wanted to meet me by the stream in the woods.

'I want to pull your knickers off and open your legs as wide as I can,' she said excitedly. 'I'm going to peel your pussy lips open and lick deep inside your sweet little hole.'

'You're making me very wet,' I whispered, closing my bedroom door so that Jackie couldn't hear me.

'I'm going to suck your clitoris into my mouth,' Amy continued. 'I'll suck it so hard that it pops out from its hood and then I'll lick it and take you to heaven.'

'My clit is hard now,' I breathed. 'I'll meet you in the woods later this morning.'

'Now – I want you *now*,' she said firmly.

'Later,' I replied. 'Be there at eleven o'clock.'

'You *do* want to meet your sister, don't you?'

'Well, I . . .'

'Meet me in the woods as soon as you can.'

'All right,' I conceded. 'I'll do my best.'

My vaginal muscles tightened and my young womb contracted as I imagined Amy sucking my clitoris into her pretty mouth. Would my sister be there? I wondered. Did I want to meet her? I was confused. I took a deep breath and composed myself before going down to the kitchen. Jackie was cooking breakfast – eggs and bacon and toast. The table was laid and there were two glasses of fresh orange juice and coffee and . . . She was brilliant, and I didn't want to lose her.

'Was that your phone I heard just now?' she asked me.

'Yes, it was John,' I replied. I gazed at her short skirt, her naked thighs. 'He wants us there this evening.'

'Great,' Jackie trilled. 'More money.'

'My sister's moving up to Birmingham and I'm hoping to meet her before she goes.'

'When did you speak to her?'

'I . . . I didn't. Amy rang me yesterday and –'

'You didn't tell me.'

'Didn't I? Sorry, I must have forgotten to mention it. That looks good,' I said as she placed my breakfast on the table. 'You're wonderful, Jackie.'

'It seems rather odd that you forgot to tell me that Amy rang you about your sister.'

'I've had a lot on my mind, Jackie.'

'Such as Amy?'

'What? No, no. There's Alan and John and his friends and my sister . . . I've been thinking about the business, not about Amy.'

'Your phone rang twice,' Jackie said, watching me closely for a reaction.

'Yes, it was my sister.'

'Why didn't you tell me?'

'Jackie, I can hardly get a word in. All this talk about Amy . . . I'm going to meet my sister after breakfast.'

'What about Alan?'

'You deal with him.'

Jackie hardly spoke as we ate our breakfast. She was great to have around and I didn't want to be without her, but I knew that I couldn't put up with her suspicious mind and continual questioning. I had an idea as I enjoyed my breakfast. If I pretended to be my twin sister and I called at the flat, I might fool Jackie. I could take Amy to the flat and . . . No, I decided, that wouldn't be a good idea. I was going to have to quell Jackie's suspicions, but I had no idea how.

Alan finally arrived. Jackie let him in and led him into the lounge. I heard them giggling as I slipped out of the front door. Jackie would be all right, I reflected as I headed for the park. She'd make Alan happy and take his money and . . . I'd let her down, I thought. We were in business together, and I'd left her alone to deal with a client. But my sister was playing on my mind. I wanted to meet Amy in the woods and have sex with her, but my thoughts were on the other Ali. I remembered the photographer as I crossed the park and wondered whether my nude pictures were on some website or other for the world to see. As I followed the path through the trees I knew that I had to sort myself out. Sneaking off to meet my lesbian lover when we had a paying client waiting, taking secret phone calls . . . I was going to have to get my act together.

'Are you alone?' I asked Amy. I'd found her sitting by the stream. 'What was that you said about meeting my sister?'

'She said that she might come here and meet you,' she replied, looking up and smiling at me.

'When?' I asked.

'Now.'

'So where is she?'

'I don't know, Ali,' she sighed. 'I saw her this morning and she said that she *might* come here.'

'She's going to Birmingham today. This is our last chance to meet.'

'Sit down,' Amy said. 'You're all wound up and –'

'Of course I'm wound up, Amy,' I interrupted as I sat on the grass beside her. 'Ali is my twin sister.'

'She might not be your sister. I know that you both look identical, but that doesn't mean to say that she's your sister.'

'Why is she playing games? She's known about me for some time, and yet . . . Surely she's intrigued?'

'Of course she is. But she's also worried. I told you before about her family history. Just have patience. While we're waiting, let me take you to heaven.'

'I can't think about sex,' I breathed. 'Besides, what if my sister turned up and found us . . .'

'I've told her that we've had sex. She won't think anything of it if she finds us loving each other.'

I shook my head as Amy slipped her shoes off and dangled her feet in the shallow stream. I didn't think that the other Ali would turn up. This was probably a ploy, I thought as I gazed at Amy's long legs. Amy had wanted to meet me in the woods for sex and had thought she'd use my sister as bait. Perhaps I should forget about the other Ali, I mused despondently. My parents hadn't even asked me how I was getting on with tracking her down and I thought it might be best to forget about her.

'She's not coming here, is she?' I finally said.

'She said that she might,' Amy replied.

'Why hasn't she phoned me? She knows my number, so why hasn't she phoned?'

'I have no idea, Ali.'

'Amy, if you've made this up just to get me here . . .'

'Of course I haven't made it up.' She grabbed her phone from her bag and punched in a number. 'Ali, it's me,' she finally said. 'Are you coming here or not? Yes, she's here with me. Well, at least ring or . . . OK, I will.'

'What did she say?' I asked Amy as she sat beside me.

'She's going to ring you.'

'When?'

'I don't know, she didn't say. Ali, I want you. Please let me love you.'

I lay back on the grass as Amy slipped her hand between my thighs and massaged the swell of my pussy lips through the tight material of my knickers. I could see her phone in her open handbag. It was within reach, I thought as she eased my wet knickers to one side and slipped her finger deep into my contracting vagina. If I could just switch it on and get Ali's number . . . Amy moved her bag out of reach and settled beside me. She pressed her full lips to mine in a passionate kiss.

221

After she'd opened my crop-top and lifted my bra clear of my young breasts, Amy massaged the firm mounds of my tits and teased the erect teats of my nipples. I felt a quiver run through my womb as she moved down and sucked a nipple into her hot mouth. Her finger moved about within the tight sheath of my vagina and her wet tongue swept repeatedly over the smooth skin of my breast. The feelings this produced freed my mind of thoughts of my sister and I knew that Amy was going to take me to my sexual heaven as my clitoris swelled and my juices of lesbian desire flowed. I realised again that I could never be without her.

After pulling my wet knickers down and slipping them off my feet, Amy parted my legs wide and massaged my hairless pussy lips. Her fingers ran up and down my creamy-wet sex crack, caressing the sensitive tip of my erect clitoris, and she sucked my nipple into her hot mouth again. My arousal rose fast and I knew that soon I'd be writhing in the grip of a beautiful orgasm. Amy quickened her massaging rhythm and I began to think that I shouldn't have rented the flat with Jackie. She was my best friend, a lifelong friend, but I knew that her continual suspicion and questioning was going to become a real problem. I was going to have to do something, I thought for the umpteenth time. But what?

Amy pulled her blouse up and offered her breasts to my mouth as I neared my orgasm. Sucking on a ripe nipple, I closed my eyes and moaned softly through my nose. Her breasts were full but firm and as I suckled I imagined that I was drinking her milk. I'd thought that I'd found love when I'd been having sex with Jackie. But I'd never felt so close and warm like this. Confused about my feelings as Amy cradled my head and begged me to come, I sucked harder on her erect nipple.

My orgasm exploded within the pulsating nub of my sensitive clitoris. I breathed heavily through my nose and shook uncontrollably. I groped between Amy's thighs and managed to slip my hand inside her wet knickers to massage her erect clitoris as I rode the crest of my climax. She whimpered as I caressed her there, and I knew that she was going to reach her orgasm quickly as my own pleasure began to fade.

'Suck me,' Amy gasped. She yanked her knickers off and knelt astride my head. 'Suck my clit and make me come.'

I opened my mouth as Amy lowered her young body and pressed her gaping vaginal slit over my face. I pushed my tongue deep into her dripping hole and lapped up her flowing cream. She rocked her hips, sliding her sex valley back and forth over my mouth as I slurped and sucked and mouthed. Sucking on her solid clit-bud, I licked its sensitive tip repeatedly as her hot quim milk streamed over my face. She tasted heavenly, and I drank deeply from her teenage body, sucking first on her open hole and then on her pulsating clitoris. Her cries of orgasm resounded through the trees as she reached her climax, shook uncontrollably and ground her open cunt flesh hard against my face as I sustained her pleasure with my tongue and gobbling mouth.

Amy's orgasmic juice poured in torrents from her yawning vaginal hole and streamed over my face. I sucked and licked her clitoris until she began to crumple and asked me to stop. She leaned to one side and finally rolled onto the ground where she lay on her back, panting for breath. I knew then that she was the girl for me. Was I in love? I wondered. I was certainly confused, I knew that much.

'Someone's coming,' I said as I heard the bushes rustling. 'It might be my sister.'

'I'll leave,' Amy said, leaping to her feet. 'You'll probably want to chat so . . . I'll ring you later.'

'Yes, ring me later and –'

I watched her as she slipped into the bushes. Now I wondered what the hell I was going to say to my sister. I heard the foliage rustling again and took a deep breath as I tried to compose myself. It would be strange to meet my identical twin, I thought anxiously. If she really was my sister to meet her at long last would be . . . I turned as I heard someone behind me.

'Simon,' I gasped, looking up at him as he towered above me. 'What are *you* doing here?'

'Which sister do we have here?' he asked me as he sat down beside me. 'Are you the whore or –'

'I'm your next-door neighbour,' I said. 'At least, I was. I moved out because you forced me to –'

'I paid you,' he cut in. 'I gave you one hundred pounds in return for sex.'

'Only because you thought that I was my sister. You forced me to –'

'Would you like to earn some more money?'

'No, I would not.'

'I've been watching you with that young girl. What would your parents say if I told them that you were a lesbian?'

'They would never believe you. Besides, I'd say that it was my sister.'

'You're getting in too deep, Ali.'

'What do you mean by that?'

'I've been doing my homework. You've been playing games with me, haven't you?'

'No, I . . .'

'You haven't got a twin sister, have you?'

'Of course I have. I've met her several times and we're getting to know each other.'

'You've been playing the role of both sisters, Ali. You were the girl I fucked here, in the woods. And you were the girl that I met behind the shed in your garden. Now, I have a little proposition for you. We wouldn't want your parents to discover the truth, would we? You're a prostitute, you're a lesbian and –'

'Go away, Simon,' I spat. 'You can't threaten me because you have no proof.'

'Take a look at this,' Simon said as he pulled a photograph from his pocket. 'That's you, here in the woods, having sex with that girl. I took that one yesterday and I've just taken some more. My camera is hidden in the bushes back there.'

'That's my sister,' I said, forcing a laugh as I gazed at the picture. 'You can't prove that that's me.'

'I have a whole series of photographs on my computer. I've been following you, making notes and taking photographs. Now, my proposition is that you have sex with me twice each week and I'll keep quiet.'

'You can't blackmail me like this. My parents would never –'

'I was talking to your dad earlier. He said that you haven't found your sister yet. He reckons that she doesn't exist. It's up to you, Ali. You either have sex with me, or your parents discover the truth.'

'You'll pay me?' I said stupidly.

'Your payment will be my keeping quiet. Now, take your clothes off and we'll have some fun.'

I had no choice – I knew that as I slipped my top off. Perhaps my dad was right and the other Ali didn't exist. She'd phone me and Amy had said that she wanted to meet me but ... I'd seen her in town, I thought as I stood naked in front of Simon. Or I'd seen someone who had looked like me. Simon grinned as he reached out and squeezed the firm mounds of my small breasts. He had me exactly where he wanted me, I thought anxiously. I'd be at his beck and call, and there was nothing I could do about it.

I followed his orders and lay on the ground with my arms and legs outstretched. He gazed at my pussy and commented on my hairless lips, my tight little sex crack. He was a crude man, an evil man, and I knew that I was in for a bad time. But my plans wouldn't be affected by this, I decided. I could still run the business and ... Had Simon discovered where I lived? I wondered. He'd said that he'd followed me and taken notes. If he knew where I was living, he could cause problems. He might talk to Jackie and ... I was thinking too far ahead. Hopefully, all he'd want would be sex with me once or twice each week.

'I always thought that you were such a sweet little thing,' Simon murmured as he settled on the grass beside me. 'It turns out that you're a devious little cow. Dreaming up a twin sister so that you can play the role of a common slut whenever it takes your fancy is very clever. You're a resourceful little whore, aren't you?'

'I *do* have a sister,' I replied futilely.

'I suppose you thought that if your parents heard that you'd been charging men for sex you'd simply blame your twin sister. It's very clever. You play the sweet little girl and then, when you want your cunt fucked and spunked, you play the common slut. Open your cunt lips for me.'

'No, I –'

'Open your cunt wide, Ali. I want to see where these men put their cocks. Open your dirty little cunt as wide as you can, or I'll do it for you.'

I peeled my hairless pussy lips apart, exposing the wet entrance to my teenage vagina, and looked up at the sun shining through the trees high above me. This had been my favourite place when I'd been younger, I thought. I'd played by the stream and ... Now it was a place of crude sex, a place of prostitution and blackmail. Jackie was waiting for me at the flat, Amy wanted me as her lesbian lover, Ali would be on her way to Birmingham, and I was fast losing my direction in life.

Simon licked the wet flesh between my splayed sex lips, muttering crude comments about my cunt and how many cocks I'd had fucking and spunking me. Amy had been gentle in her lesbian loving but Simon was vulgar and cold. Still, I was used to men fucking me to satisfy their base desires. I was in the business of sex, I was a prostitute, and there was nothing that Simon could do to shock me.

He looked up, grinned at me, and ordered me to finger-fuck my wet cunt. I slipped a hand beneath my thighs and eased a finger into my tight vagina as he watched eagerly. It was strange to think that I'd been such an innocent girl before I'd discovered the existence of Ali. Simon had been my neighbour for years. He'd always greeted me with a smile and had been pleasant and polite. I'd had no idea of the crude thoughts lurking in the depths of his depraved mind. He must have looked at me a thousand times and imagined my pussy, my pert breasts, and thought the vulgar things he'd like to do to my naked body.

'Put a finger in your arse,' Simon said. He spread my legs wide, parted my firm buttocks and exposed the tight hole of my anus. 'I want to watch you push your finger deep into your tight little arse, Ali. Open it up ready for my cock. Go on, finger-fuck both holes.'

I managed to ease a finger into the tight duct of my bottom and pushed it into my rectum as far as I could. Simon was breathing heavily as he watched my crude act, and I knew that his cock would be as hard as granite. Once he'd fucked me I'd be free to go back to the flat. But he had my mobile number, and I knew that he'd be ringing me constantly and demanding crude sex. I'd probably be opening my legs to him every day, and getting nothing in return apart from his silence.

Simon ordered me to force a second finger into my bottom-hole as he held my thighs open as wide as they'd go. I could hear my pussy juice squelching as I managed to drive another finger into my tight rectum. As I moved my fingers in and out of my hot holes I could hear my cunt milk squelching as my clitoris swelled. Simon's tongue swept repeatedly over the solid tip of my sensitive clitoris and my vaginal muscles tightened, gripping my thrusting finger. I knew that I'd be writhing in orgasm before long.

I was a slut, I thought. I was being blackmailed, forced to finger my tight holes, and yet I was on the verge of reaching my climax. Even blackmail couldn't stop my arousal from soaring out of control. Blackmail, I thought as my young womb contracted. Simon couldn't prove that I didn't have a sister. I couldn't prove that the other Ali existed and, equally, he couldn't prove that she didn't. Would I ever get to meet her? I wondered. More to the point, did she really exist?

My orgasm erupted within the pulsating bulb of my erect clitoris, my vaginal muscles tightened, my anal sphincter gripped my thrusting fingers – I writhed on the grass like a snake in agony. My naked body shook uncontrollably and I could hear my cries of sexual satisfaction echoing through the woods as Simon sucked on my orgasming clit-bud and I finger-fucked my spasming holes faster.

'Filthy slut,' Simon gasped as he licked my rock-hard clitoris. 'All you're good for is fucking. Come on, keep it going. I want to see your cunt juice spurting out over your hand, you dirty whore.'

His crude words heightened my arousal as my orgasm peaked again, rocking my young body to its depths. I'd have three cocks fucking me that evening, I mused in my sexual delirium. John and his cronies would fuck Jackie and me senseless and fill us with spunk. They'd fuck our tight bottom-holes and our mouths and we'd enjoy orgasm after orgasm. I loved my young body and the pleasure it brought me, I thought happily as my orgasm began to fade. My body also earned me a lot of money, even if Simon wasn't going to pay me.

Simon stood and tugged his trousers down before he knelt astride my head, pressed his purple glans against my lips and ordered me to suck it. I parted my lips, sucked his bulbous knob into my wet mouth and savoured the taste of his salt. I was hooked on cocksucking, I thought dreamily as I ran my tongue over the velveteen surface of his cock-tip. I also loved swallowing spunk, but I wasn't getting paid for this. Far from getting paid, I was being blackmailed.

'Suck out my spunk, you filthy slut,' Simon gasped, pushing his knob to the back of my throat. 'I'm going to fuck your mouth every day, Ali. I'm going to fuck your mouth and spunk down your throat and . . .'

As he rambled on, I knew that I'd never be free of him. He'd be phoning me and pestering me for sex every day. I was already sneaking out and having sex with Amy behind Jackie's back. If I had to meet Simon in the woods every day, Jackie would become really suspicious. I wouldn't dare to tell her that I was being blackmailed. I could have called Simon's bluff, but I didn't dare risk him running to my parents with the photographs.

His spunk jetted from his throbbing knob and flooded my mouth. I repeatedly swallowed hard as his balls battered my chin. I wanted to get back to the flat to see Jackie. We had John and his friends to entertain that evening and I didn't want to spend half the day in the woods with Simon. I swallowed the last of his spunk and sat upright as he pulled his cock out of my mouth and lay gasping on the grass beside me.

'You're good,' he said, turning his head and grinning at me. 'Come and sit on my face, Ali. I want to drink from your hot little cunt.'

'I have to go now,' I said firmly. 'I have to get back and –'

'Just do it, Ali,' Simon sighed.

'If I don't you'll go running to my parents with your tales?'

'Yes, I will.'

'OK, so that might get me into trouble. At the very least, it will be awkward for me.'

'Indeed it will,' Simon replied, chuckling wickedly.

'But where will that get *you*?'

'What do you mean?'

'Well, for a start, you can forget about having sex with me.'

'Let's hope that I don't have to go to your parents. Now, sit on my face like a good girl.'

'This is what you'll be missing,' I said, kneeling astride Simon's head and settling the wet lips of my vulval entrance over his mouth.

Sure that I'd given him something to think about, I reckoned that my idea might work. Simon stood to lose the pleasure of my young body if he went blabbing his mouth off to my parents and showing them the photographs. I felt his tongue enter my tight vaginal sheath as I thought about the situation. He licked deep inside my hot pussy, sucked out my sex milk and drank deeply from my young body. He wouldn't be doing this again if he carried out his threat, I thought as he

230

sucked and slurped between the hairless lips of my vagina. Not unless he paid me, of course.

'I have a couple of young friends,' I said as my clitoris swelled. 'I could have introduced them to you, but –'

'I know your game,' Simon cut in through a mouthful of wet vaginal flesh.

'I don't play games.'

'You play the role of your twin sister.'

'I can't prove that I have a sister, but it's true.'

'All I want is you, Ali. I don't want your friends, I only want you. If you force me to go to your parents, don't you think that they'll find it odd that your twin wears your clothes? I have photos of you in the clothes you've had for ages. Your mum will know that it's you in the photos.'

Simon was right, I knew as he once more pushed his tongue deep into my wet vagina. I'd never met my sister, and neither had my parents, so they were bound to believe that I was the girl in the incriminating photographs. I was going to have to meet Simon regularly for sex, and I decided that it would be best to explain the situation to Jackie. I could use Simon as an excuse, I thought as he sucked my solid clitoris into his hot mouth. I could tell Jackie that I was going to meet him, and then spend some time with Amy. Perhaps my predicament wasn't so bad after all.

'Piss in my mouth,' Simon grunted. 'A filthy little slut like you should love pissing.'

'With pleasure,' I said.

I squeezed my muscles and let out a gush of hot liquid as he pressed his mouth between my fleshy sex lips. I could hear the splashing sound as Simon's mouth filled with my urine, and I could hear him gulping, drinking my hot pee. He was a truly dirty old man, I thought as the flow continued. I looked down and watched his mouth overflow as the golden liquid ran down to his ears. My arousal soared, my clitoris pulsating in the beginning of an orgasm, and I reached down to massage the sensitive protrusion.

I cried out as my orgasm erupted, threw my head back and closed my eyes. Simon's mouth was still flooding with my golden piss as I shuddered and writhed in the grip of my powerful climax, and I knew that he'd never go running to my parents with his tales. If he did, he'd lose the hottest teenage slut he was ever likely to meet. There was no way he'd risk that, I thought happily as I massaged my clitoris faster and sustained my incredible pleasure.

'Filthy whore,' Simon spluttered as the flow finally began to lessen and my orgasm faded. 'God, you're a dirty little slut.'

'That's why you like me,' I said. My eyes rolled as I recovered. 'And that's why you won't say anything to my parents.'

'Don't think that I won't talk to them if you mess me about,' he retorted as I collapsed onto the grass next to him.

'If you do that you'll never see me again.'

'I know where you're living,' Simon said, chuckling evilly and grinning at me. 'I also know that you're living with Jackie, your old school friend. What would her parents say if they discovered that she was a prostitute?'

'They wouldn't believe your lies, Simon. Why are you doing all this?'

'Because I want to fuck you every week.'

'You could have done that without resorting to blackmail.'

'I want to fuck you for free, Ali. I won't pay you for it.'

I grabbed my clothes and got dressed as Simon

tugged his trousers back on. I reckoned that he might carry out his threat. The last thing I needed was Jackie's mother turning up at the flat and accusing her of being a prostitute. Her mother knew my parents and . . . This could turn out to be a dangerous situation, I knew as Simon chuckled wickedly again. I picked up my bag and was about to leave when he grabbed my arm.

'Be here this evening,' he said. 'And bring Jackie with you. I want to fuck both of you.'

'No, I can't,' I said, wondering what the hell to say. 'Not this evening.'

'OK then, I'll talk to both sets of parents and –'

'Simon, please . . . I'll give you whatever you want, but don't involve Jackie.'

'Be here at six o'clock, both of you, or there'll be trouble.'

'Are you blackmailing my sister?' Ali asked as she emerged from the bushes.

I stared open-mouthed at her, dumbfounded for several seconds. 'Ali, I . . . are you . . .' I stammered.

'Don't worry about him,' she said, brushing her long blonde hair away from her face. 'If I have to, I'll meet your parents and tell them that I was the girl in the photographs. I'll also tell his wife what he gets up to.'

I watched Simon clamber to his feet and walk away. Then I stared hard at the girl. 'You're just like me,' I said, shaking my head in disbelief. 'So, you are my sister?'

'No, I'm not,' she said. She stood in front of me. 'It's incredible, Ali. It's no wonder that people mixed us up. But I'm not your sister.'

'You might be,' I suggested.

'Anything's possible, but I'm sure that we're not related. As far as I know, I was born in Sheffield where

I lived with my mother for a couple of years. She was a whore and I was taken away and put in a home.'

'So you don't remember if there was another child in the house?' I asked her hopefully.

'I was only two years old so I don't remember much. There was another girl who ... I think she was a neighbour's kid.'

'You don't remember her name?'

'No, I don't. So, we meet at last. I'm going to Birmingham later today, so this will be our only meeting.'

'I feel as though I'm looking at myself in a mirror,' I said softly, shaking my head again. 'It's uncanny. We *must* be sisters.'

'Whether we are or not doesn't matter, does it? Besides, if you are my twin, then your birth mother was a whore.'

'Do you have any contact with your real mother?'

'No, and I don't want to. I've heard that she's still a whore. Mind you, so am I. Like mother, like daughter,' she quipped, giggling. 'That's what they say, isn't it?'

'I'm a whore too,' I confessed. 'Maybe it runs in the family.'

'Are you actually on the game? I've heard that you are, but I wasn't sure.'

'Yes, yes, I am.'

'In that case, take this.' Ali opened her bag and passed me a small diary. 'Names, phone numbers, times, addresses ... it's a list of my clients.'

'Why are you giving this to me?'

'As I said, I'm moving away. You might as well take on my clients.'

'Thanks – thanks very much.'

'Don't take any crap from them. Make them pay up front and charge them over the top. They all have money so they'll pay whatever you ask.'

'Ali, we need to talk,' I sighed. 'There are so many unanswered questions.'

'Hang on, I'm just going into the bushes for a pee.'

I sat on the grass by the stream and flicked through the diary. There were dozens of names and addresses, all of them local, and I knew that I was now fully set up in business. I also knew that I wouldn't be hearing from Simon again. Ali had saved the day, I thought happily. By threatening to go to his wife she'd sent him scurrying off like a frightened rabbit. Things were turning out far better than I could ever have hoped for.

I slipped the diary into my bag and decided to ask Ali for her phone number. Even though she was moving to Birmingham we could at least keep in touch. I was sure that she was my sister, and there were ways of proving it if she agreed. The likeness was incredible. In a way it had been quite frightening to stand in front of her and look at myself. I rose to my feet and began to wonder where she'd got to. I called out for her. As I made my way through the bushes I knew that she'd gone. She was elusive, I thought. Would she phone me? Would she ever make contact with me again?

I walked through the woods to the park, looking around, but there was no sign of Ali. I'd been thinking about her for so long and when I'd finally got to meet her all we'd had was a two-minute chat. As I made my way home I felt despondent. I'd met my twin sister, or my lookalike. At last I'd met her, and yet ... I wasn't sure what I felt as I neared the flat. I had Amy to think about, and Jackie. What did the future hold? I wondered as I let myself in and found Jackie sitting in the lounge.

'You were a long time,' she said, looking up at me from the sofa.

'Was I?' I said softly.

'Where have you been?'

'Out and about, that's where I've been. How did it go with Alan?'

'He was disappointed because you weren't here, but it went all right. The money's on the mantelpiece.'

'Oh, OK.'

'Are you all right?' Jackie asked me. 'You seem . . .'

'I've just met my sister,' I told her.

'God, what did she say?'

My mobile phone rang and I answered it. I was pleased to hear Amy's voice. 'Hi,' I said. 'How are things?'

'Can you meet me tomorrow morning in the woods?'

'Yes, I'll be there at nine.'

'Is Jackie with you?'

'Yes, that's right.'

'I want to suck your clitoris, Ali. I want to suck it and –'

'That would be wonderful,' I sighed as my young womb contracted.

'I'll take you to heaven with my fingers and my tongue and –'

'OK, I'll see you tomorrow.'

I dropped my phone back into my bag and smiled at Jackie. 'That was my sister,' I lied. 'I'm seeing her tomorrow morning.'

'That's great,' Jackie said, beaming. 'Will I ever get to meet her?'

'No, I don't think so. She . . . she's a funny girl. I hope to be seeing quite a lot of her.'

'I'm sorry that I went on about Amy.'

'That's all right, Jackie. I'm not interested in Amy. I have my sister now. And you, of course.'

'Shall we go to bed?'

'Yes,' I said softly, grinning at her. 'Let's go to bed.'

nexus

The leading publisher of fetish and adult fiction

TELL US WHAT YOU THINK!

Readers' ideas and opinions matter to us so please take a few minutes to fill in the questionnaire below.

1. Sex: Are you male ☐   female ☐   a couple ☐?

2. Age: Under 21 ☐   21–30 ☐   31–40 ☐   41–50 ☐   51–60 ☐   over 60 ☐

3. Where do you buy your Nexus books from?

☐ A chain book shop. If so, which one(s)?

_____

☐ An independent book shop. If so, which one(s)?

_____

☐ A used book shop/charity shop
☐ Online book store. If so, which one(s)?

_____

4. How did you find out about Nexus books?

☐ Browsing in a book shop
☐ A review in a magazine
☐ Online
☐ Recommendation
☐ Other _____

5. In terms of settings, which do you prefer? (Tick as many as you like.)

☐ Down to earth and as realistic as possible
☐ Historical settings. If so, which period do you prefer?

_____

☐ Fantasy settings – barbarian worlds
☐ Completely escapist/surreal fantasy
☐ Institutional or secret academy

☐ Futuristic/sci fi
☐ Escapist but still believable
☐ Any settings you dislike?

_____

☐ Where would you like to see an adult novel set?

_____

6. In terms of storylines, would you prefer:
☐ Simple stories that concentrate on adult interests?
☐ More plot and character-driven stories with less explicit adult
activity?
☐ We value your ideas, so give us your opinion of this book:

_____

_____

_____

7. In terms of your adult interests, what do you like to read about? (Tick as many as you like.)
☐ Traditional corporal punishment (CP)
☐ Modern corporal punishment
☐ Spanking
☐ Restraint/bondage
☐ Rope bondage
☐ Latex/rubber
☐ Leather
☐ Female domination and male submission
☐ Female domination and female submission
☐ Male domination and female submission
☐ Willing captivity
☐ Uniforms
☐ Lingerie/underwear/hosiery/footwear (boots and high heels)
☐ Sex rituals
☐ Vanilla sex
☐ Swinging
☐ Cross-dressing/TV
☐ Enforced feminisation

☐ Others – tell us what you don't see enough of in adult fiction:

_____

_____

_____

8. Would you prefer books with a more specialised approach to your interests, i.e. a novel specifically about uniforms? If so, which subject(s) would you like to read a Nexus novel about?

_____

_____

_____

9. Would you like to read true stories in Nexus books? For instance, the true story of a submissive woman, or a male slave? Tell us which true revelations you would most like to read about:

_____

_____

_____

10. What do you like best about Nexus books?

_____

_____

11. What do you like least about Nexus books?

_____

_____

12. Which are your favourite titles?

_____

_____

13. Who are your favourite authors?

_____

_____

14. Which covers do you prefer? Those featuring:
(Tick as many as you like.)

- ☐ Fetish outfits
- ☐ More nudity
- ☐ Two models
- ☐ Unusual models or settings
- ☐ Classic erotic photography
- ☐ More contemporary images and poses
- ☐ A blank/non-erotic cover
- ☐ What would your ideal cover look like?

_____

15. **Describe your ideal Nexus novel in the space provided:**

_____

_____

_____

_____

16. **Which celebrity would feature in one of your Nexus-style fantasies? We'll post the best suggestions on our website – anonymously!**

_____

THANKS FOR YOUR TIME

Now simply write the title of this book in the space below and cut out the questionnaire pages. Post to: Nexus, Marketing Dept., Thames Wharf Studios, Rainville Rd, London W6 9HA

Book title: _____

NEXUS NEW BOOKS

To be published in July 2008

NEIGHBOURHOOD WATCH
Lisette Ashton

Cedar View looks like any other sleepy cul-de-sac in the heart of suburbia. Trees line the sides of the road. The gardens are neat and well maintained. But behind the tightly drawn curtains of each house the neighbours indulge their lewdest and bawdiest appetites. It's not just the dominatrix at number 5, the swingers at number 6 or the sadistically sinister couple at number 4 who have secrets. There's also the curious relationship between the Smiths, the open marriage of the Graftons, not to mention the strange goings-on at the home of Denise, a woman whose lust seems never to be sated. Everyone on Cedar View has a secret – and they're all about to be exposed.

£6.99   ISBN 978 0 352 34190 7

NEXUS CONFESSIONS VOLUME 4
Various

Swinging, dogging, group sex, cross-dressing, spanking, female domination, corporal punishment, and extreme fetishes . . . Nexus Confessions explores the length and breadth of erotic obsession, real experience and sexual fantasy. This is an encyclopaedic collection of the bizarre, the extreme, the utterly inappropriate, the daring and the shocking experiences of ordinary men and women driven by their extraordinary desires. Collected by the world's leading publisher of fetish fiction, these are true stories and shameful confessions, never-before-told or published.

£6.99   ISBN 978 0 352 34136 5

To be published in August 2008

INDECENT PURSUIT
Ray Gordon

When young and sexually vivacious Sheena is dumped by her snobbish older boyfriend, she decides to get her revenge. So using her sexual prowess she sets out to seduce his three brothers. Her lewd language and loose behaviour prove irresistible to the men and before long she has bedded them all. But her goal of marrying into the wealthy family remains as distant as ever. In desperation, Sheena sets her sights on the father; but 'the Boss', as he is known by his sons, is determined to regain his family's honour and at the same time teach the wanton young woman a lesson in respect.

£6.99   ISBN 978 0 352 34196 9

If you would like more information about Nexus titles, please visit our website at www.nexus-books.co.uk, or send a large stamped addressed envelope to:

Nexus, Thames Wharf Studios,
Rainville Road, London W6 9HA

NEXUS BOOKLIST

Information is correct at time of printing. To avoid disappointment, check availability before ordering. Go to www.nexus-books.co.uk.

All books are priced at £6.99 unless another price is given.

NEXUS

☐ ABANDONED ALICE	Adriana Arden	ISBN 978 0 352 33969 0
☐ ALICE IN CHAINS	Adriana Arden	ISBN 978 0 352 33908 9
☐ AMERICAN BLUE	Penny Birch	ISBN 978 0 352 34169 3
☐ AQUA DOMINATION	William Doughty	ISBN 978 0 352 34020 7
☐ THE ART OF CORRECTION	Tara Black	ISBN 978 0 352 33895 2
☐ THE ART OF SURRENDER	Madeline Bastinado	ISBN 978 0 352 34013 9
☐ BEASTLY BEHAVIOUR	Aishling Morgan	ISBN 978 0 352 34095 5
☐ BEING A GIRL	Chloë Thurlow	ISBN 978 0 352 34139 6
☐ BELINDA BARES UP	Yolanda Celbridge	ISBN 978 0 352 33926 3
☐ BIDDING TO SIN	Rosita Varón	ISBN 978 0 352 34063 4
☐ BLUSHING AT BOTH ENDS	Philip Kemp	ISBN 978 0 352 34107 5
☐ THE BOOK OF PUNISHMENT	Cat Scarlett	ISBN 978 0 352 33975 1
☐ BRUSH STROKES	Penny Birch	ISBN 978 0 352 34072 6
☐ CALLED TO THE WILD	Angel Blake	ISBN 978 0 352 34067 2
☐ CAPTIVES OF CHEYNER CLOSE	Adriana Arden	ISBN 978 0 352 34028 3
☐ CARNAL POSSESSION	Yvonne Strickland	ISBN 978 0 352 34062 7
☐ CITY MAID	Amelia Evangeline	ISBN 978 0 352 34096 2
☐ COLLEGE GIRLS	Cat Scarlett	ISBN 978 0 352 33942 3
☐ COMPANY OF SLAVES	Christina Shelly	ISBN 978 0 352 33887 7
☐ CONCEIT AND CONSEQUENCE	Aishling Morgan	ISBN 978 0 352 33965 2
☐ CORRECTIVE THERAPY	Jacqueline Masterson	ISBN 978 0 352 33917 1
☐ CORRUPTION	Virginia Crowley	ISBN 978 0 352 34073 3

NEXUS ENTHUSIAST

NEXUS NON FICTION

------ ✂ --------------------------------

Please send me the books I have ticked above.

Name   ....

Address   ....

                ....

                ....

                .... Post code ....

Send to: **Virgin Books Cash Sales, Thames Wharf Studios, Rainville Road, London W6 9HA**

US customers: for prices and details of how to order books for delivery by mail, call 888-330-8477.

Please enclose a cheque or postal order, made payable to **Nexus Books Ltd**, to the value of the books you have ordered plus postage and packing costs as follows:

UK and BFPO – £1.00 for the first book, 50p for each subsequent book.

Overseas (including Republic of Ireland) – £2.00 for the first book, £1.00 for each subsequent book.

If you would prefer to pay by VISA, ACCESS/MASTERCARD, AMEX, DINERS CLUB or SWITCH, please write your card number and expiry date here:

....

Please allow up to 28 days for delivery.

Signature ....

Our privacy policy

We will not disclose information you supply us to any other parties. We will not disclose any information which identifies you personally to any person without your express consent.

From time to time we may send out information about Nexus books and special offers. Please tick here if you do *not* wish to receive Nexus information. ☐

------ ✂ --------------------------------